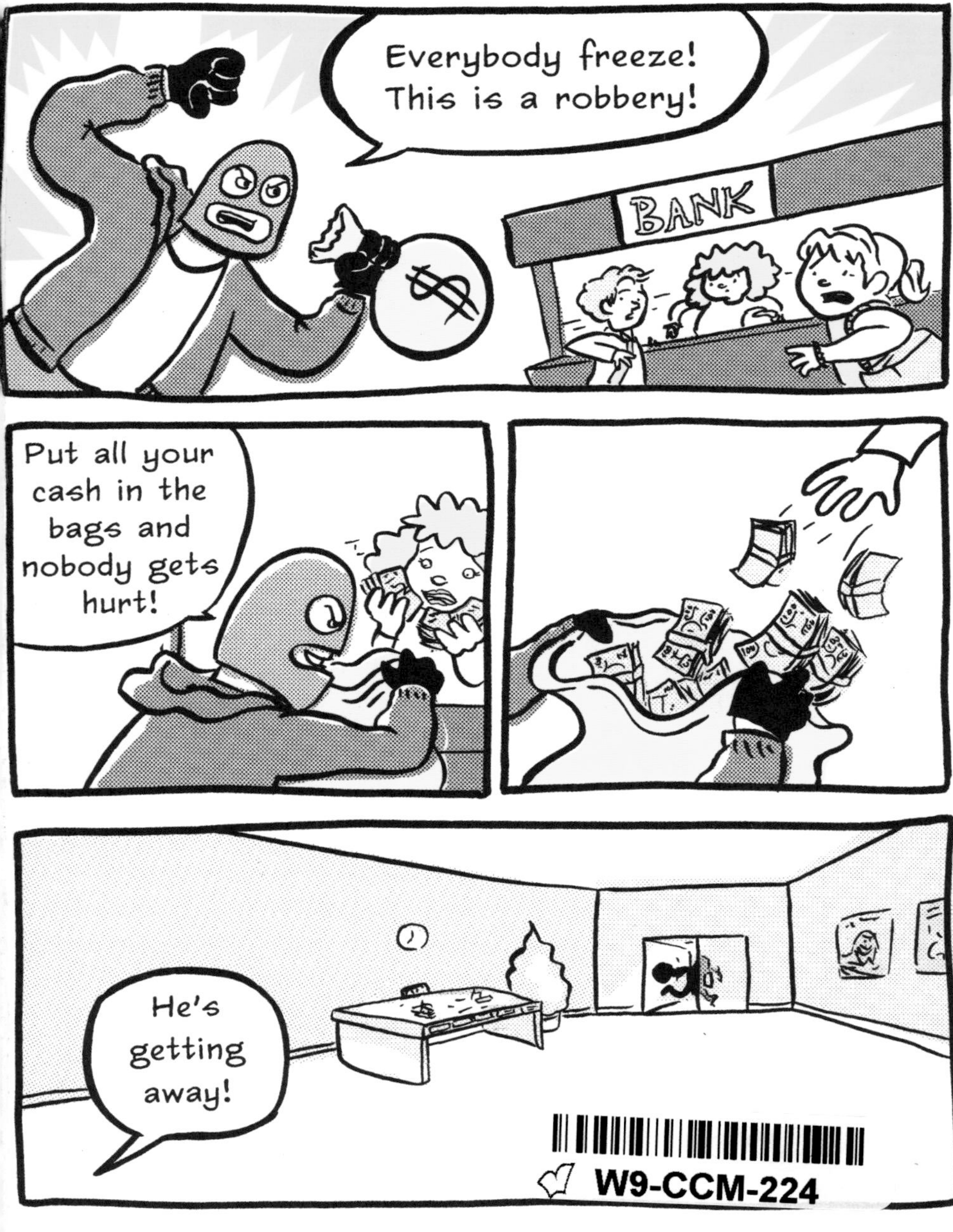
Everybody freeze! This is a robbery!
BANK
Put all your cash in the bags and nobody gets hurt!
He's getting away!

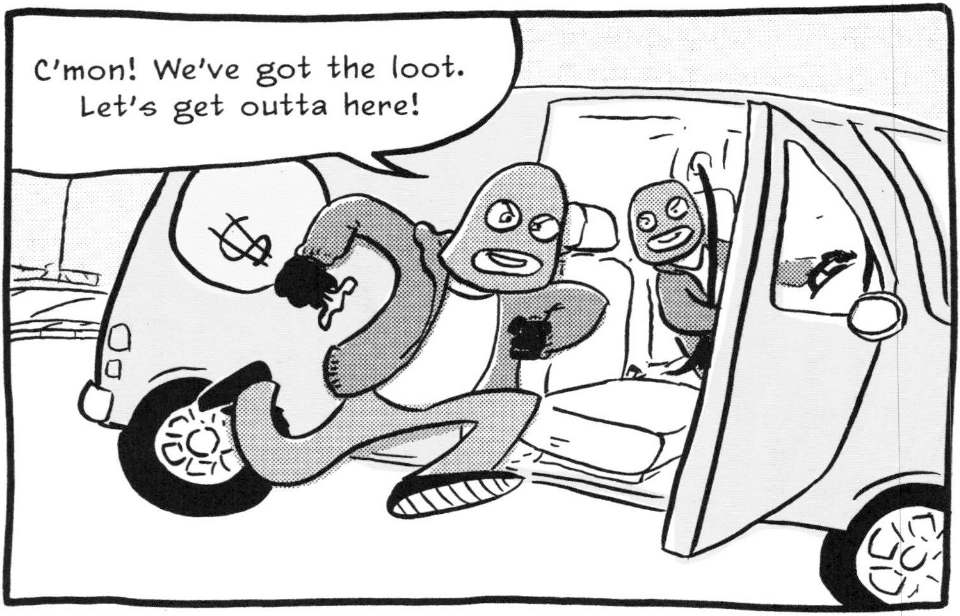
C'mon! We've got the loot.
Let's get outta here!

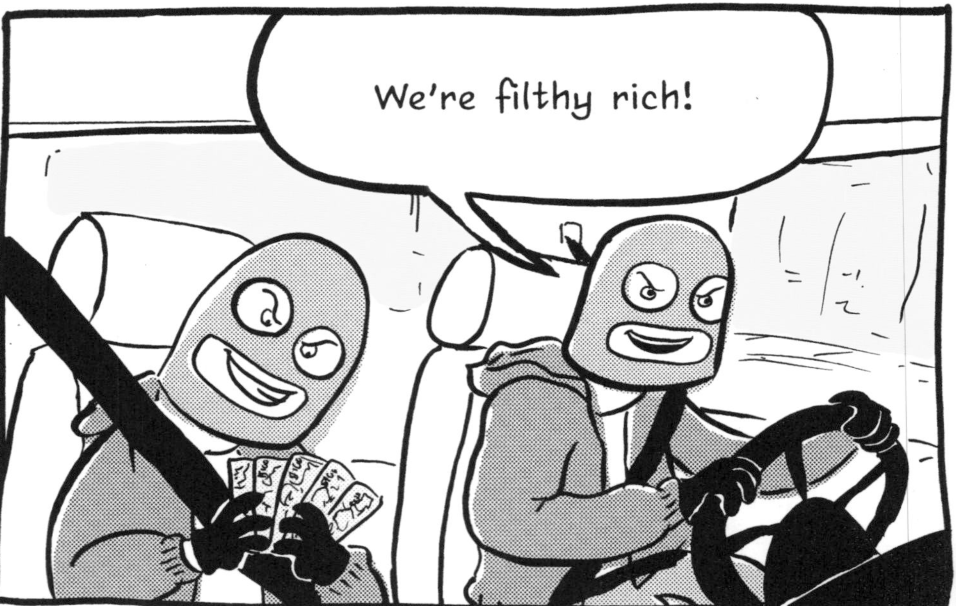
We're filthy rich!

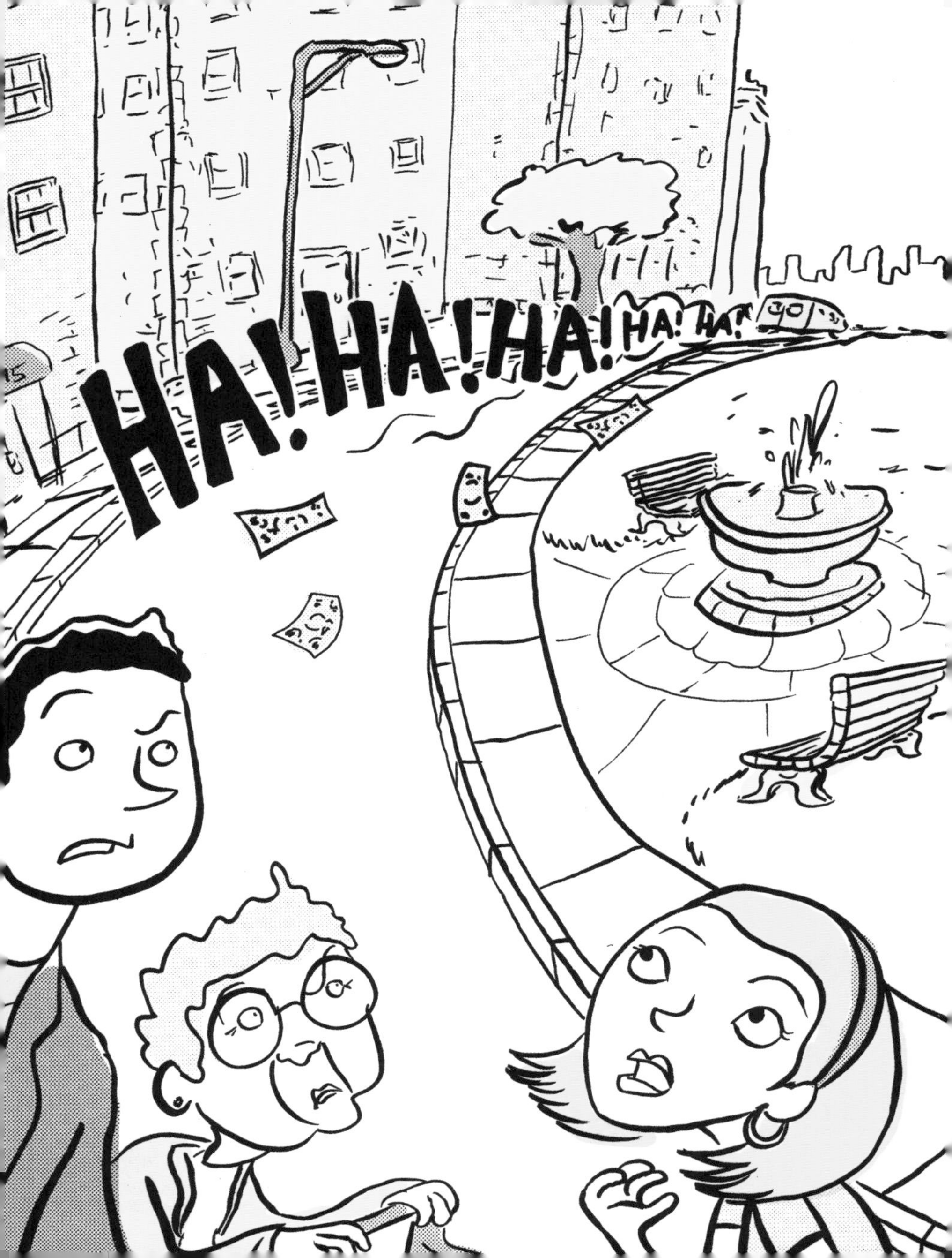
HA! HA! HA! HA! HA!

LUNCH

Jarrett J. Krosoczka

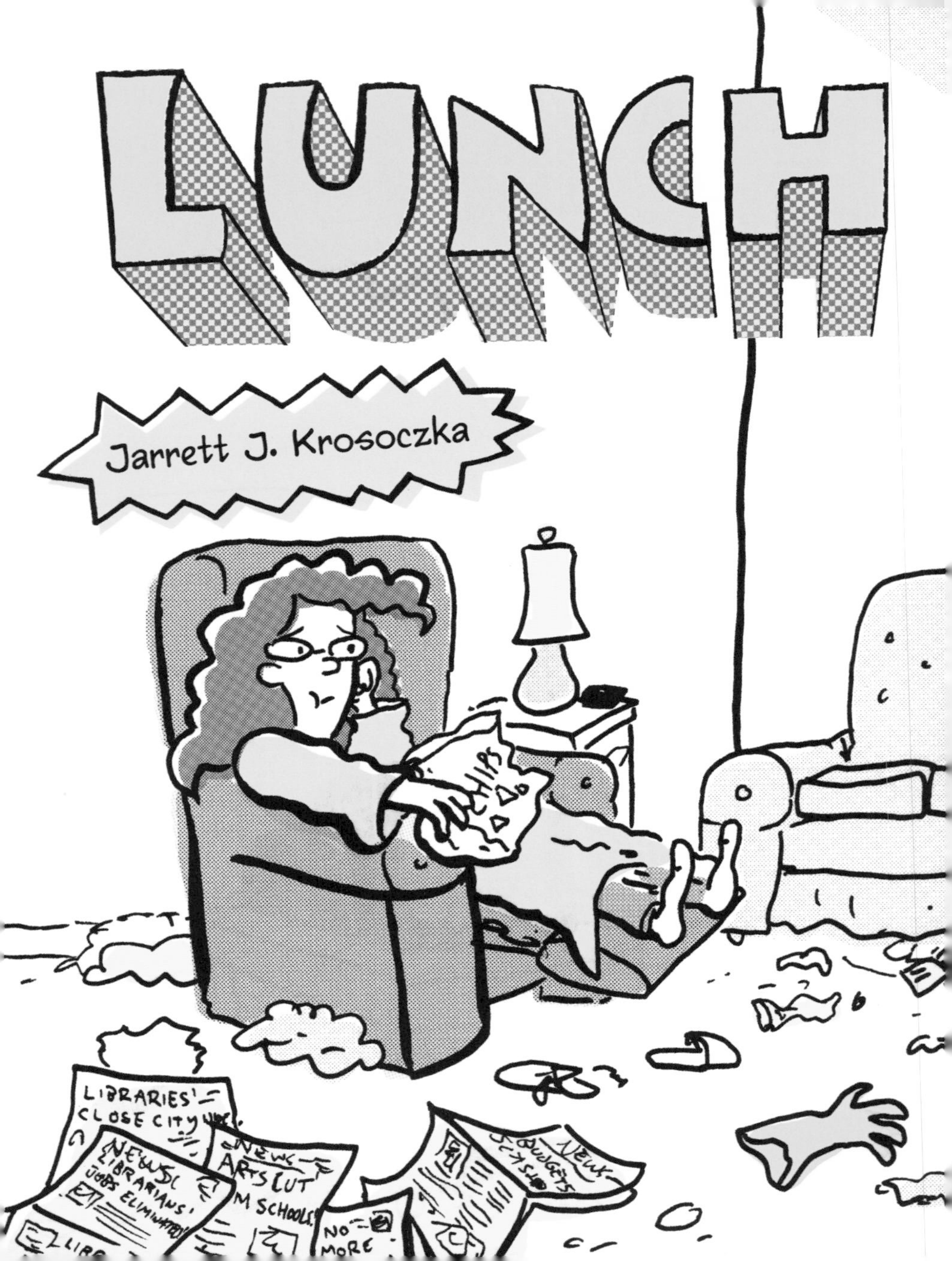

CHIPS
LIBRARIES'
CLOSE CITY
NEWS
LIBRARIANS'
JOBS ELIMINATED
NEWS
ARTS CUT
M SCHOOLS
NO MORE
NEWS
BUDGETS

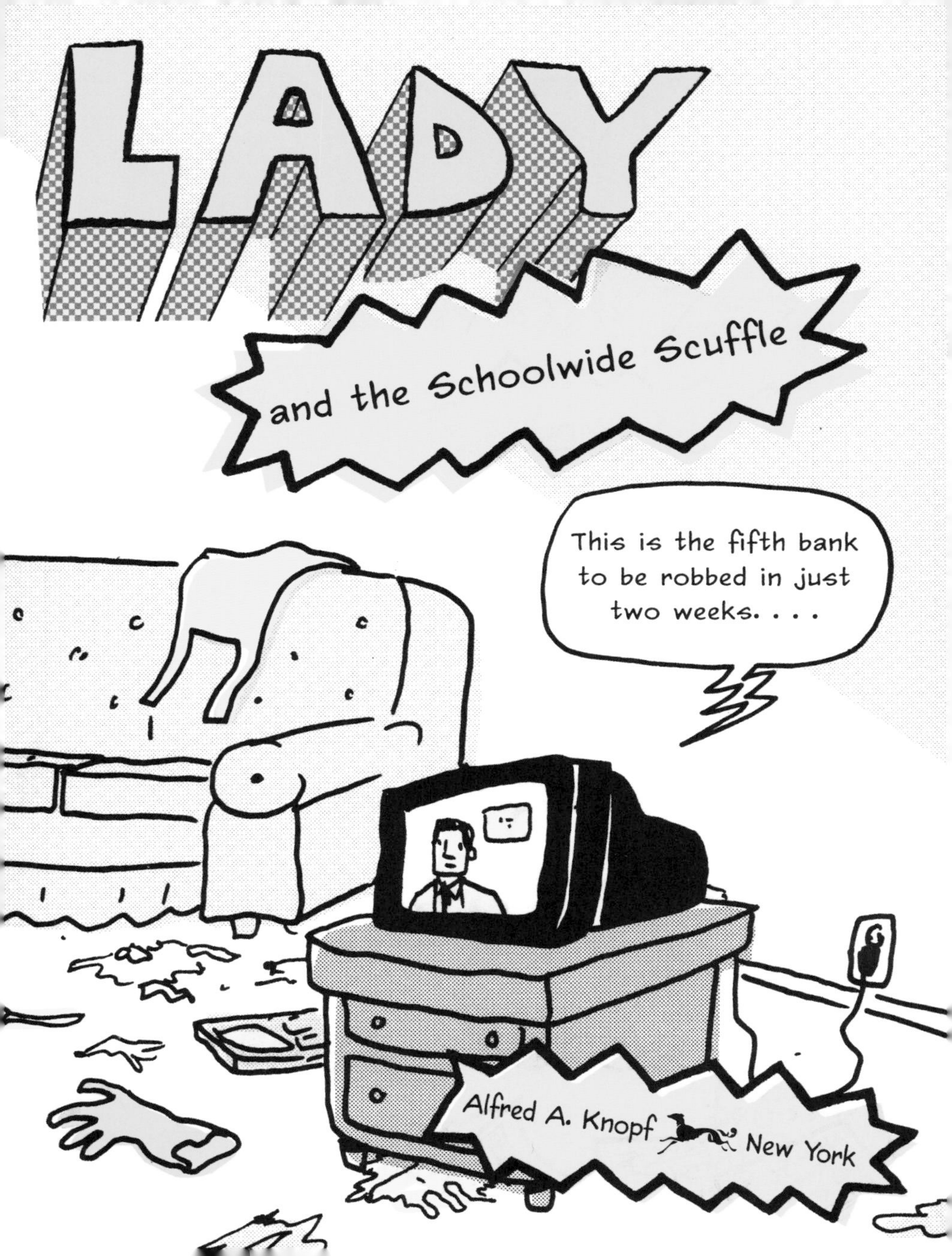
LADY
and the Schoolwide Scuffle
This is the fifth bank to be robbed in just two weeks. . . .
Alfred A. Knopf New York

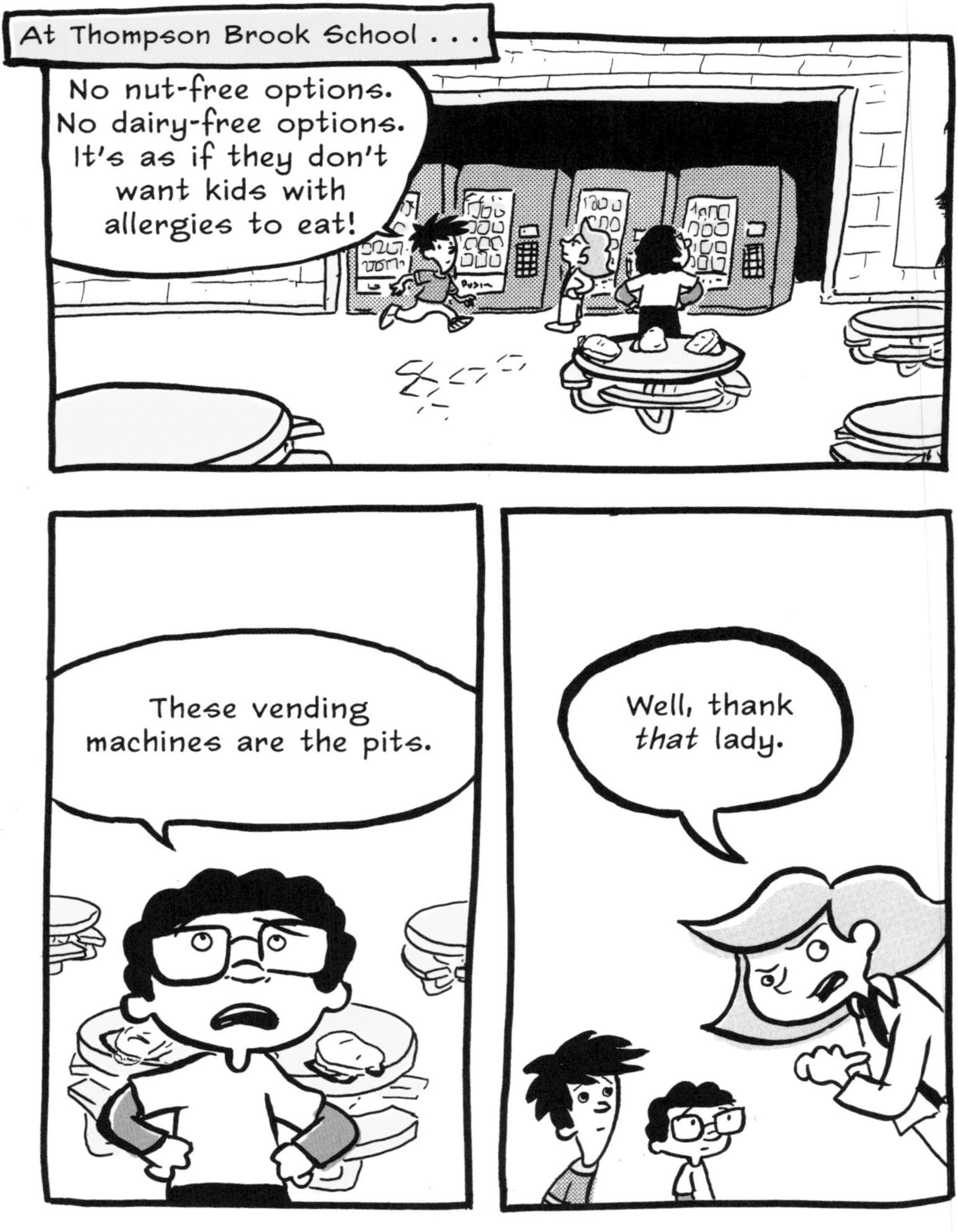
At Thompson Brook School . . .
No nut-free options. No dairy-free options. It's as if they don't want kids with allergies to eat!
These vending machines are the pits.
Well, thank *that* lady.

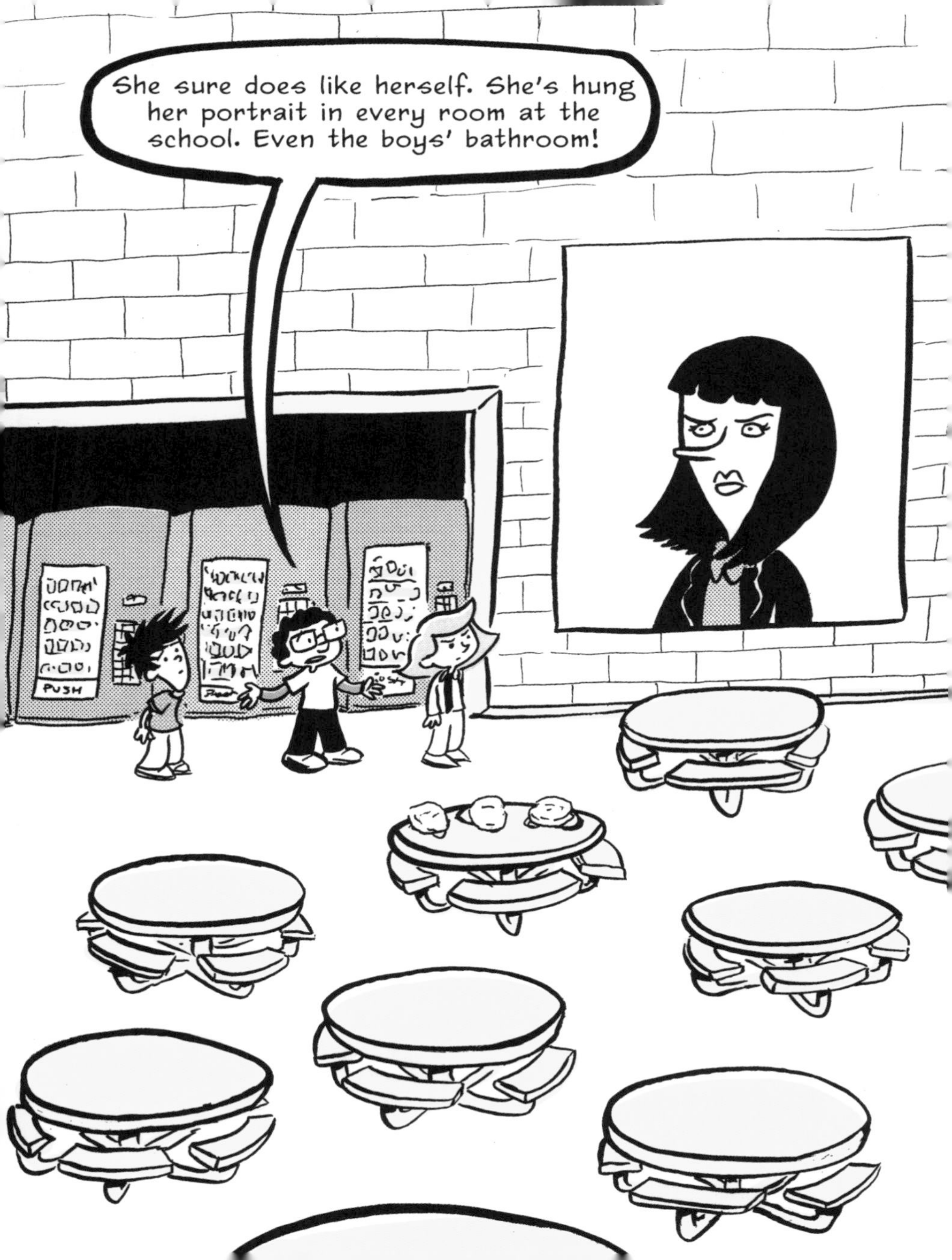
She sure does like herself. She's hung her portrait in every room at the school. Even the boys' bathroom!
PUSH

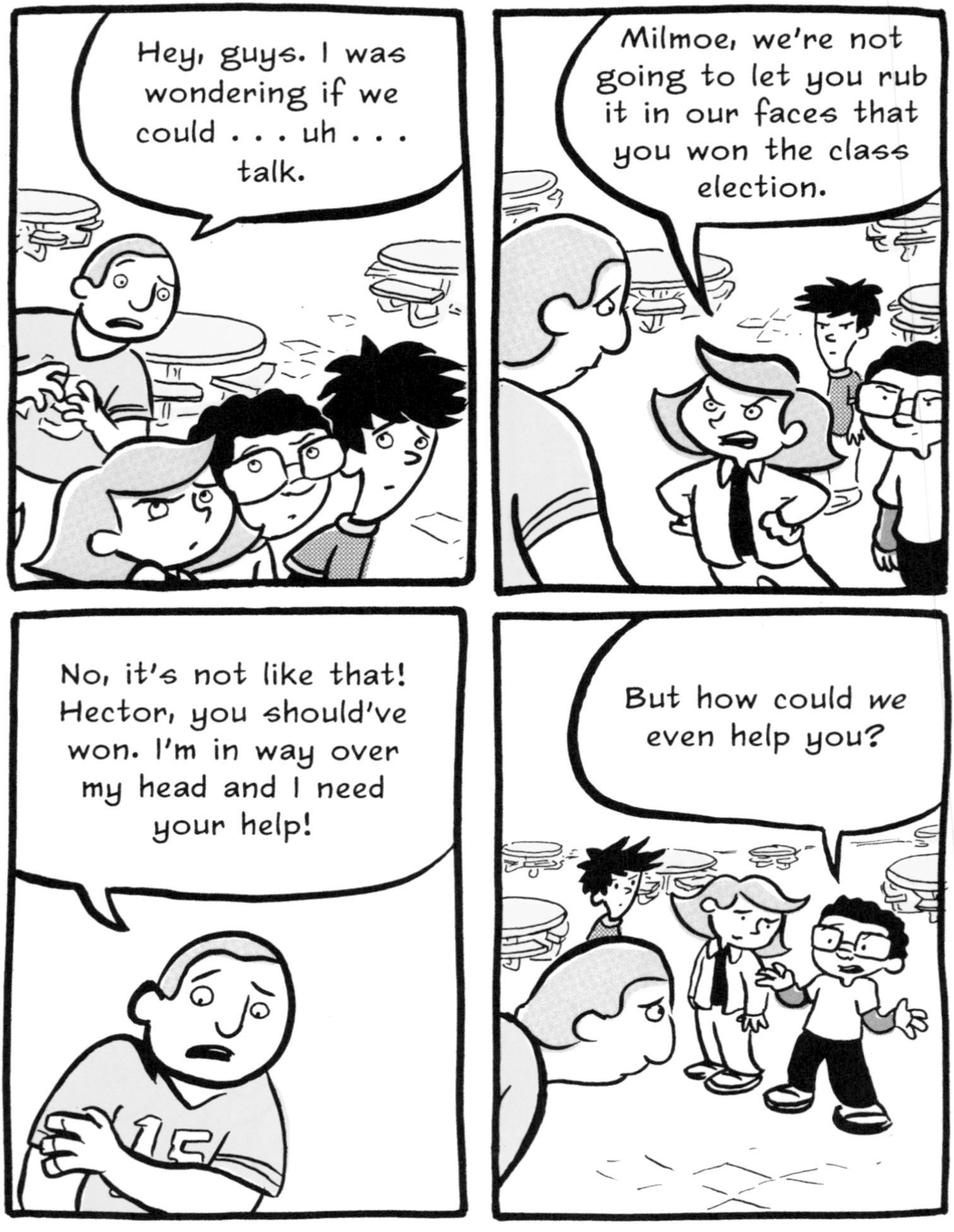
Hey, guys. I was wondering if we could . . . uh . . . talk.
Milmoe, we're not going to let you rub it in our faces that you won the class election.
No, it's not like that! Hector, you should've won. I'm in way over my head and I need your help!
But how could we even help you?

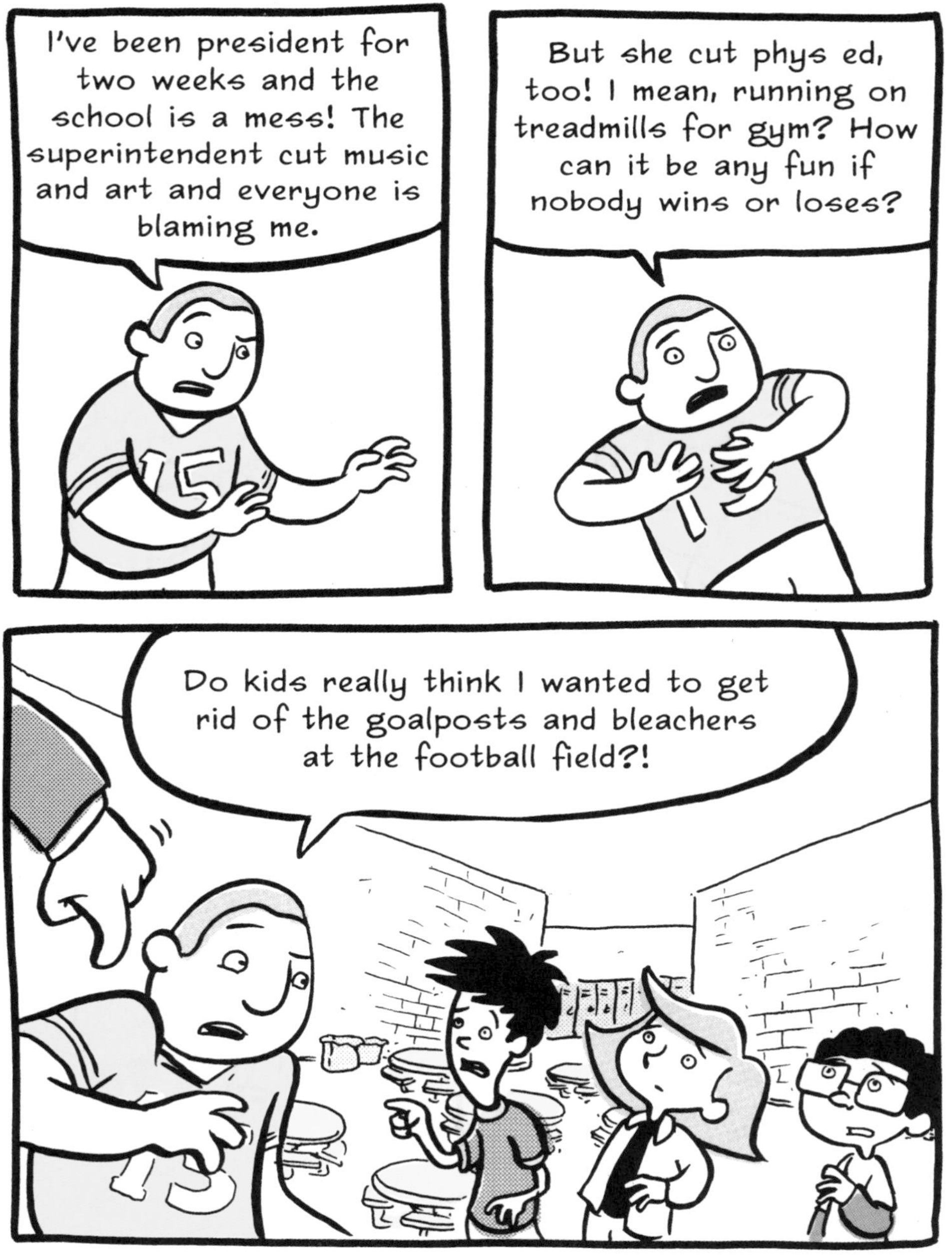
I've been president for two weeks and the school is a mess! The superintendent cut music and art and everyone is blaming me.
But she cut phys ed, too! I mean, running on treadmills for gym? How can it be any fun if nobody wins or loses?
Do kids really think I wanted to get rid of the goalposts and bleachers at the football field?!

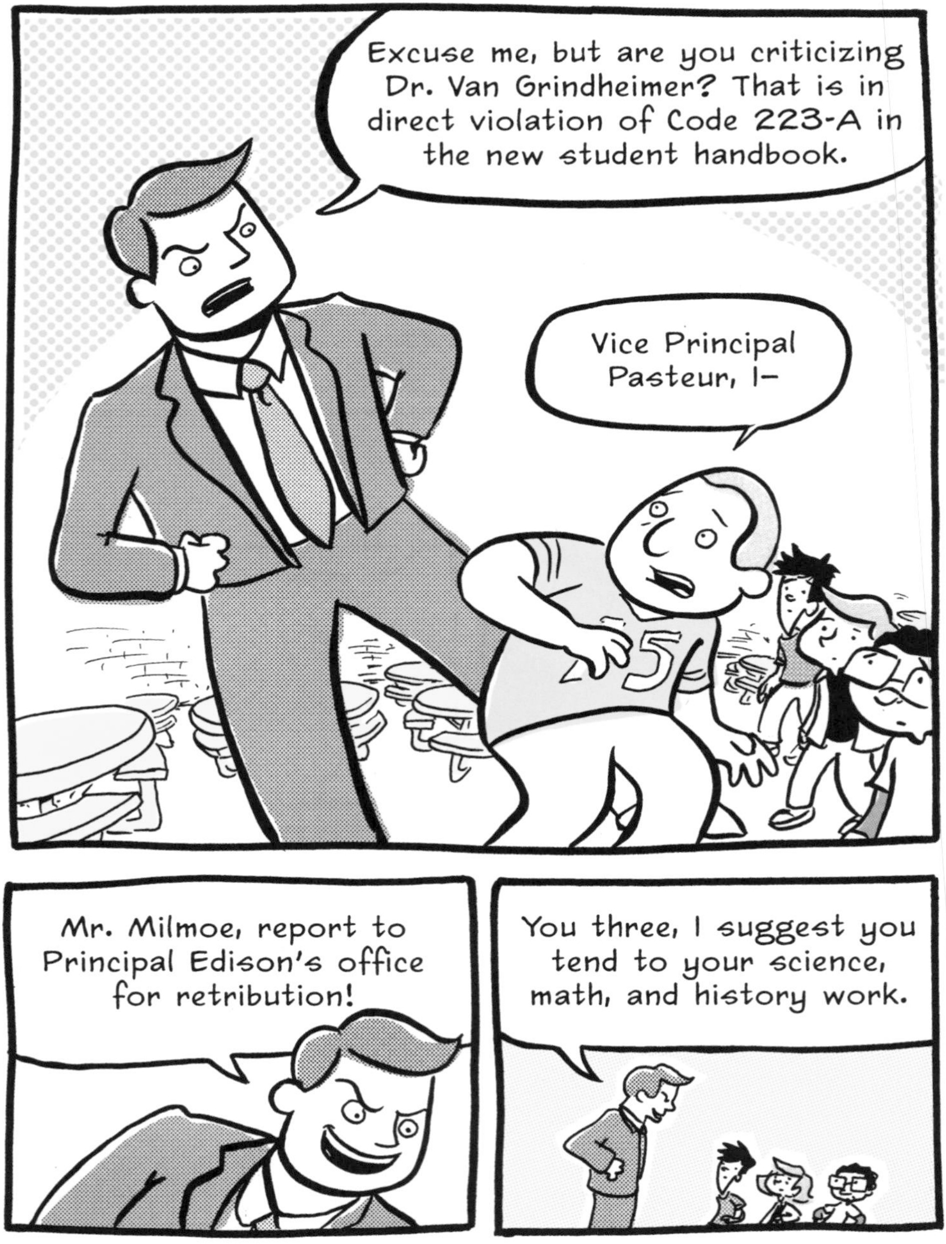
Excuse me, but are you criticizing Dr. Van Grindheimer? That is in direct violation of Code 223-A in the new student handbook.
Vice Principal Pasteur, I–
Mr. Milmoe, report to Principal Edison's office for retribution!
You three, I suggest you tend to your science, math, and history work.

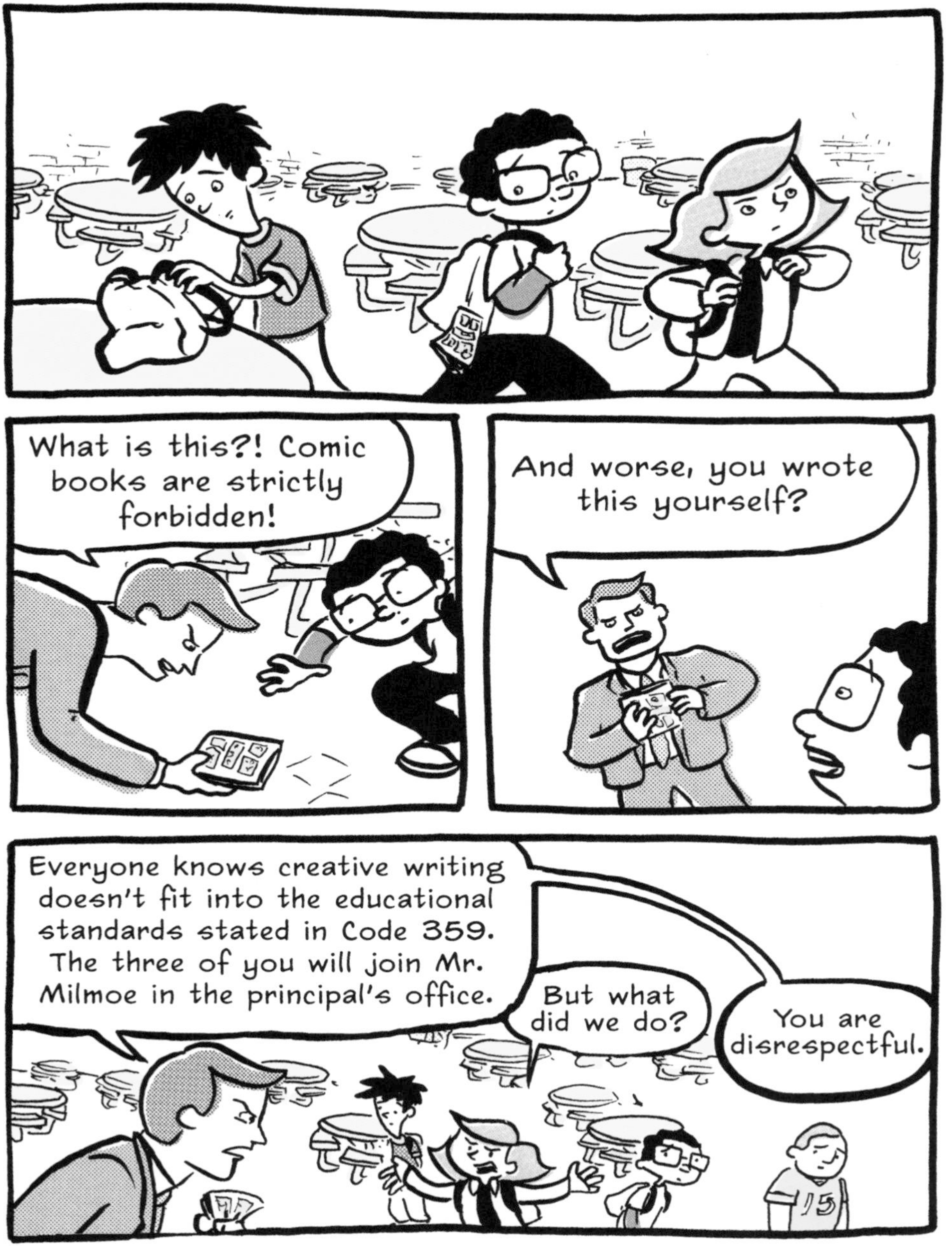
What is this?! Comic books are strictly forbidden!
And worse, you wrote this yourself?
Everyone knows creative writing doesn't fit into the educational standards stated in Code 359. The three of you will join Mr. Milmoe in the principal's office.
But what did we do?
You are disrespectful.

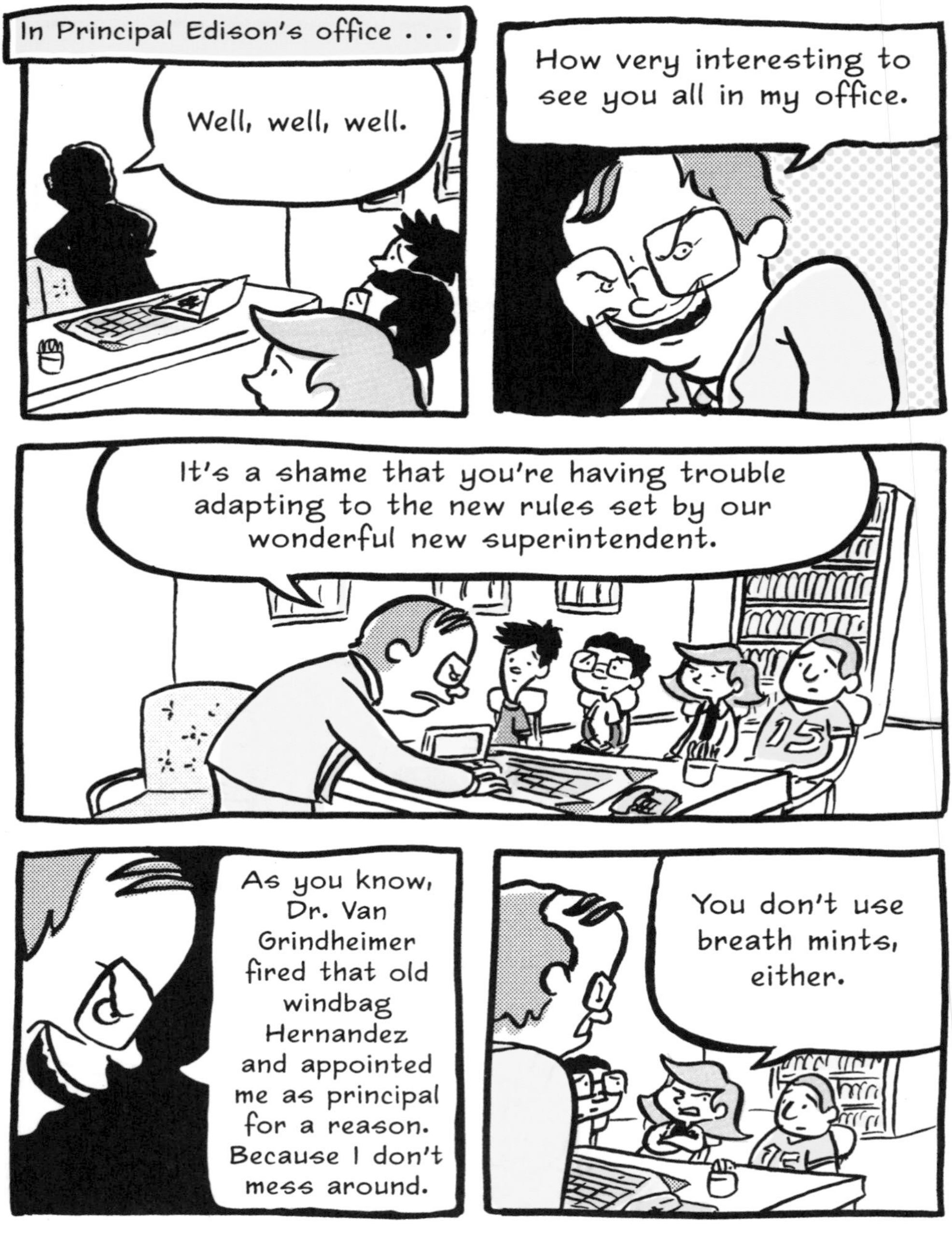
In Principal Edison's office . . .
Well, well, well.
How very interesting to see you all in my office.
It's a shame that you're having trouble adapting to the new rules set by our wonderful new superintendent.
As you know, Dr. Van Grindheimer fired that old windbag Hernandez and appointed me as principal for a reason. Because I don't mess around.
You don't use breath mints, either.

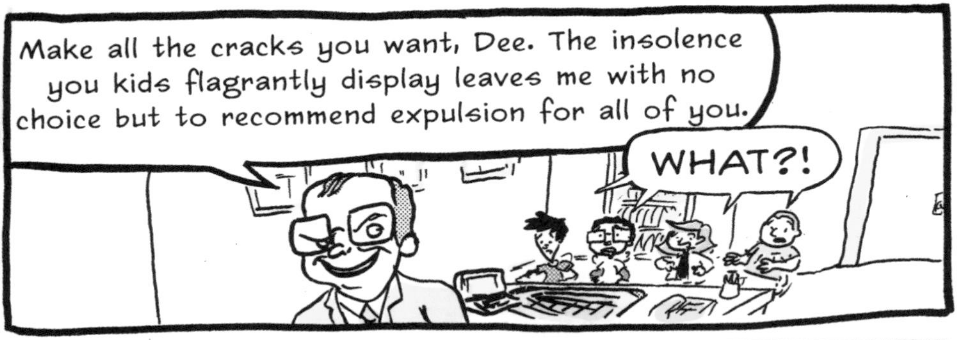
Make all the cracks you want, Dee. The insolence you kids flagrantly display leaves me with no choice but to recommend expulsion for all of you.
WHAT?!

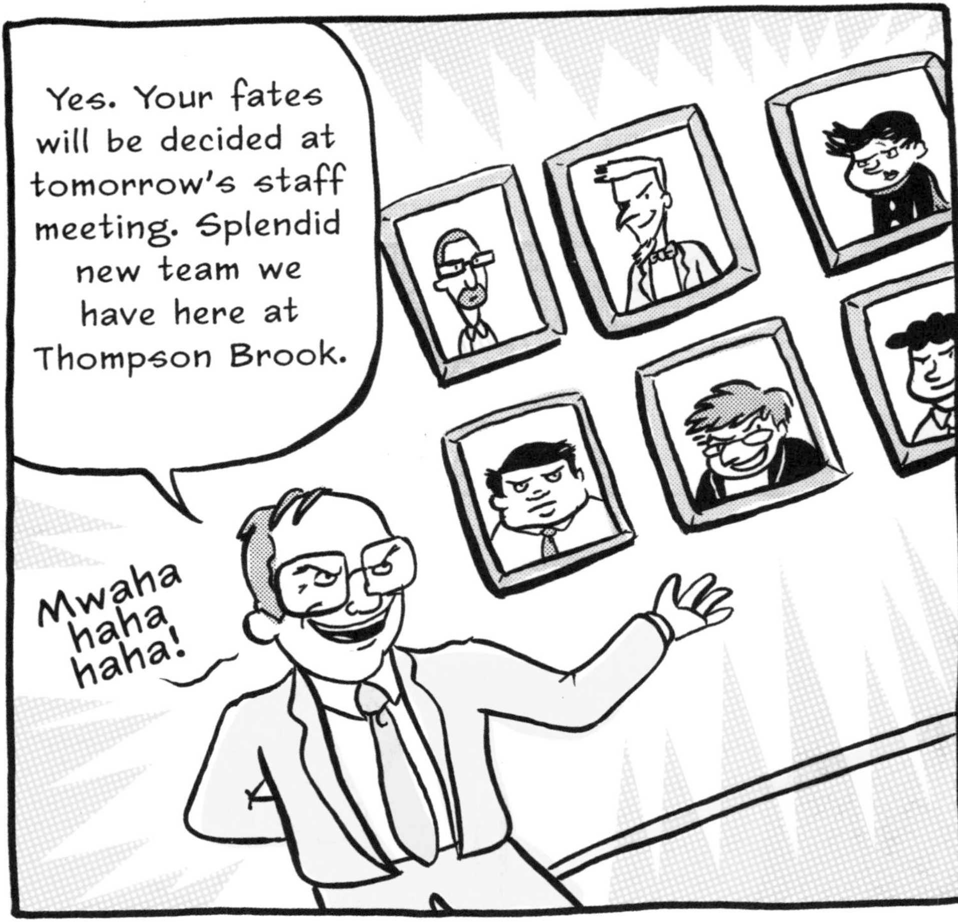
Yes. Your fates will be decided at tomorrow's staff meeting. Splendid new team we have here at Thompson Brook.
Mwaha haha haha!

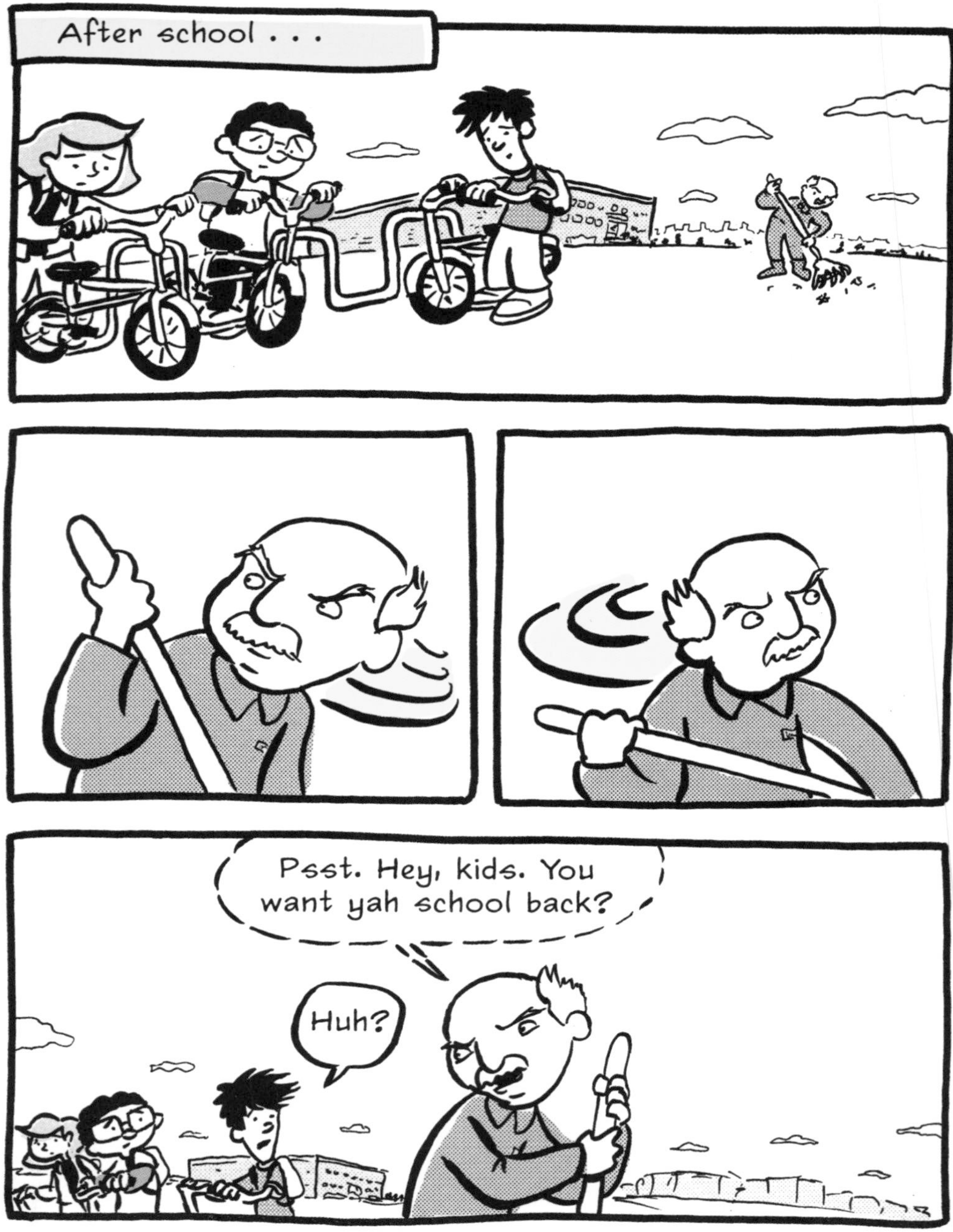
After school . . .
Psst. Hey, kids. You want yah school back?
Huh?

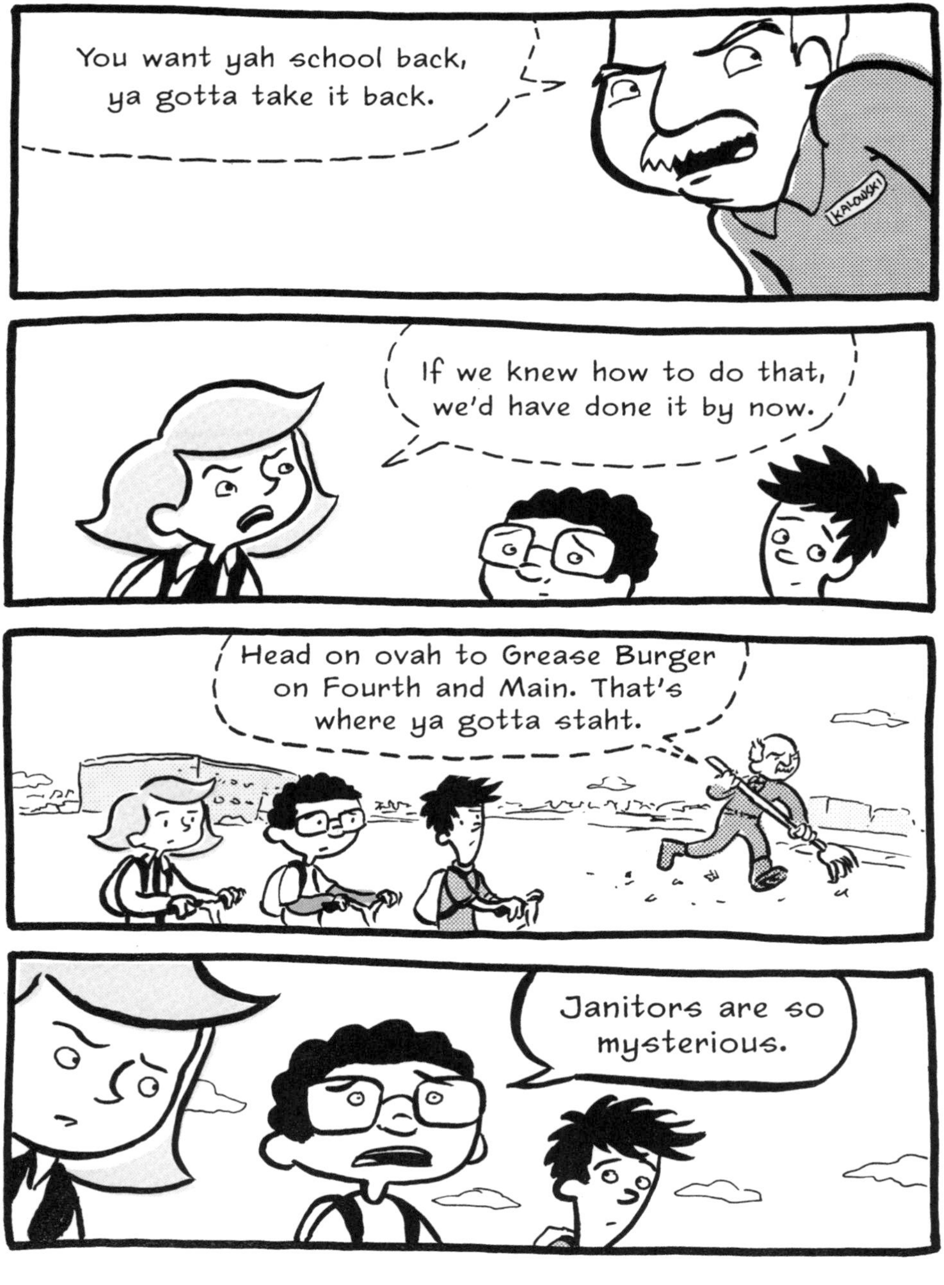
You want yah school back, ya gotta take it back.
KALOWSKI
If we knew how to do that, we'd have done it by now.
Head on ovah to Grease Burger on Fourth and Main. That's where ya gotta staht.
Janitors are so mysterious.

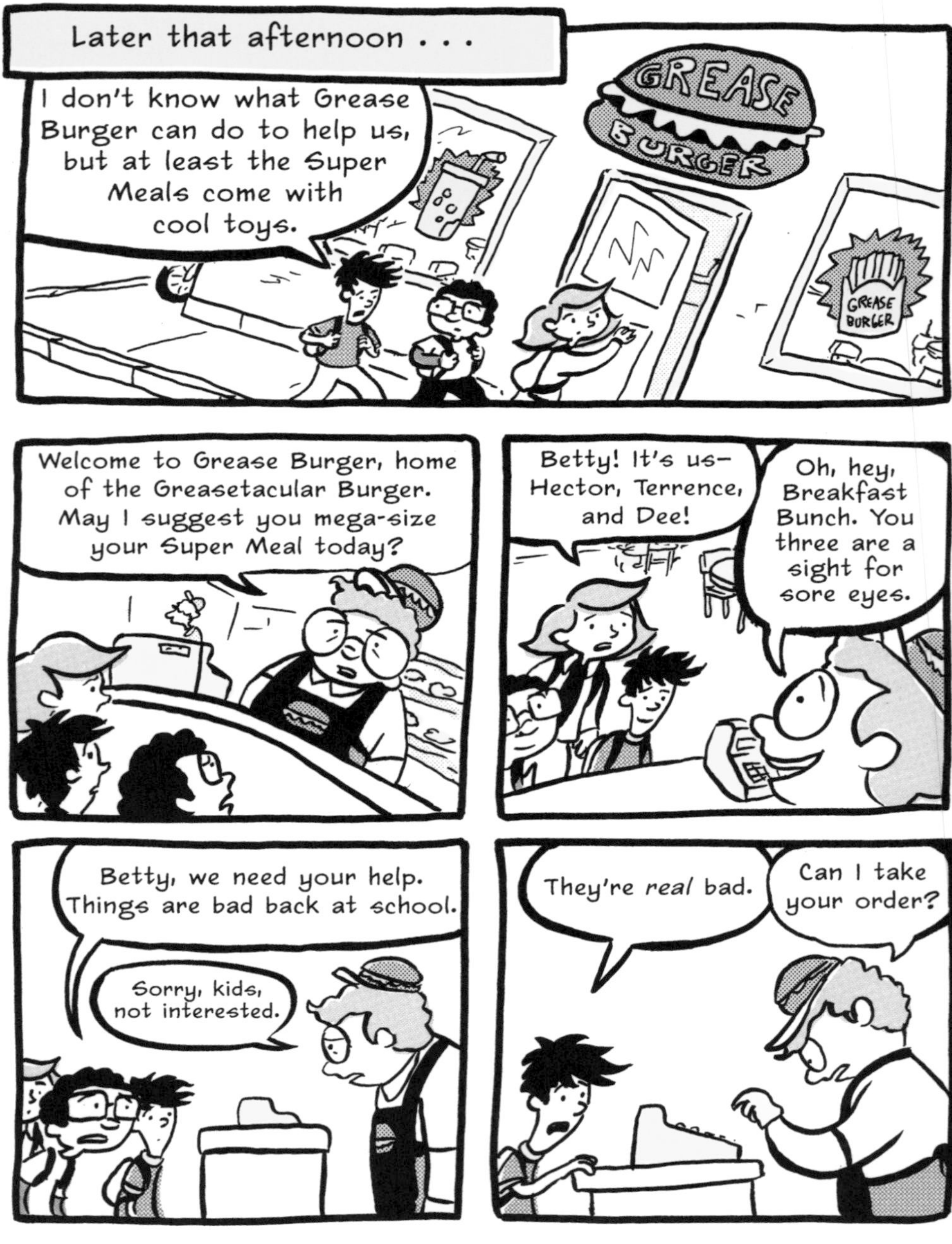
Later that afternoon . . .
I don't know what Grease Burger can do to help us, but at least the Super Meals come with cool toys.
GREASE BURGER
GREASE BURGER
Welcome to Grease Burger, home of the Greasetacular Burger. May I suggest you mega-size your Super Meal today?
Betty! It's us—Hector, Terrence, and Dee!
Oh, hey, Breakfast Bunch. You three are a sight for sore eyes.
Betty, we need your help. Things are bad back at school.
Sorry, kids, not interested.
They're *real* bad.
Can I take your order?

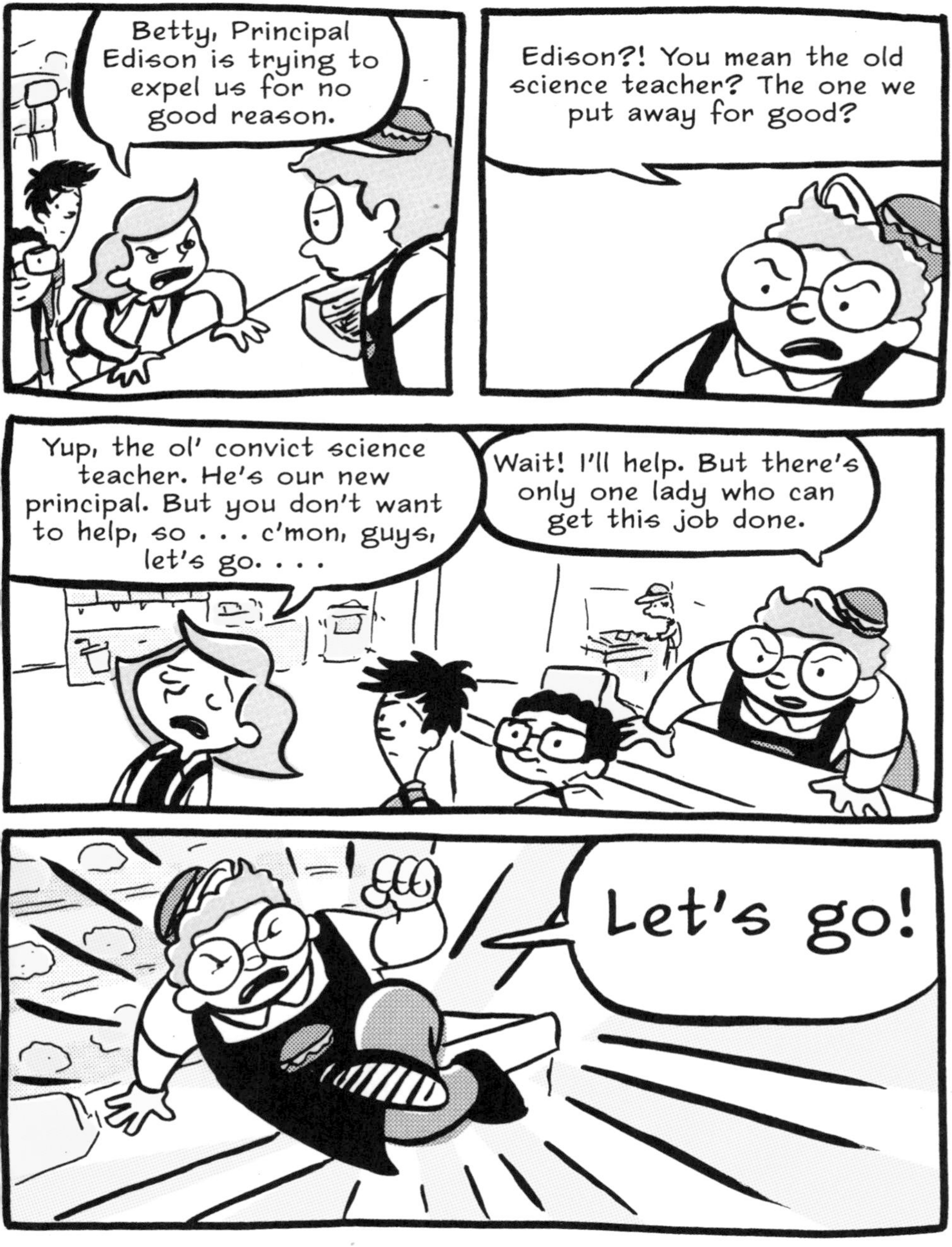

Betty, Principal Edison is trying to expel us for no good reason.
Edison?! You mean the old science teacher? The one we put away for good?
Yup, the ol' convict science teacher. He's our new principal. But you don't want to help, so . . . c'mon, guys, let's go. . . .
Wait! I'll help. But there's only one lady who can get this job done.
Let's go!

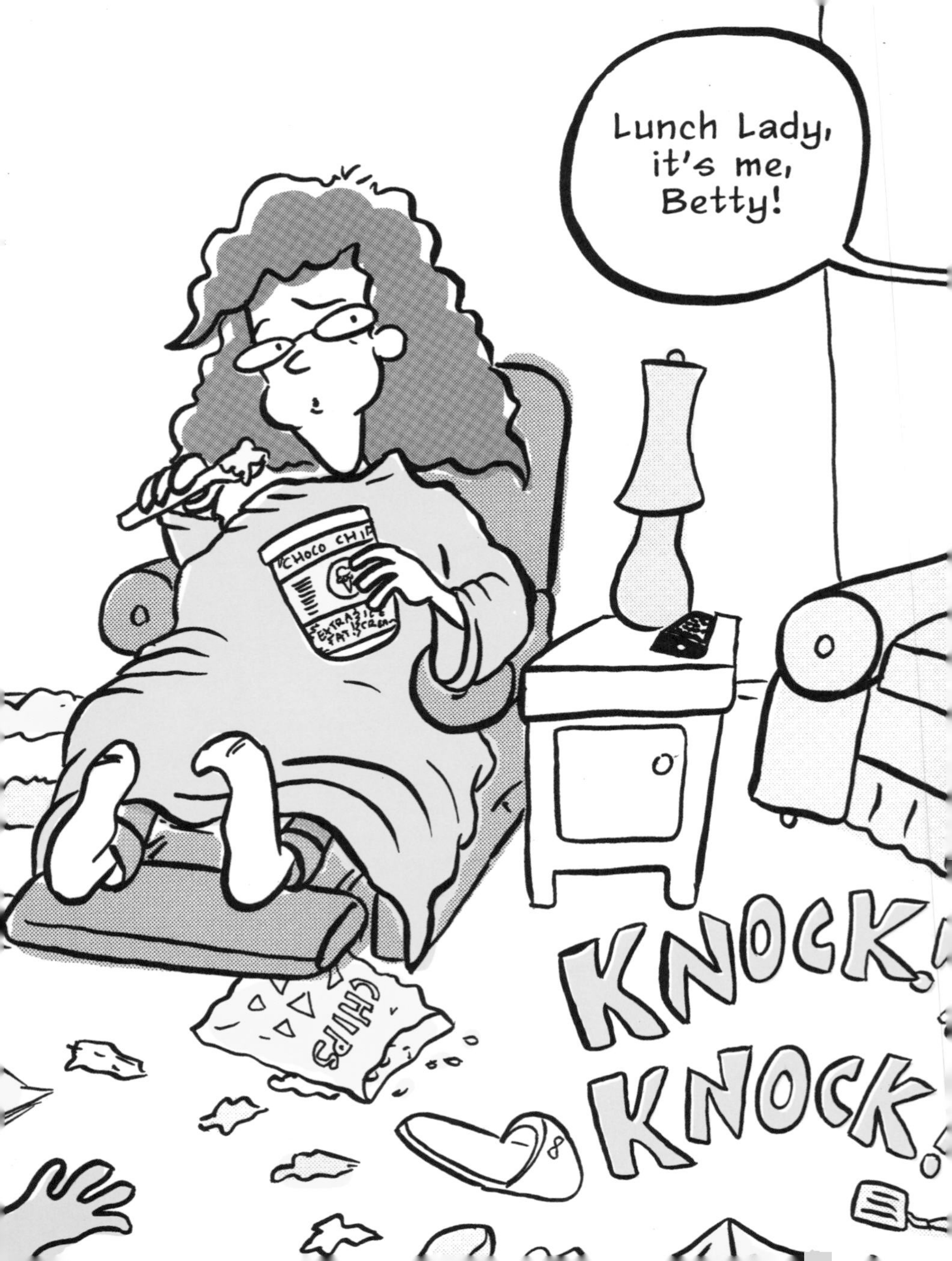

Lunch Lady, it's me, Betty!
KNOCK! KNOCK!

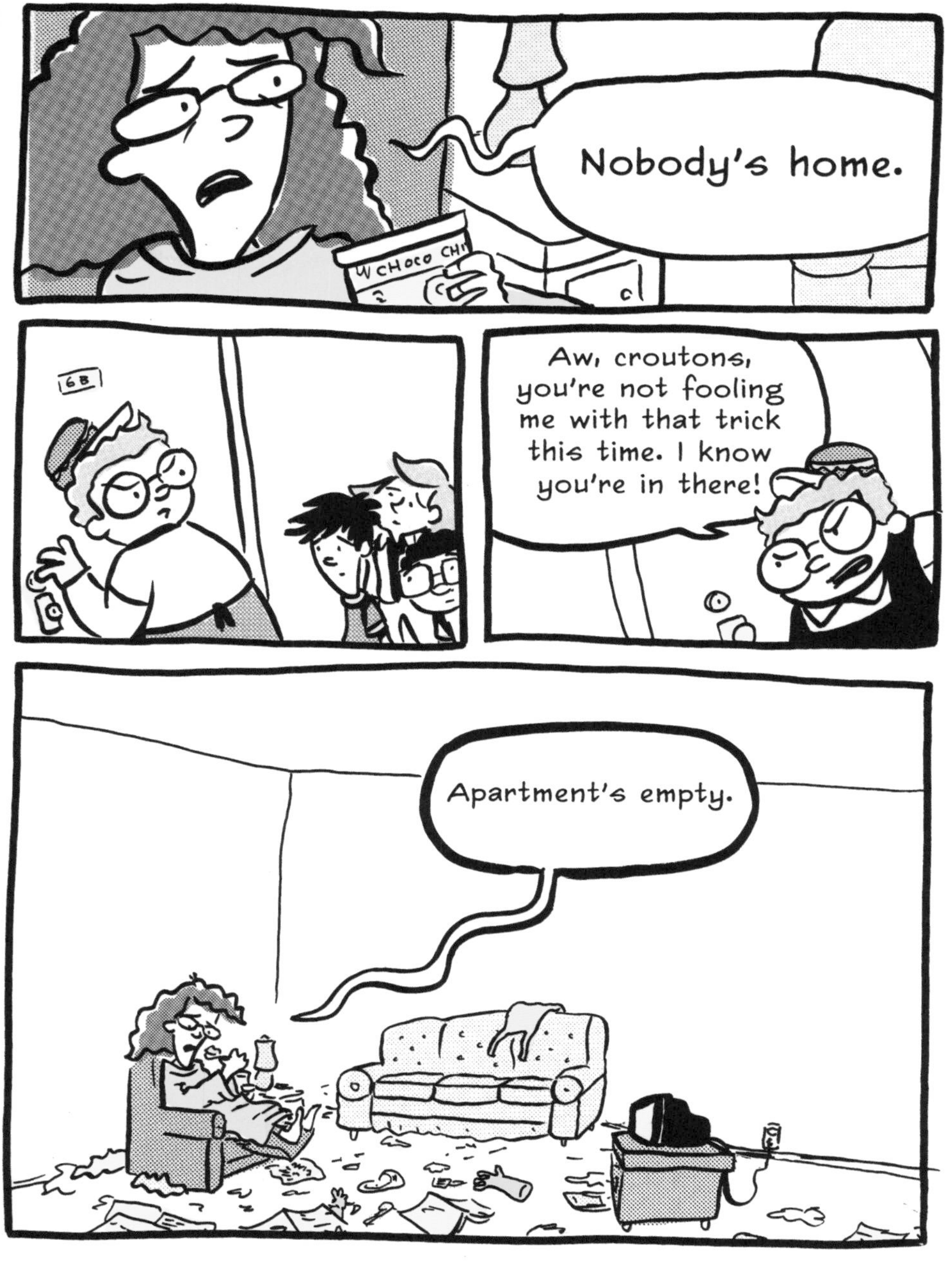
Nobody's home.
W CHOCO CH
6B
Aw, croutons, you're not fooling me with that trick this time. I know you're in there!
Apartment's empty.

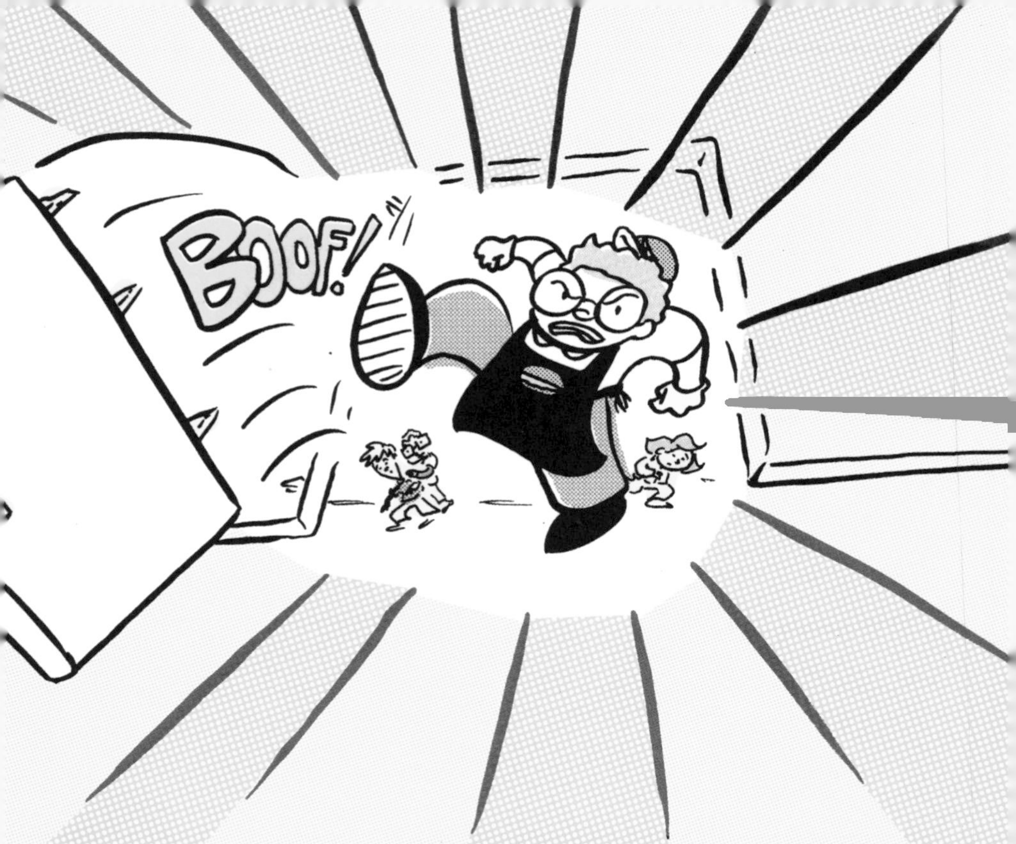
BOOF!

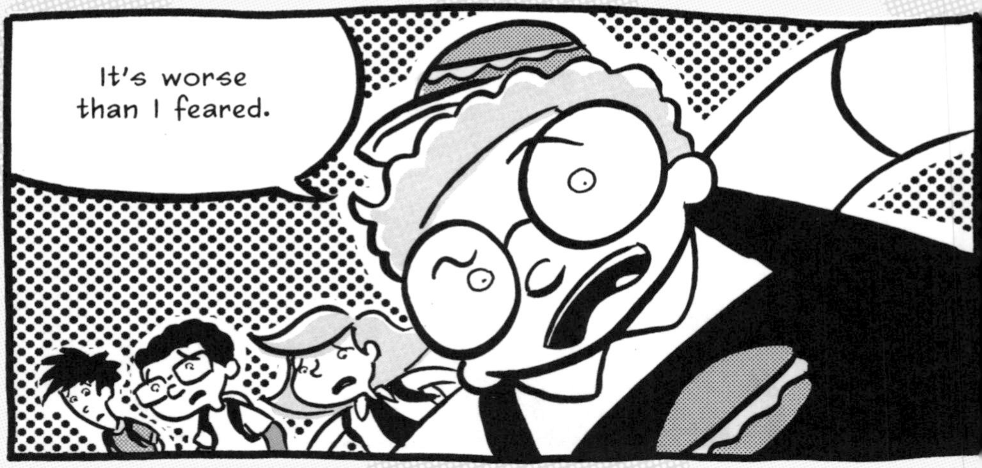
It's worse than I feared.

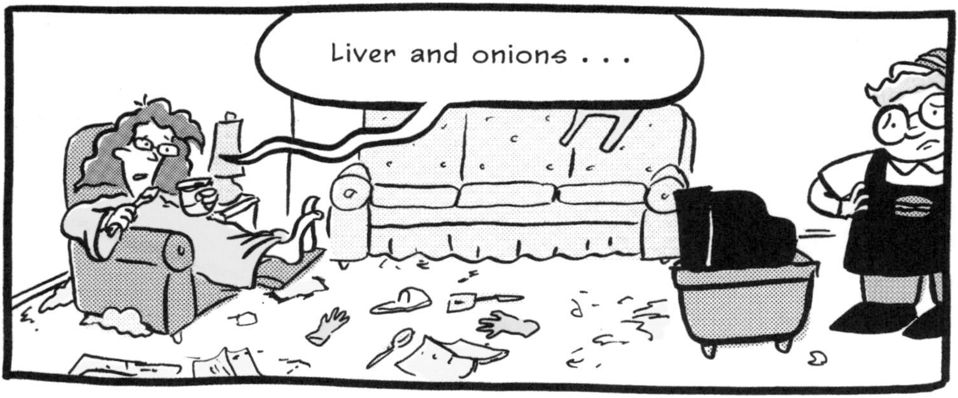
Liver and onions . . .

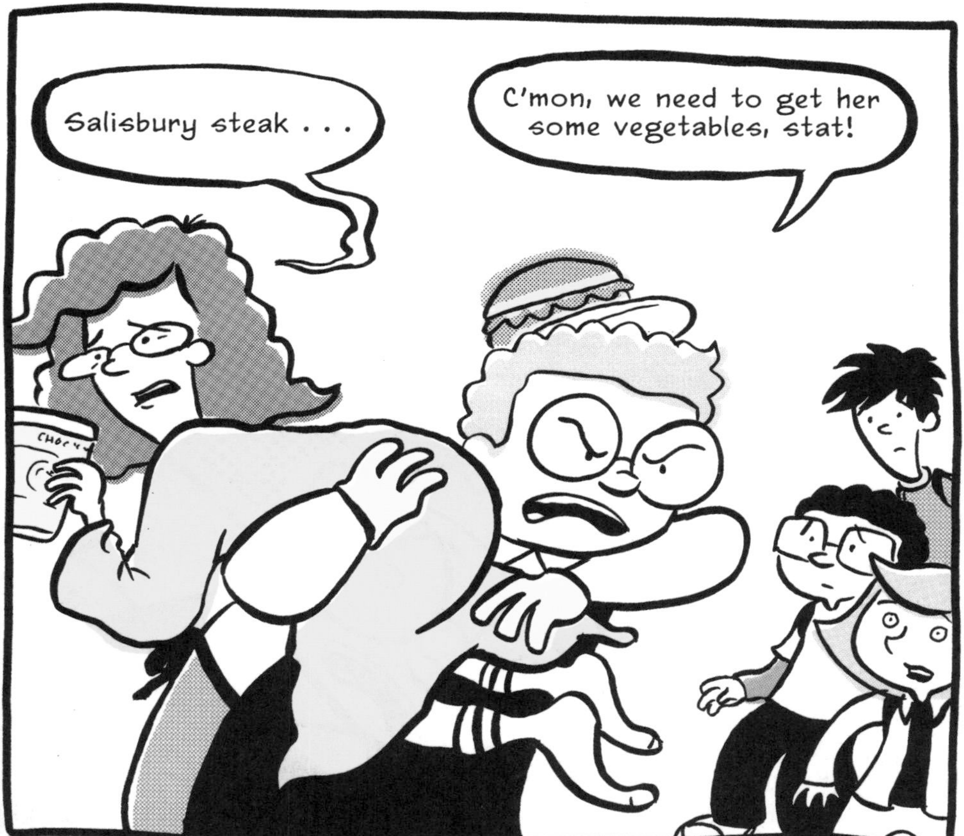
Salisbury steak . . .
C'mon, we need to get her some vegetables, stat!

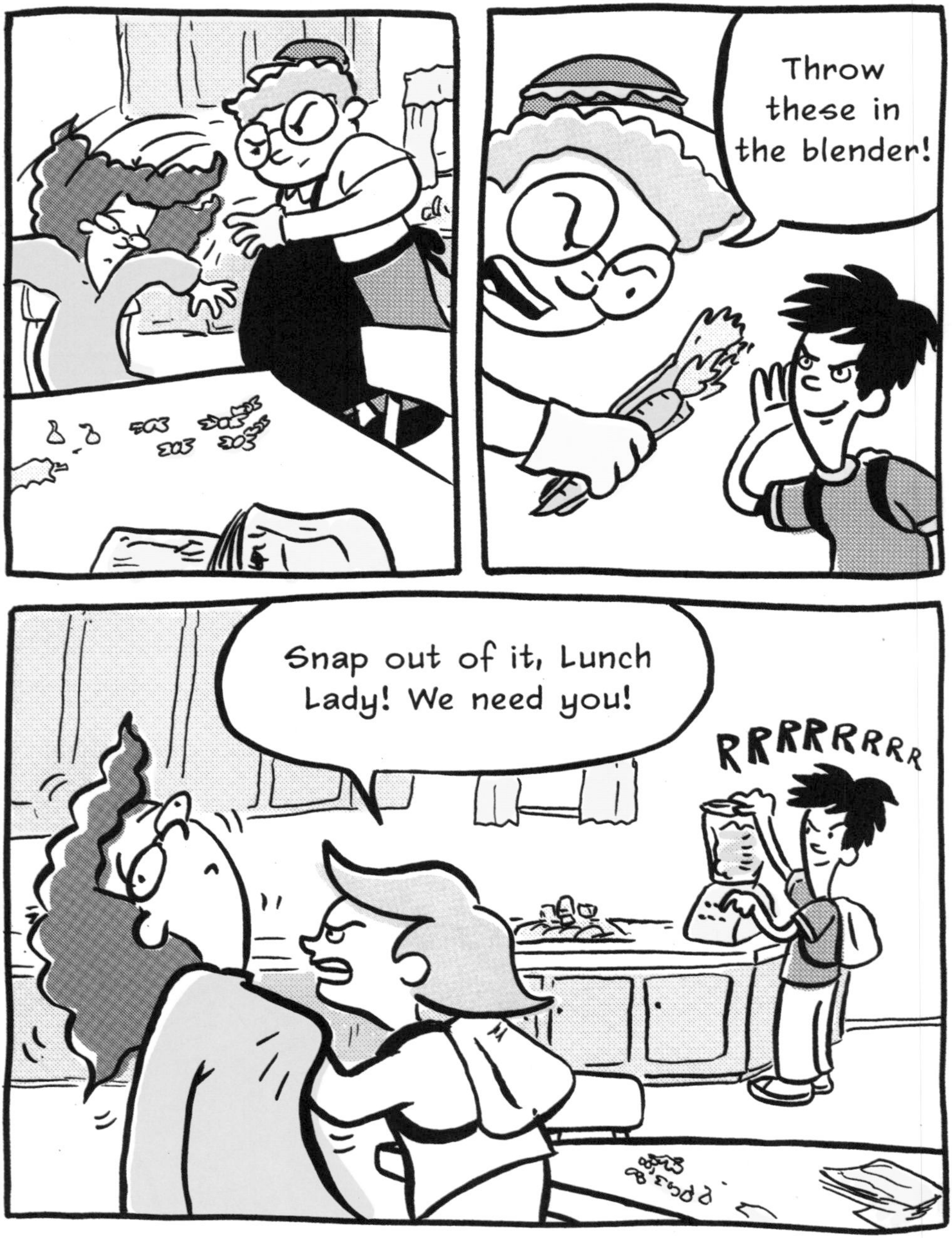
Throw these in the blender!
Snap out of it, Lunch Lady! We need you!
RRRRRRRRR

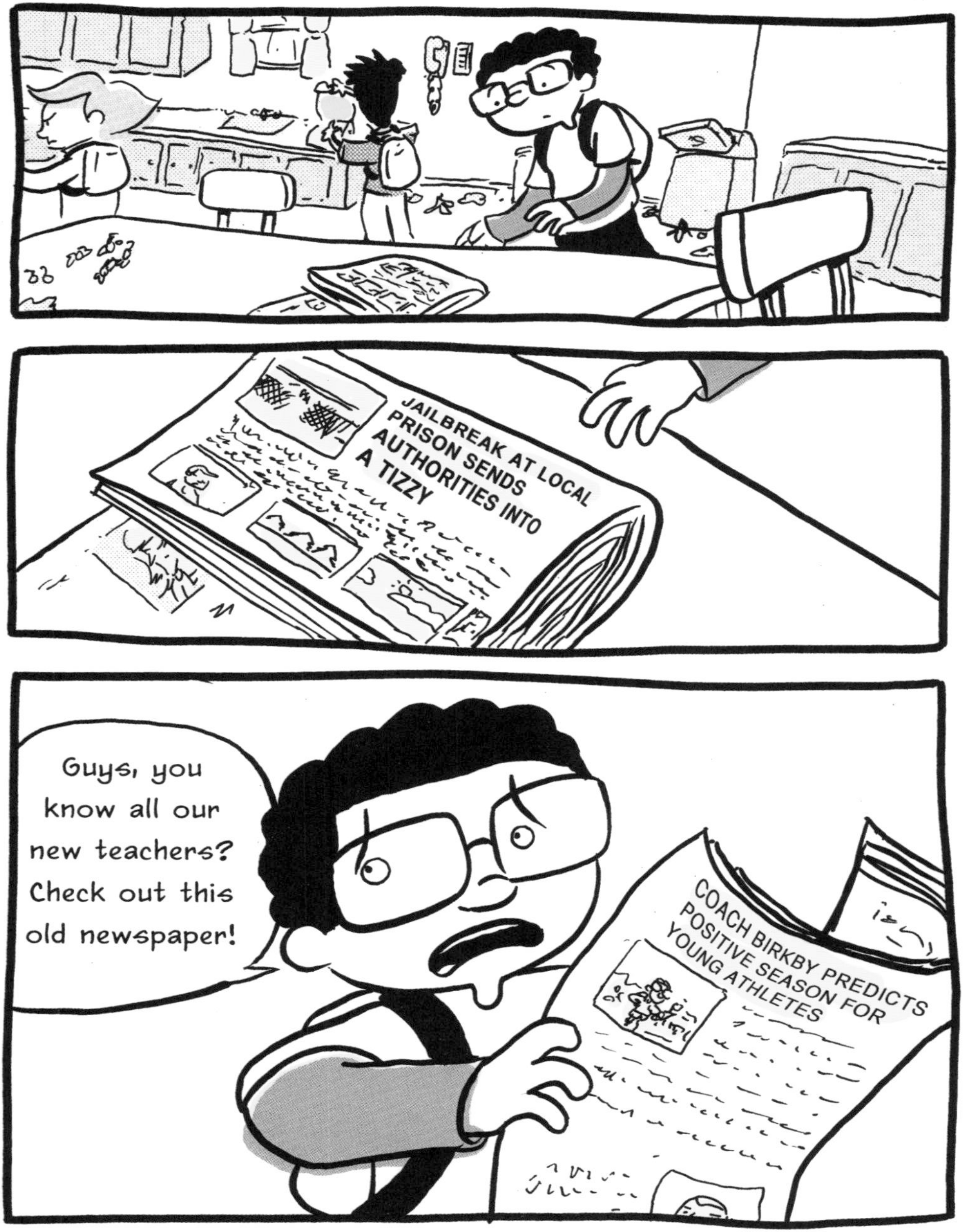
JAILBREAK AT LOCAL PRISON SENDS AUTHORITIES INTO A TIZZY
Guys, you know all our new teachers? Check out this old newspaper!
COACH BIRKBY PREDICTS POSITIVE SEASON FOR YOUNG ATHLETES

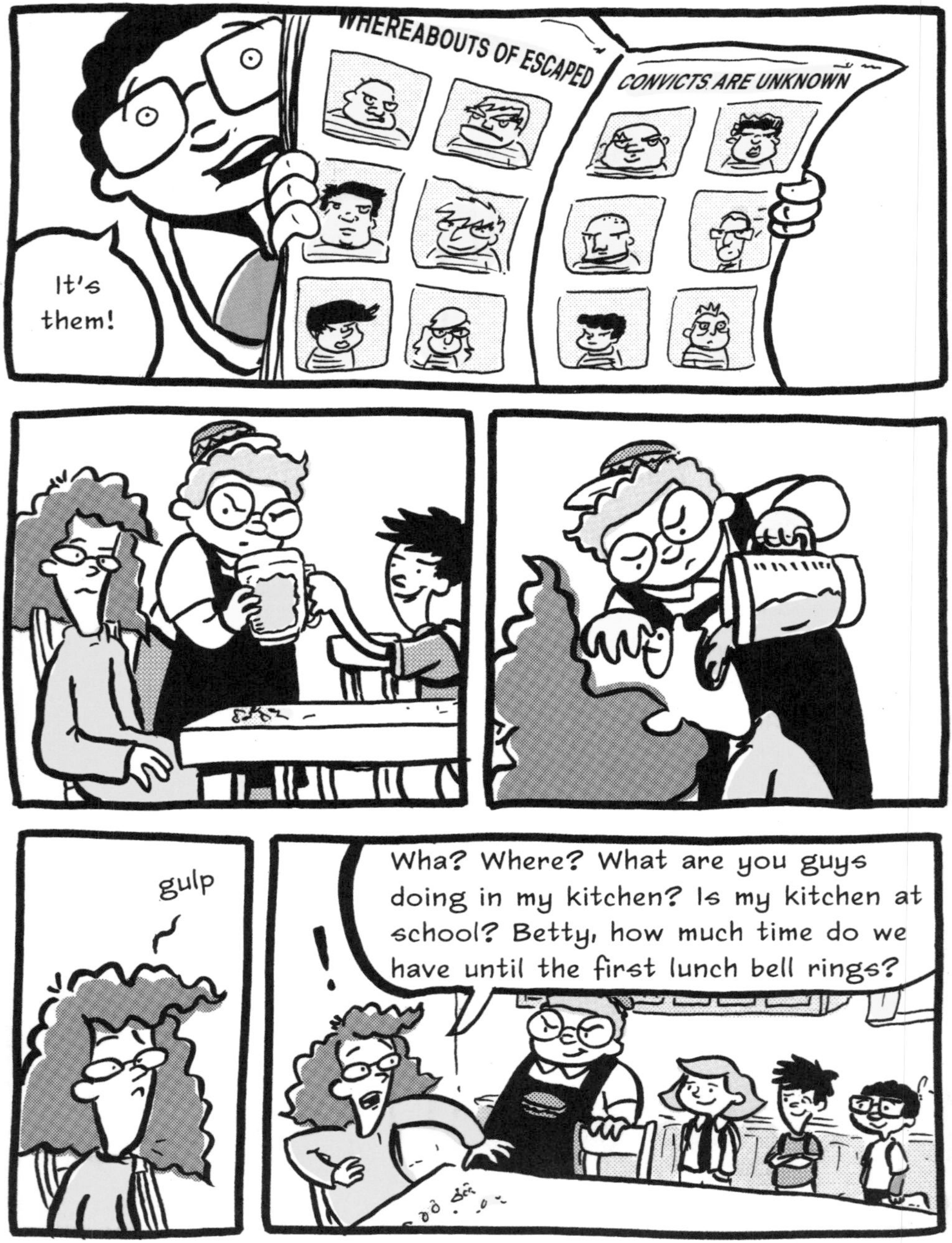
WHEREABOUTS OF ESCAPED
CONVICTS ARE UNKNOWN
It's them!
gulp
!
Wha? Where? What are you guys doing in my kitchen? Is my kitchen at school? Betty, how much time do we have until the first lunch bell rings?

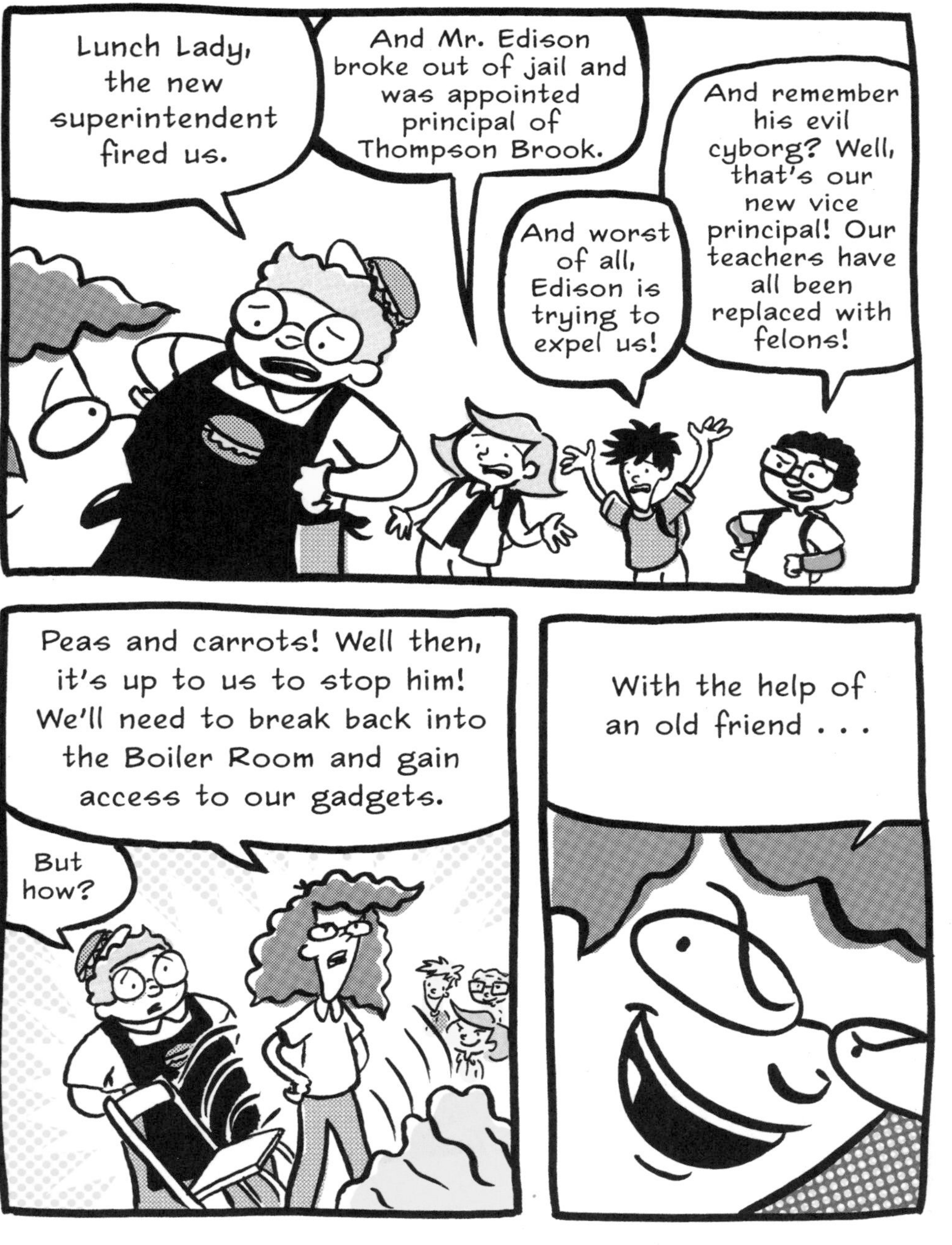
Lunch Lady, the new superintendent fired us.
And Mr. Edison broke out of jail and was appointed principal of Thompson Brook.
And worst of all, Edison is trying to expel us!
And remember his evil cyborg? Well, that's our new vice principal! Our teachers have all been replaced with felons!
Peas and carrots! Well then, it's up to us to stop him! We'll need to break back into the Boiler Room and gain access to our gadgets.
But how?
With the help of an old friend . . .

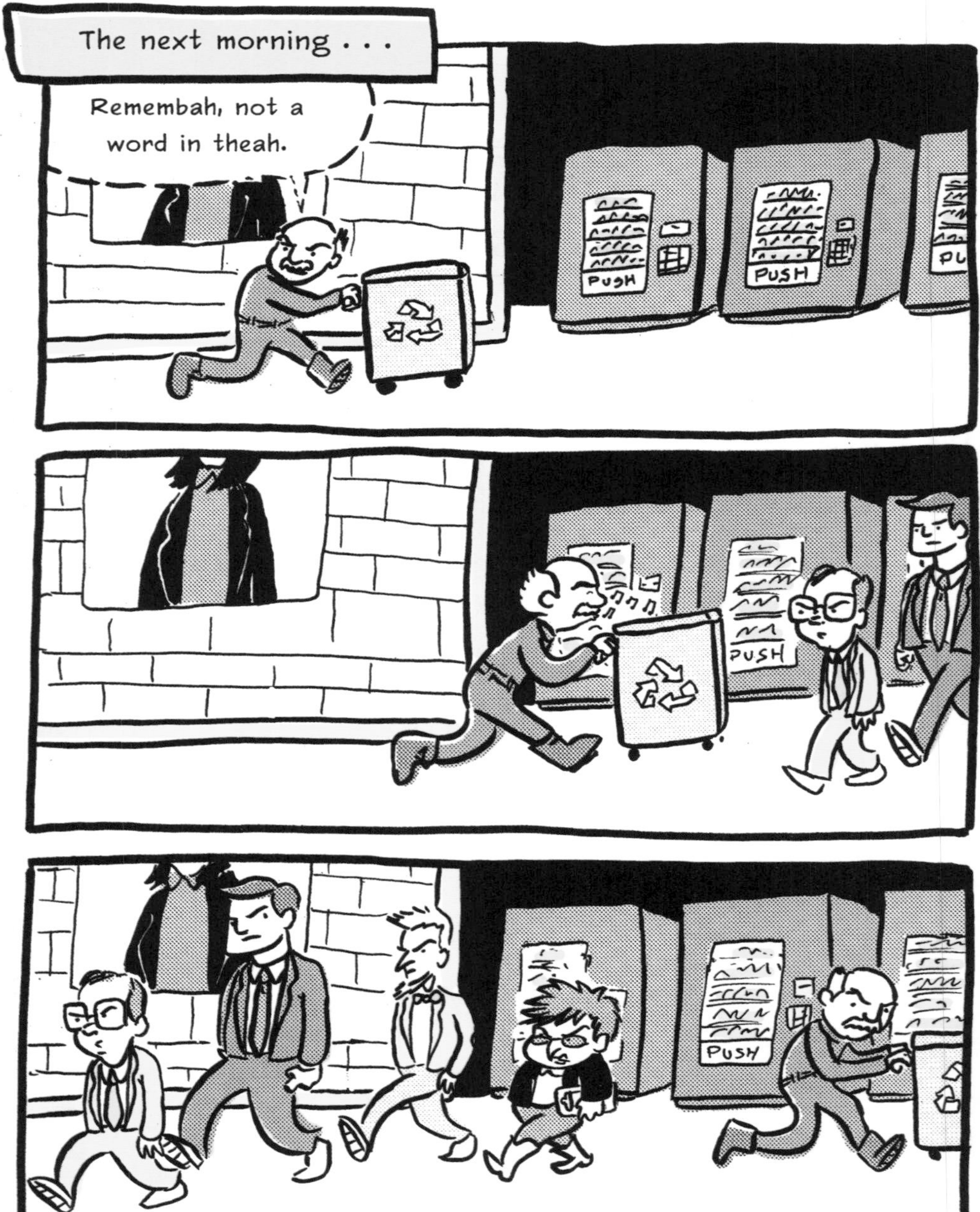
The next morning . . .
Remembah, not a word in theah.
PUSH
PUSH
PUSH
PUSH

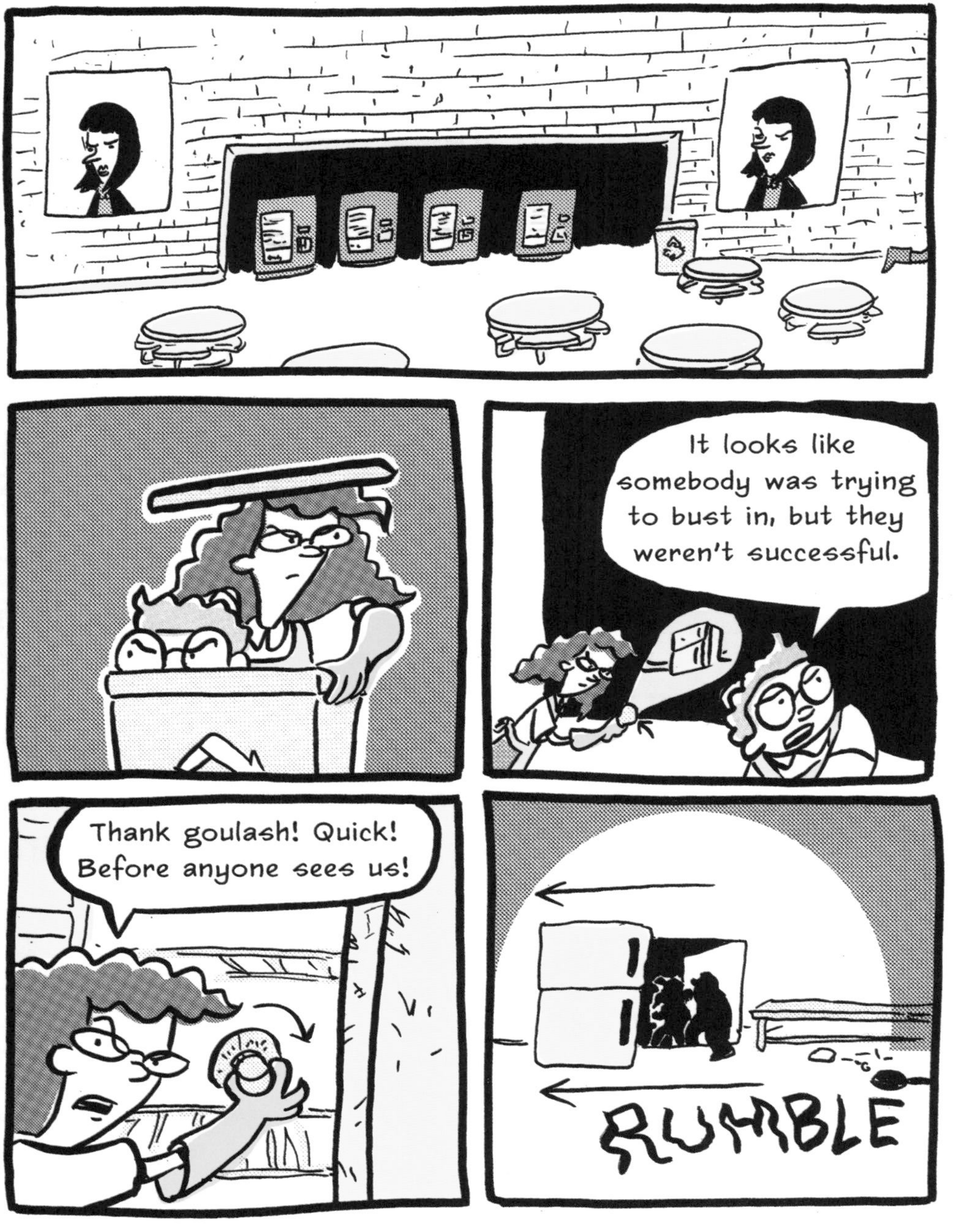
It looks like somebody was trying to bust in, but they weren't successful.
Thank goulash! Quick! Before anyone sees us!
RUMBLE

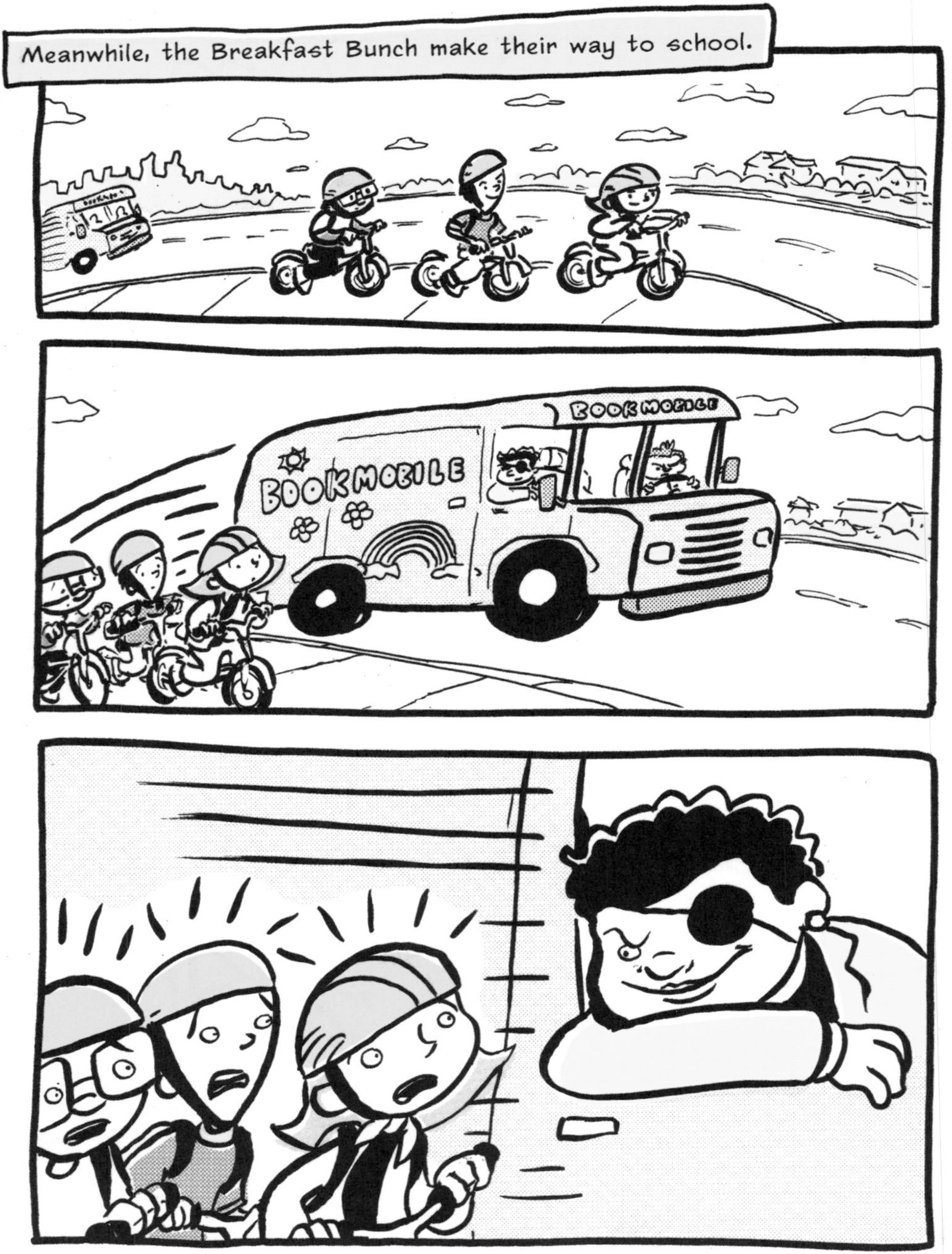
Meanwhile, the Breakfast Bunch make their way to school.
BOOKMOBILE
BOOKMOBILE

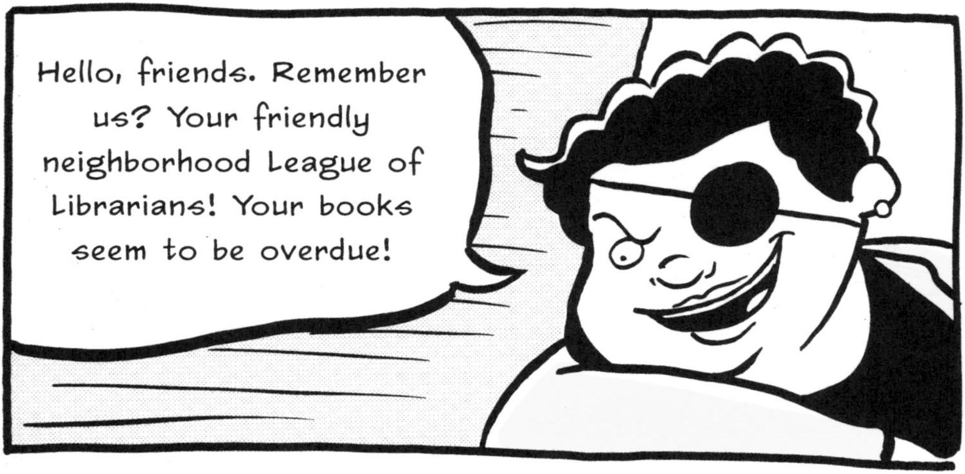
Hello, friends. Remember us? Your friendly neighborhood League of Librarians! Your books seem to be overdue!

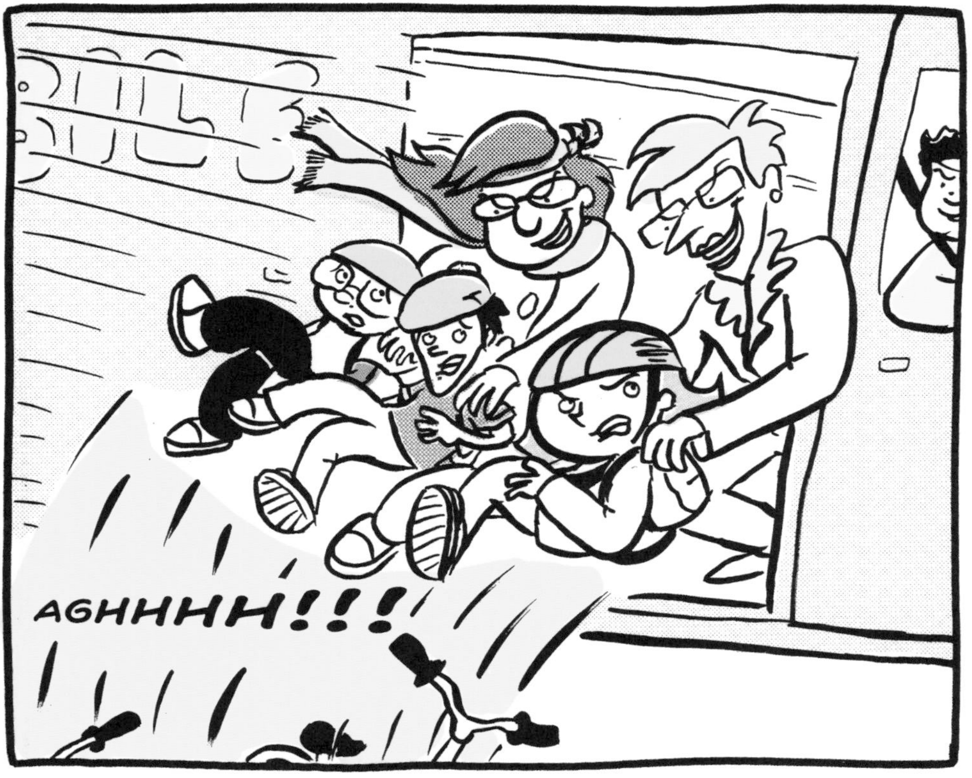
AGHHHH!!!!

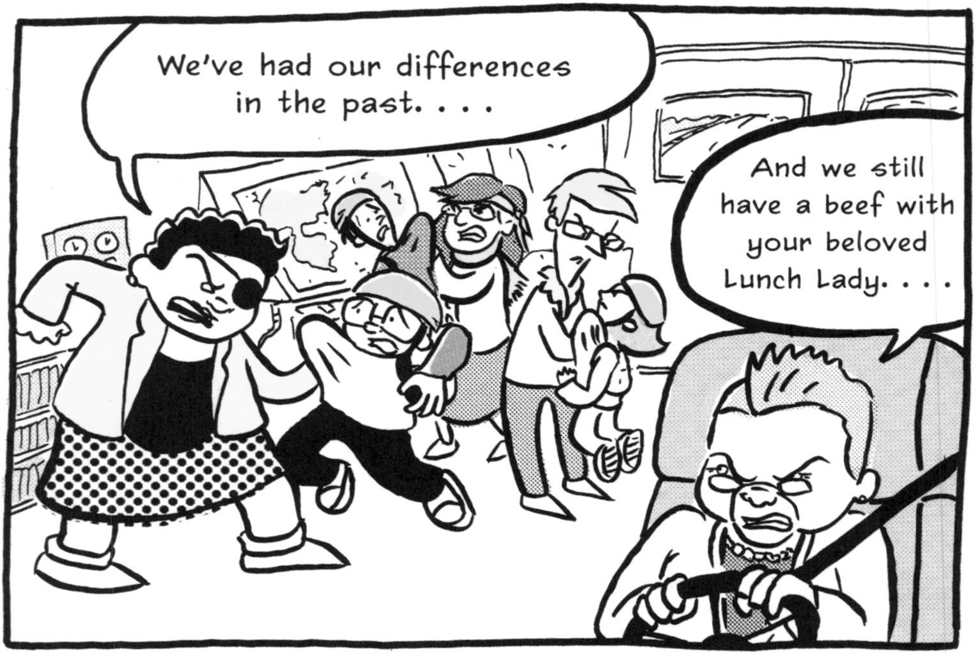
We've had our differences in the past. . . .
And we still have a beef with your beloved Lunch Lady. . . .

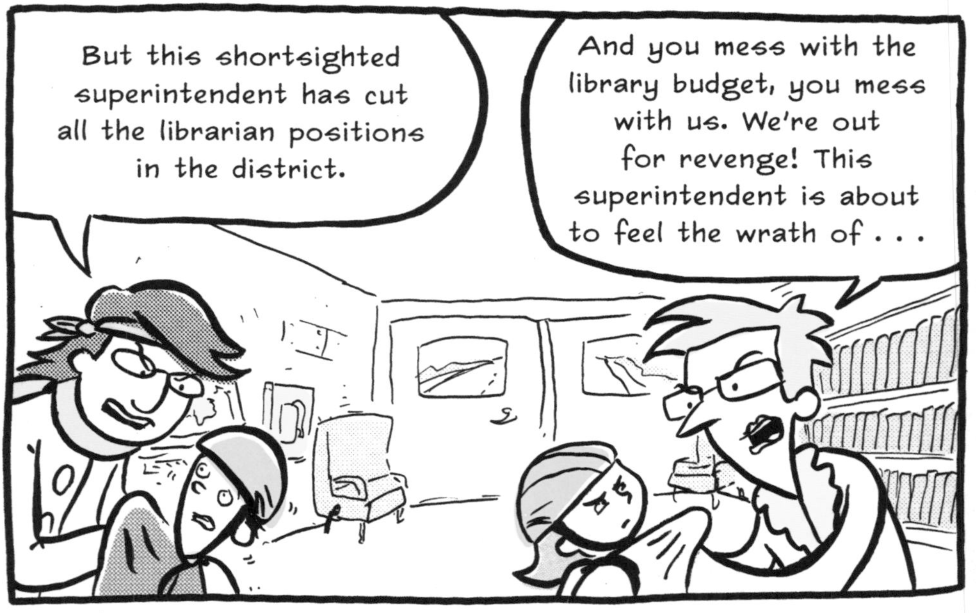
But this shortsighted superintendent has cut all the librarian positions in the district.
And you mess with the library budget, you mess with us. We're out for revenge! This superintendent is about to feel the wrath of . . .

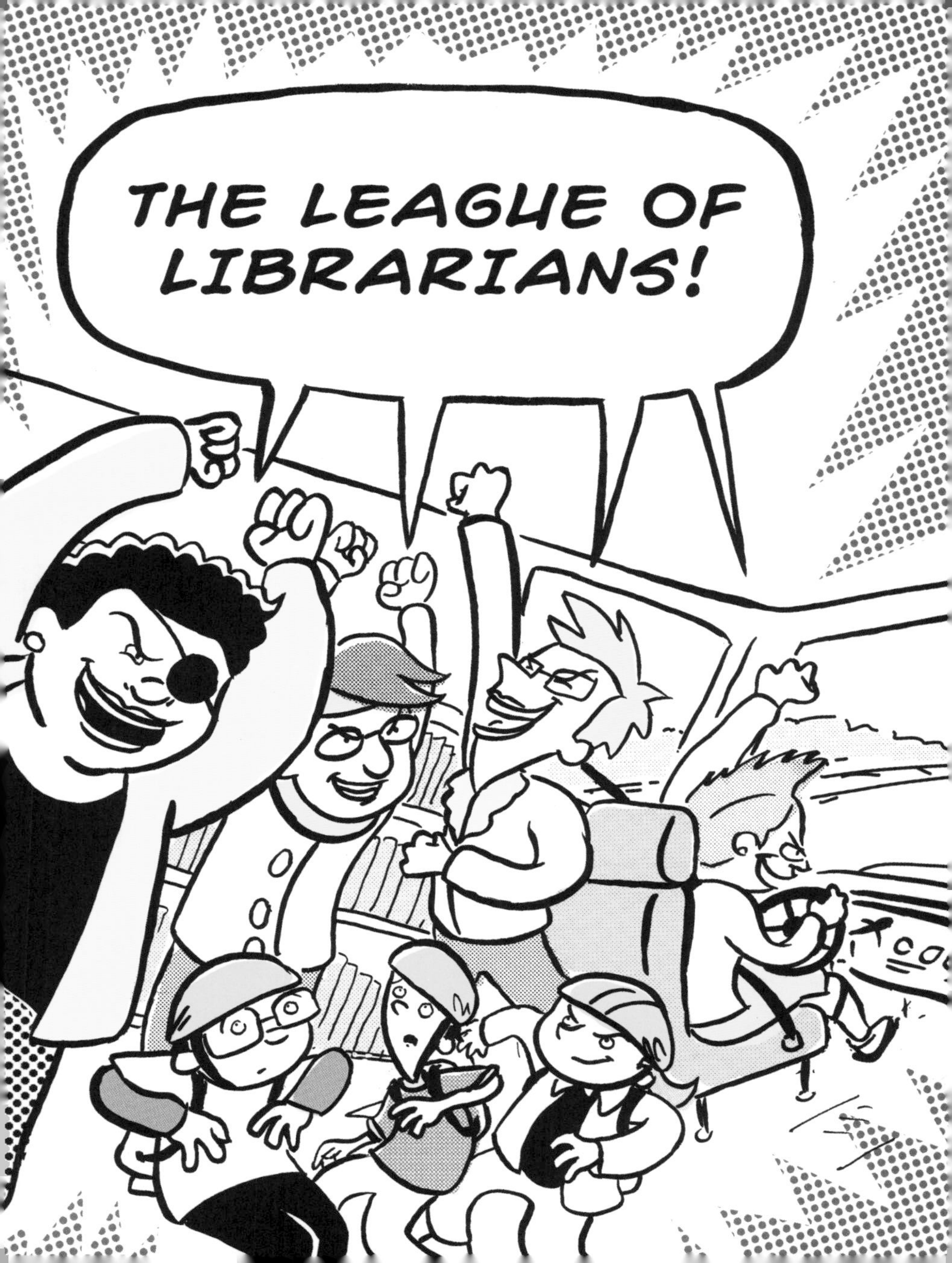
THE LEAGUE OF LIBRARIANS!

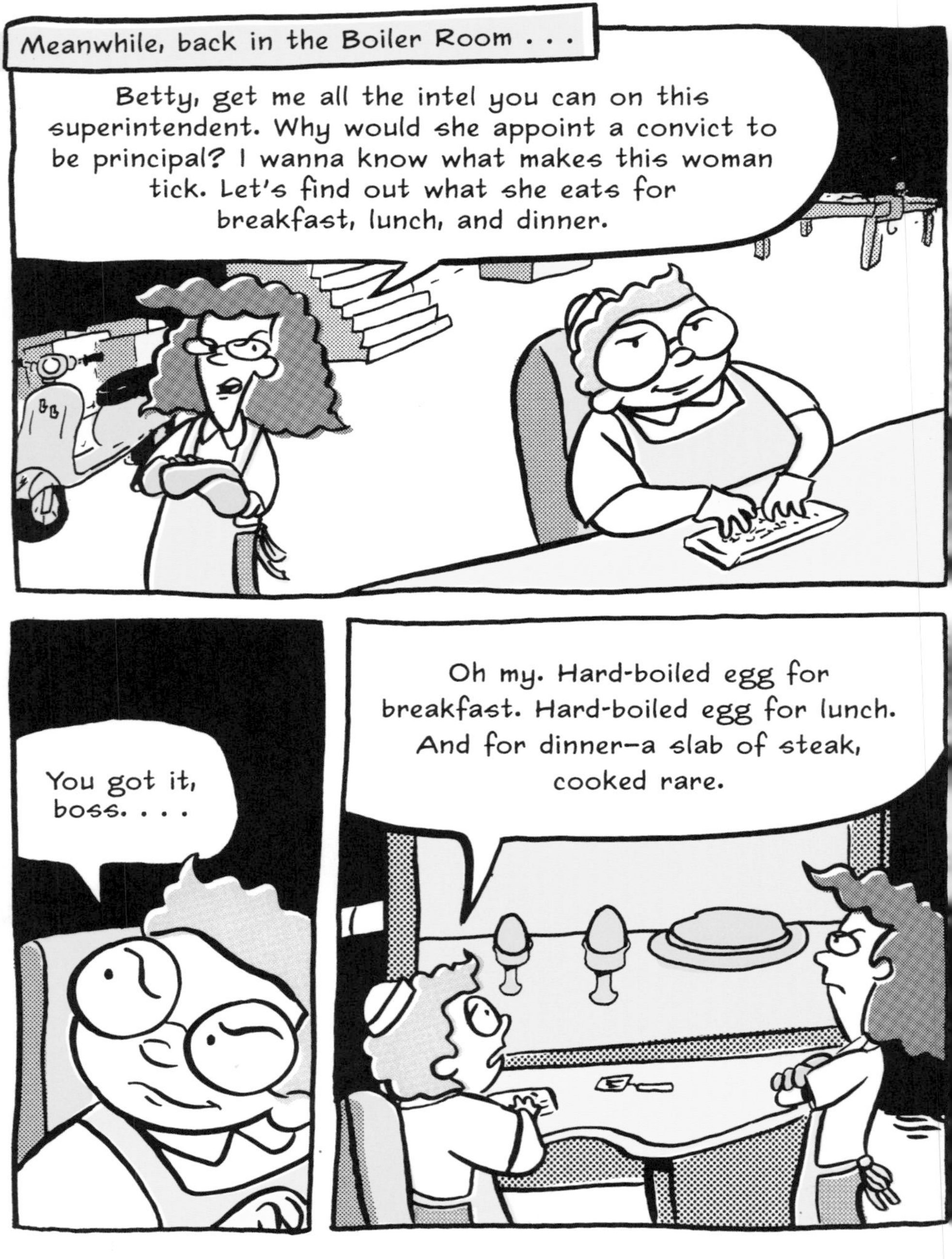
Meanwhile, back in the Boiler Room . . .
Betty, get me all the intel you can on this superintendent. Why would she appoint a convict to be principal? I wanna know what makes this woman tick. Let's find out what she eats for breakfast, lunch, and dinner.
You got it, boss. . . .
Oh my. Hard-boiled egg for breakfast. Hard-boiled egg for lunch. And for dinner—a slab of steak, cooked rare.

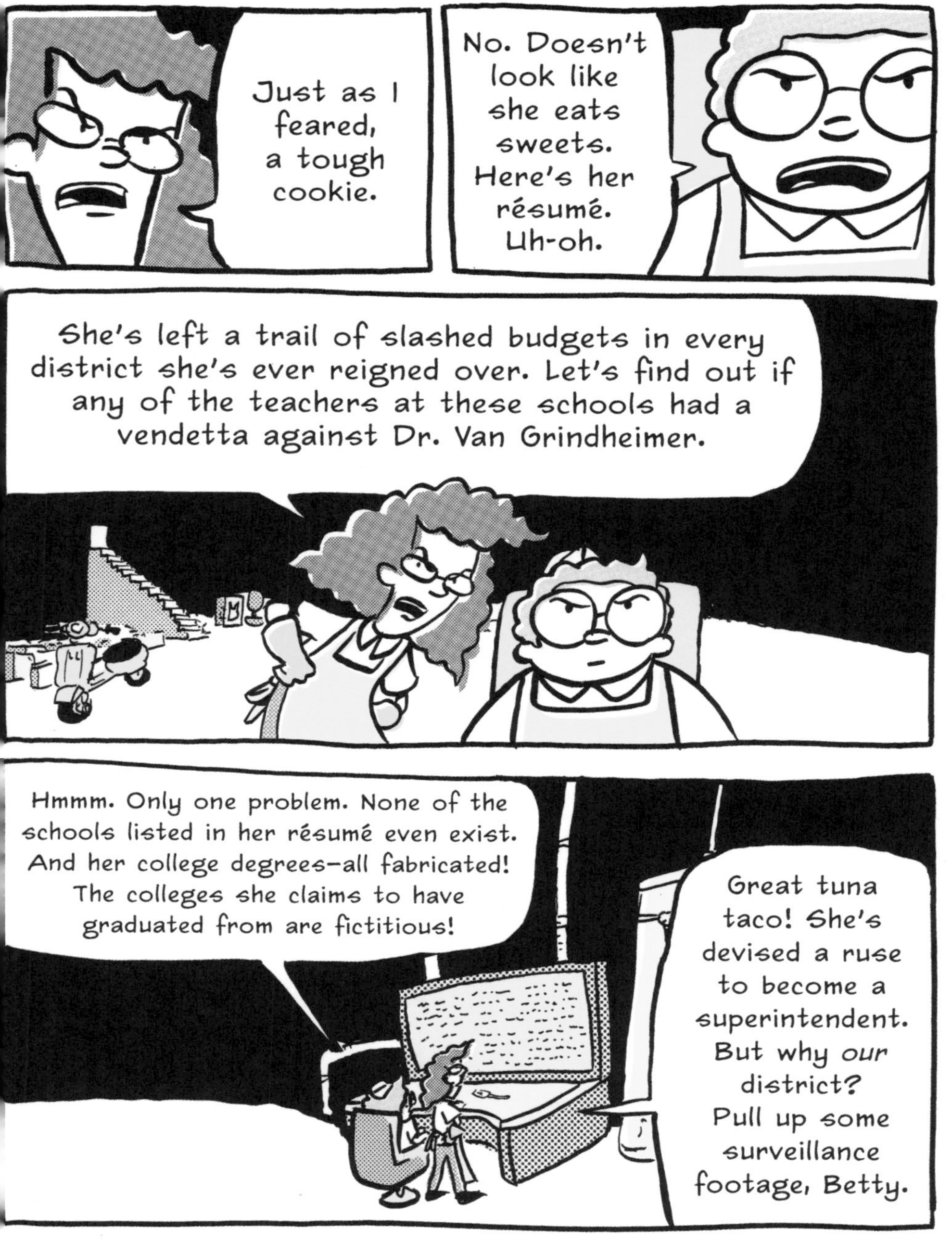

Just as I feared, a tough cookie.
No. Doesn't look like she eats sweets. Here's her résumé. Uh-oh.
She's left a trail of slashed budgets in every district she's ever reigned over. Let's find out if any of the teachers at these schools had a vendetta against Dr. Van Grindheimer.
Hmmm. Only one problem. None of the schools listed in her résumé even exist. And her college degrees—all fabricated! The colleges she claims to have graduated from are fictitious!
Great tuna taco! She's devised a ruse to become a superintendent. But why *our* district? Pull up some surveillance footage, Betty.

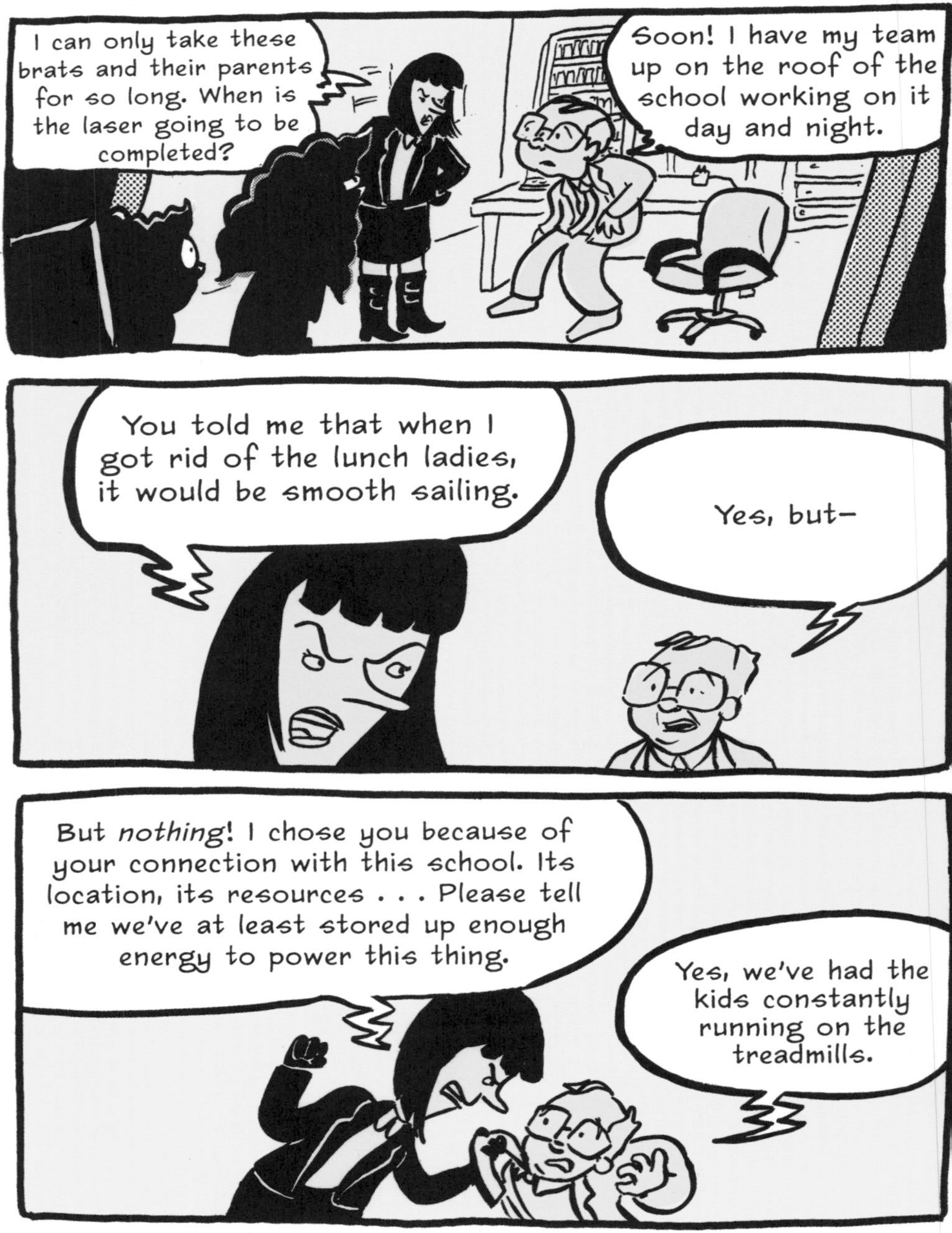
I can only take these brats and their parents for so long. When is the laser going to be completed?
Soon! I have my team up on the roof of the school working on it day and night.
You told me that when I got rid of the lunch ladies, it would be smooth sailing.
Yes, but–
But *nothing*! I chose you because of your connection with this school. Its location, its resources . . . Please tell me we've at least stored up enough energy to power this thing.
Yes, we've had the kids constantly running on the treadmills.

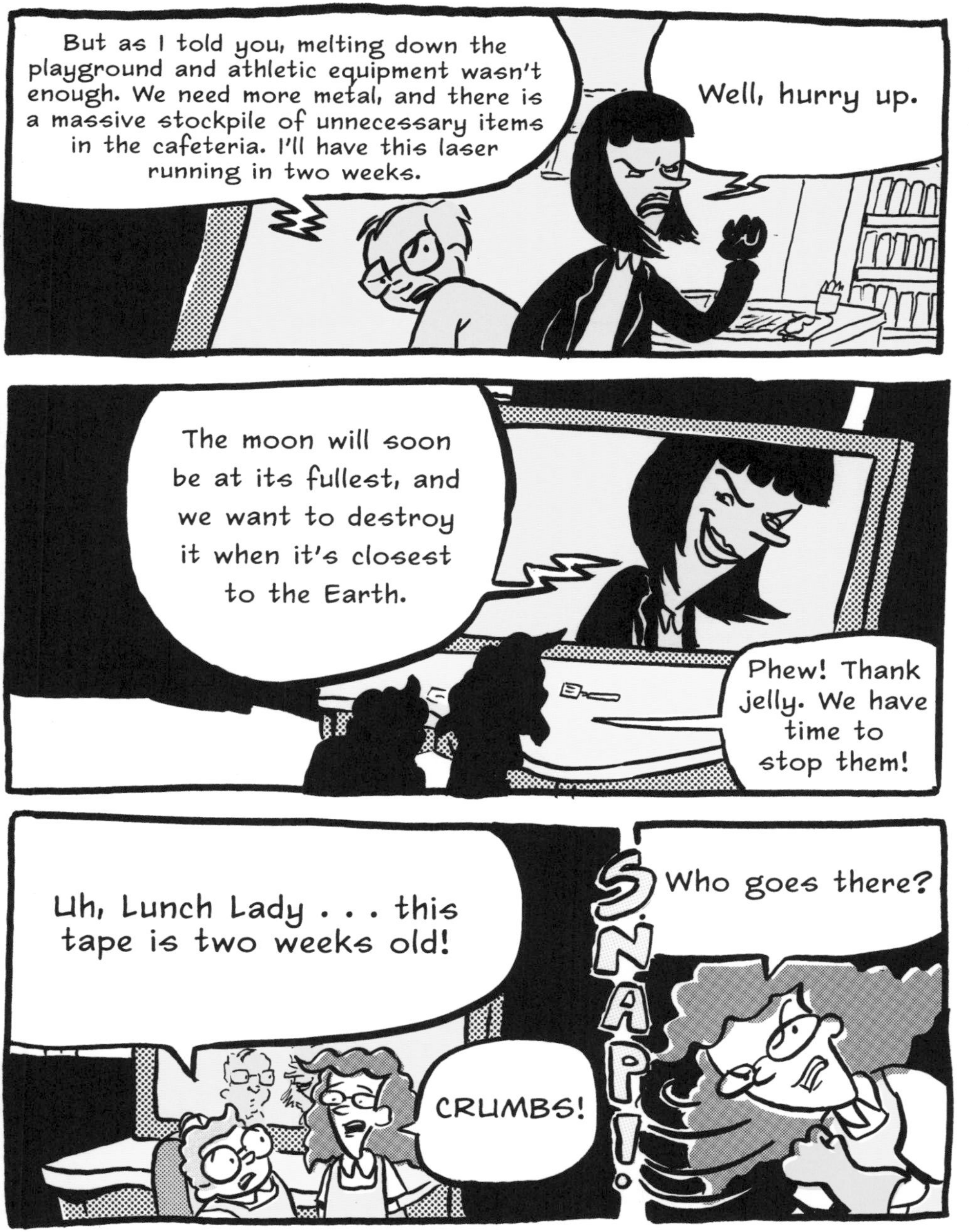
But as I told you, melting down the playground and athletic equipment wasn't enough. We need more metal, and there is a massive stockpile of unnecessary items in the cafeteria. I'll have this laser running in two weeks.
Well, hurry up.
The moon will soon be at its fullest, and we want to destroy it when it's closest to the Earth.
Phew! Thank jelly. We have time to stop them!
Uh, Lunch Lady . . . this tape is two weeks old!
CRUMBS!
SNAP!
Who goes there?

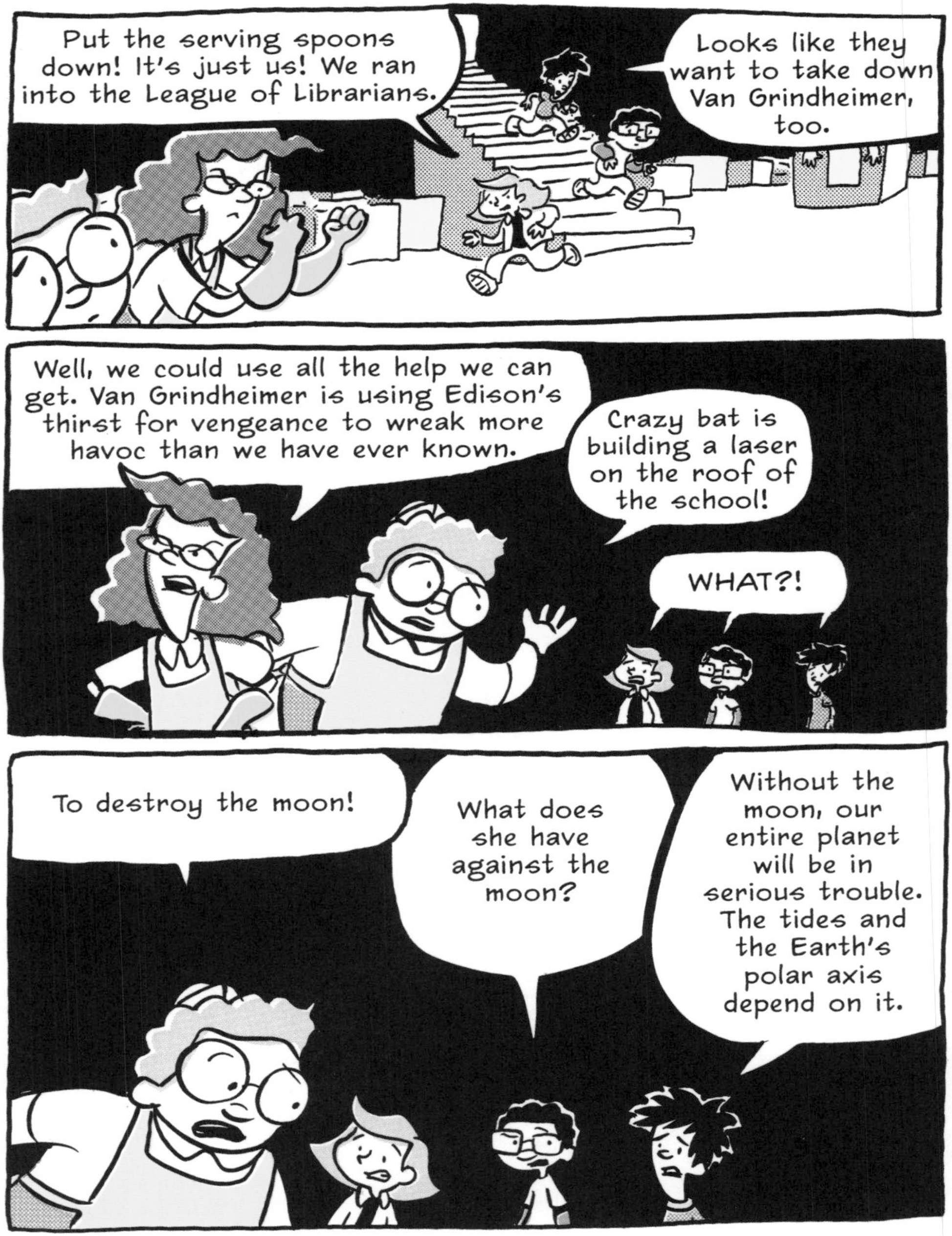
Put the serving spoons down! It's just us! We ran into the League of Librarians.
Looks like they want to take down Van Grindheimer, too.
Well, we could use all the help we can get. Van Grindheimer is using Edison's thirst for vengeance to wreak more havoc than we have ever known.
Crazy bat is building a laser on the roof of the school!
WHAT?!
To destroy the moon!
What does she have against the moon?
Without the moon, our entire planet will be in serious trouble. The tides and the Earth's polar axis depend on it.

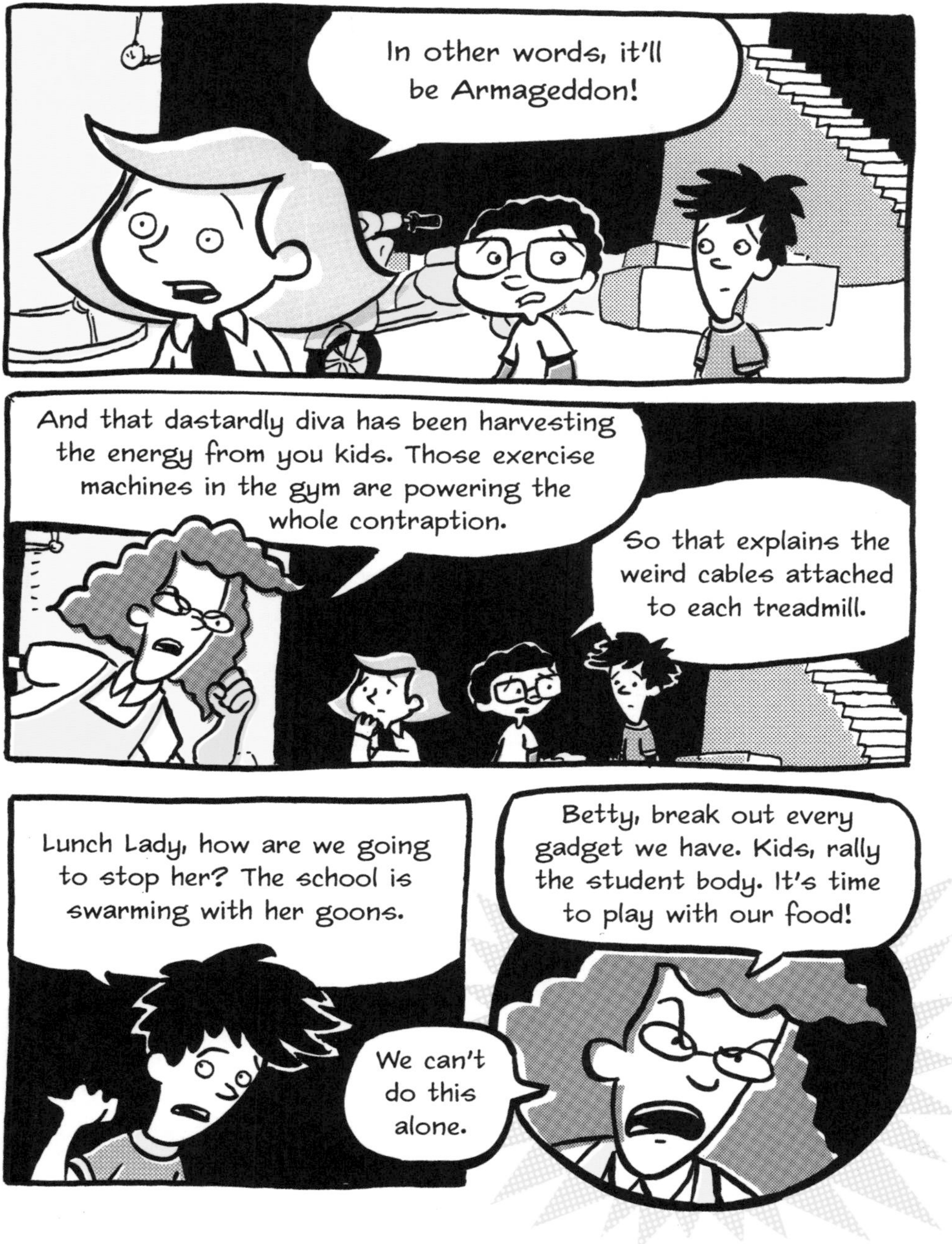
In other words, it'll be Armageddon!
And that dastardly diva has been harvesting the energy from you kids. Those exercise machines in the gym are powering the whole contraption.
So that explains the weird cables attached to each treadmill.
Lunch Lady, how are we going to stop her? The school is swarming with her goons.
We can't do this alone.
Betty, break out every gadget we have. Kids, rally the student body. It's time to play with our food!

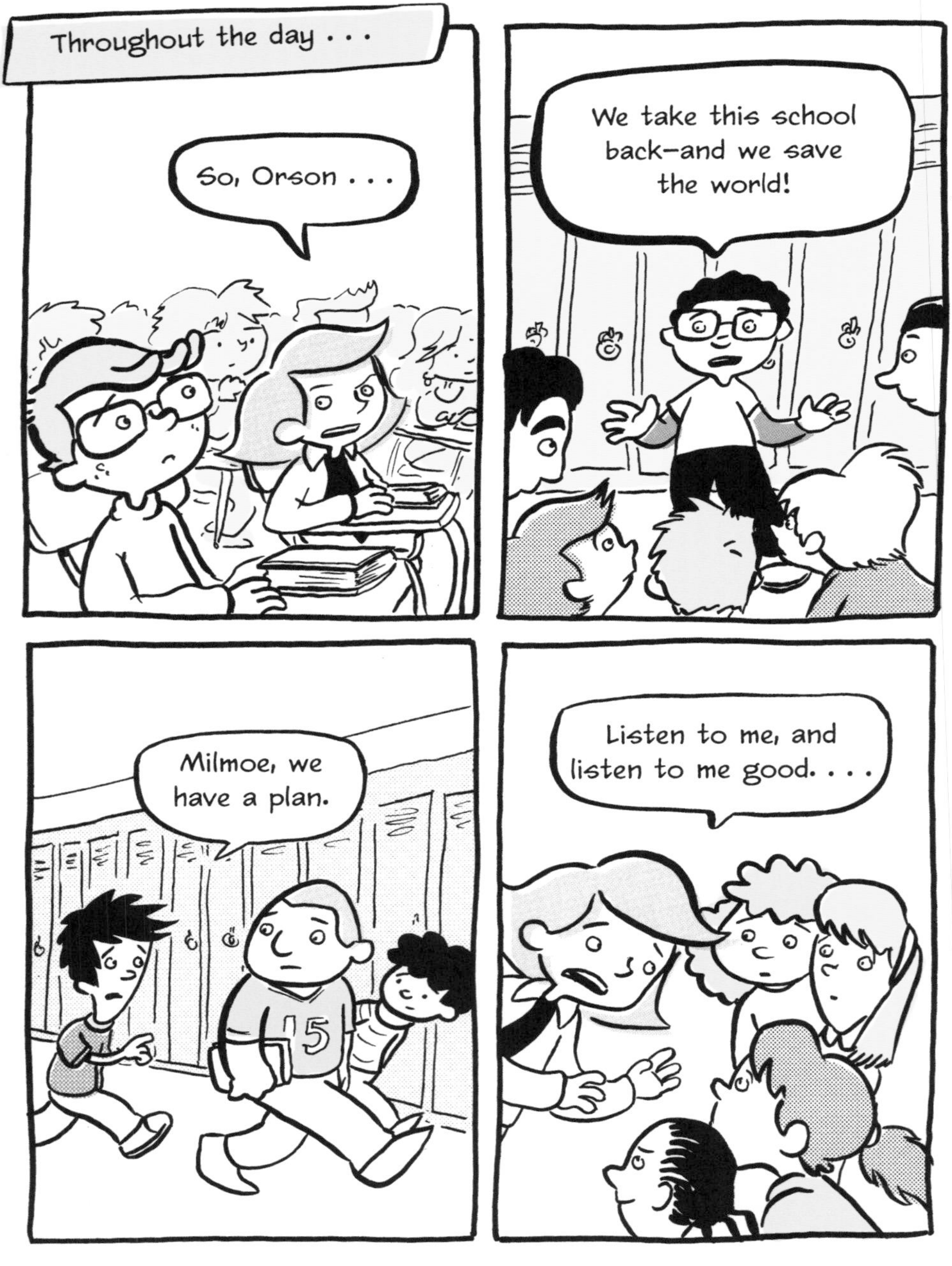
Throughout the day . . .
So, Orson . . .
We take this school back—and we save the world!
Milmoe, we have a plan.
15
Listen to me, and listen to me good. . . .

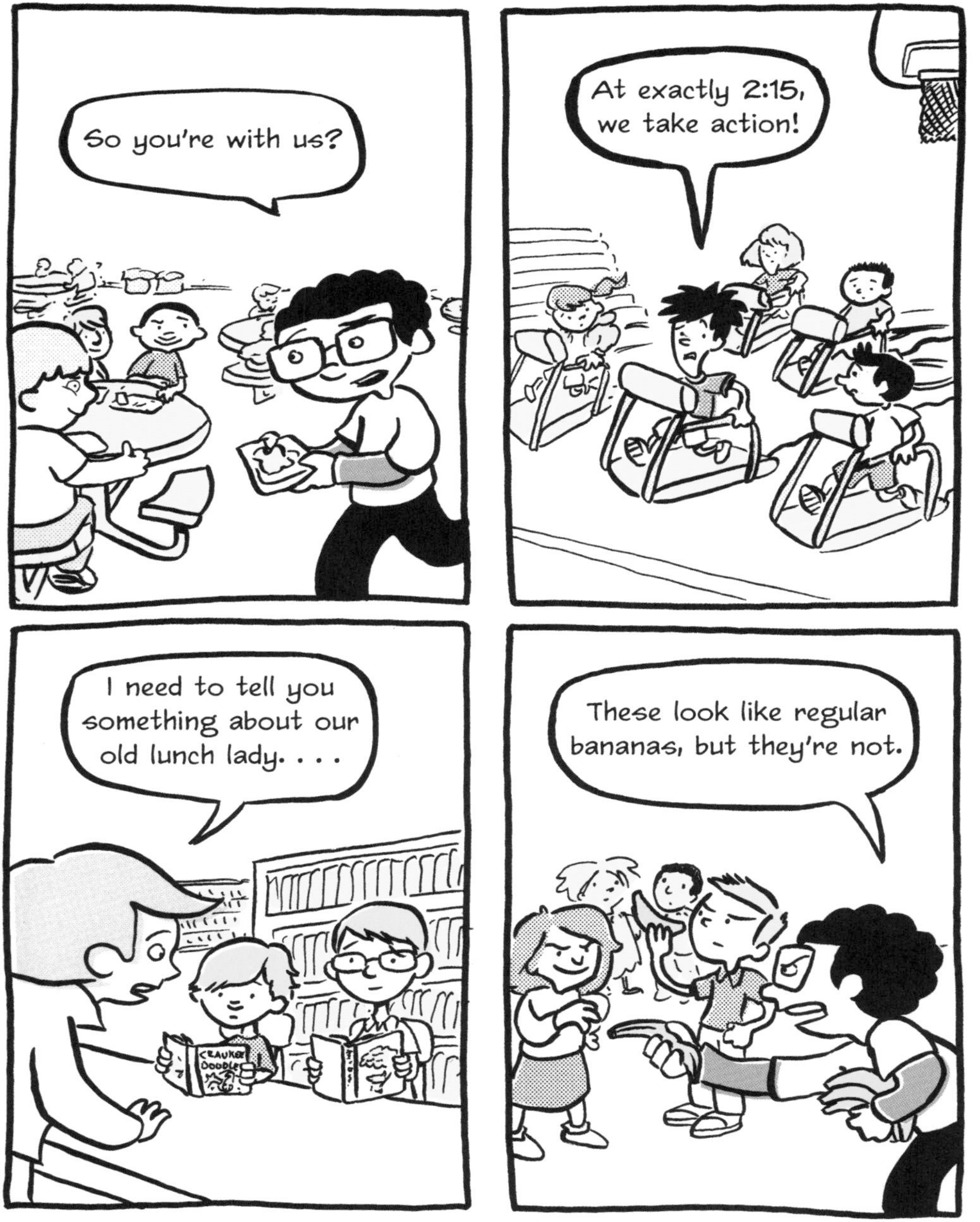
So you're with us?
At exactly 2:15, we take action!
I need to tell you something about our old lunch lady. . . .
These look like regular bananas, but they're not.

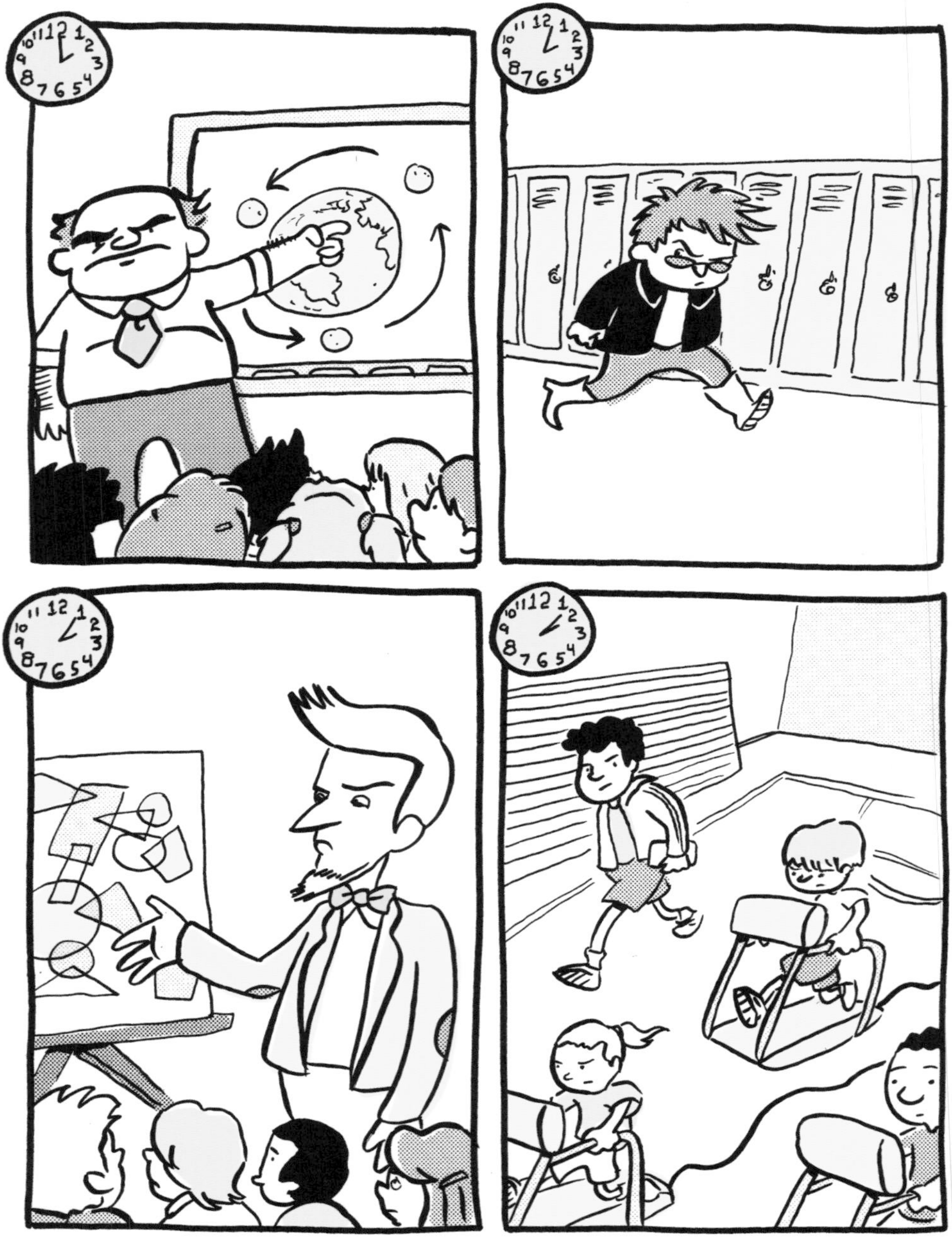

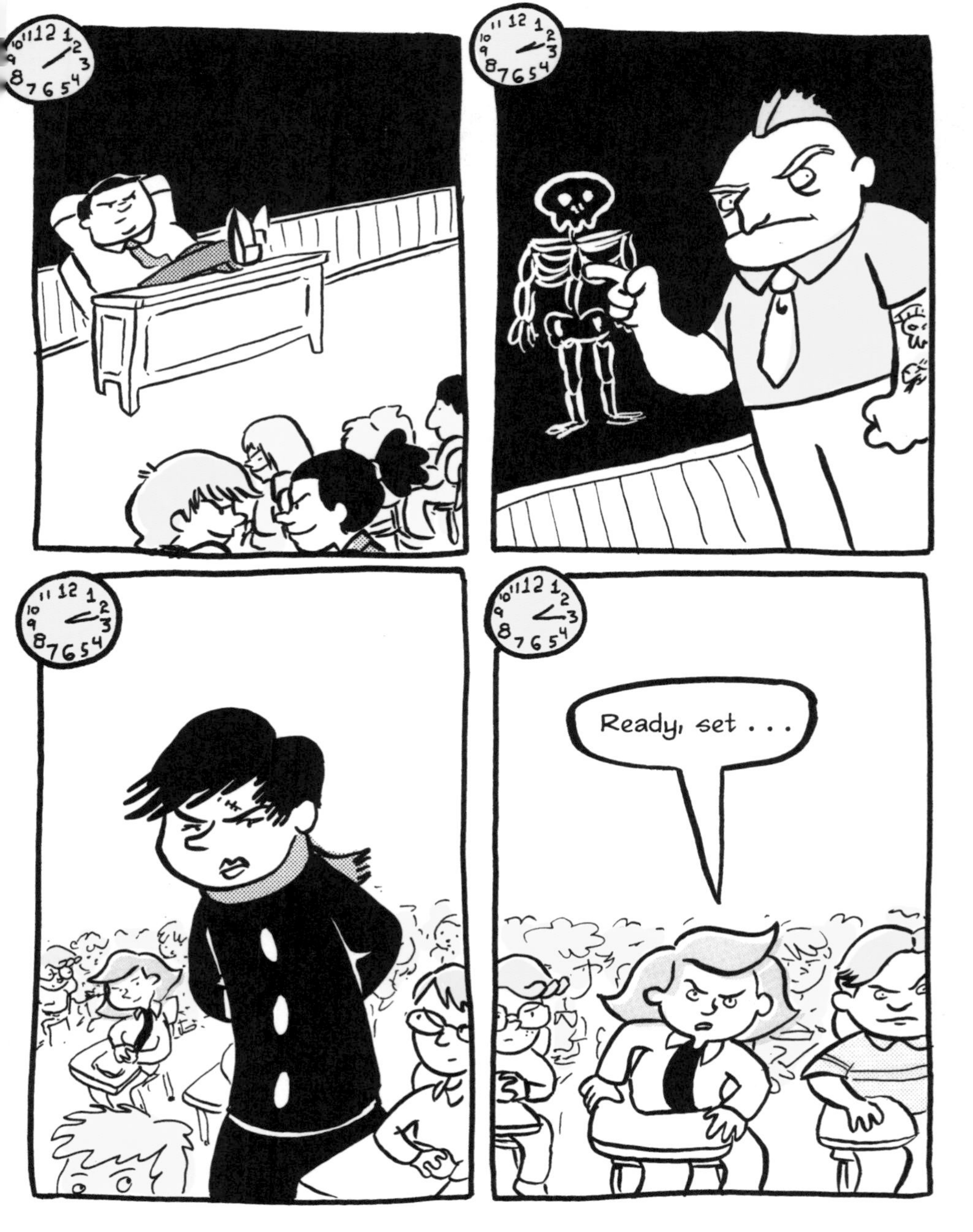
Ready, set . . .

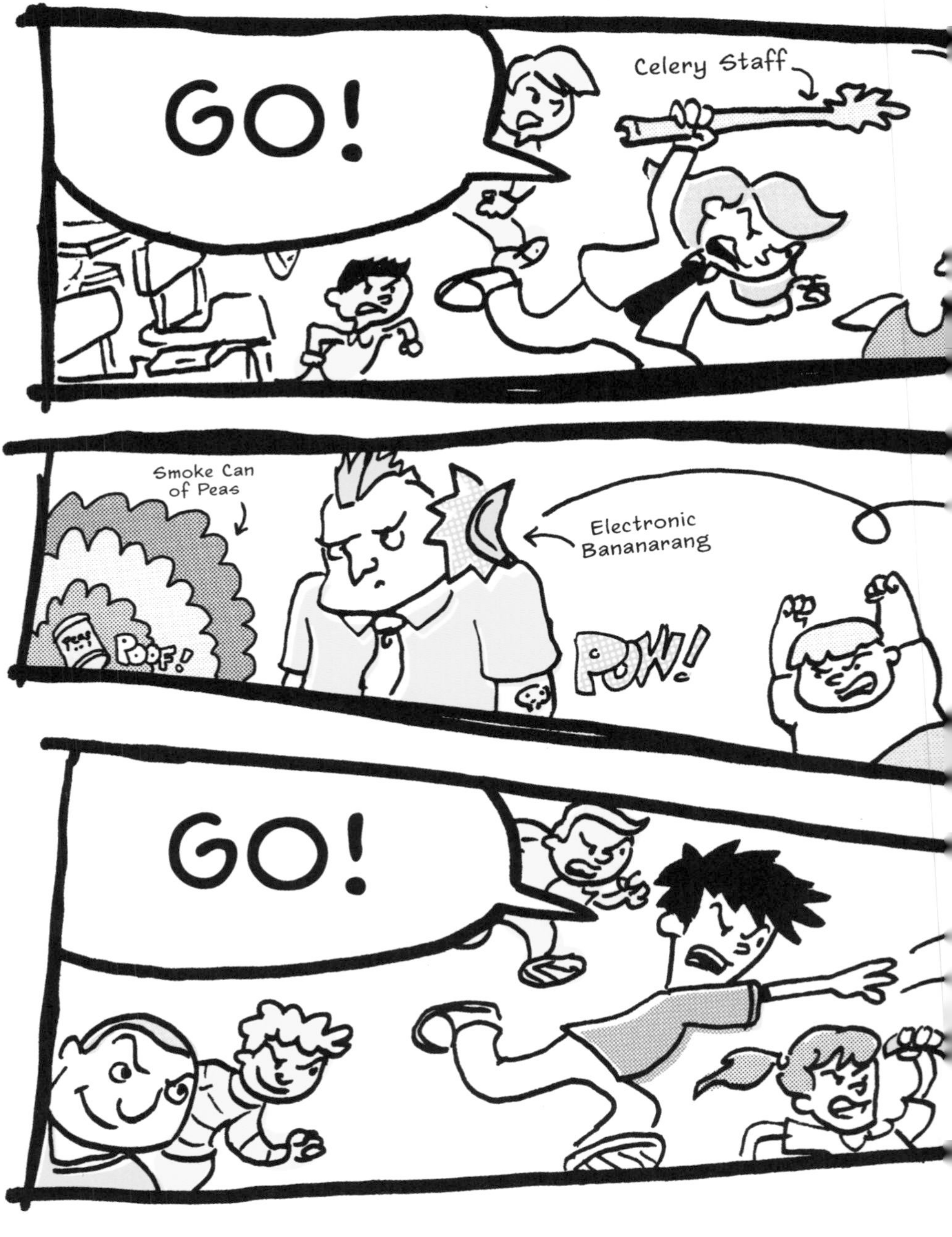
GO!
Celery Staff
Smoke Can of Peas
PEAS
POOF!
Electronic Bananarang
POW!
GO!

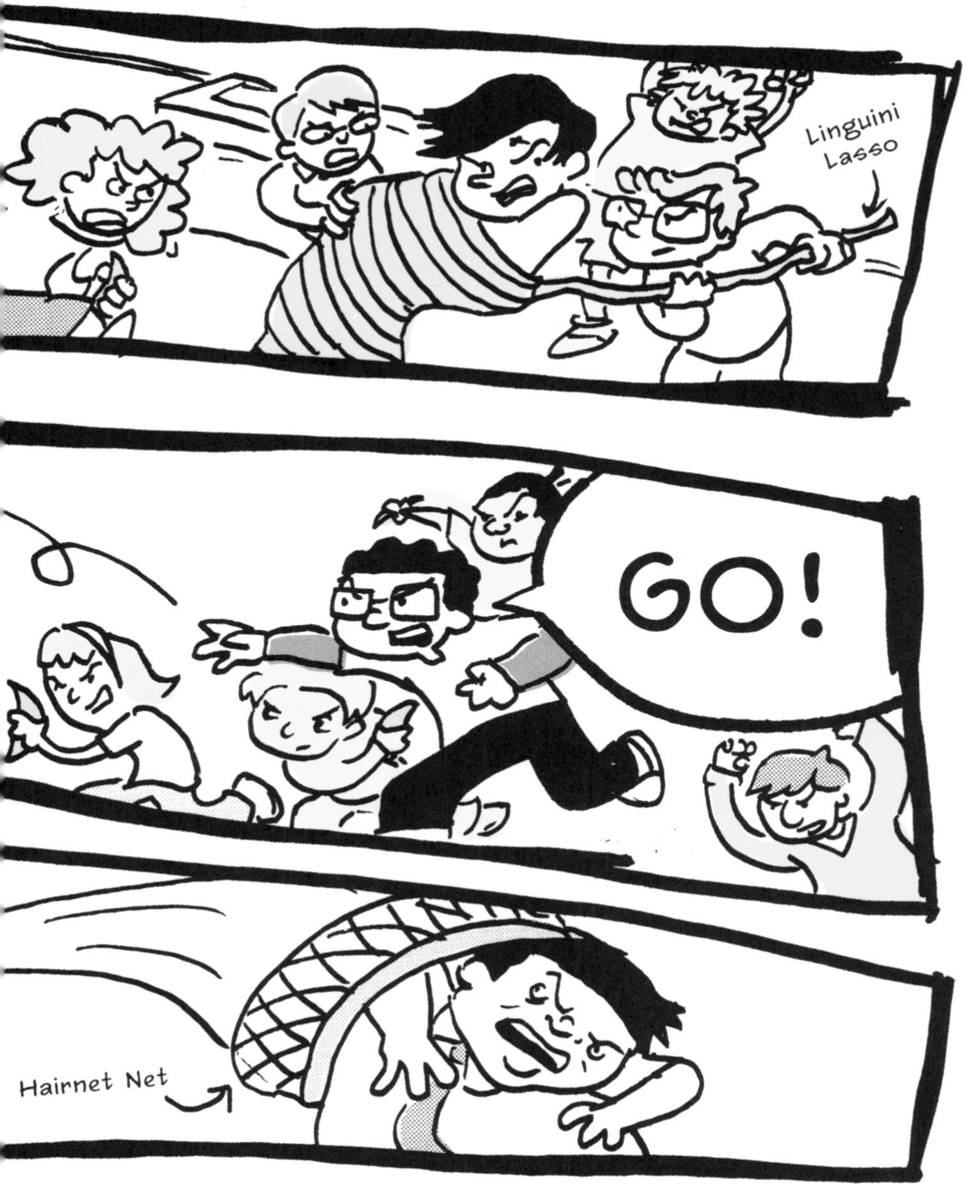

Linguini Lasso
GO!
Hairnet Net

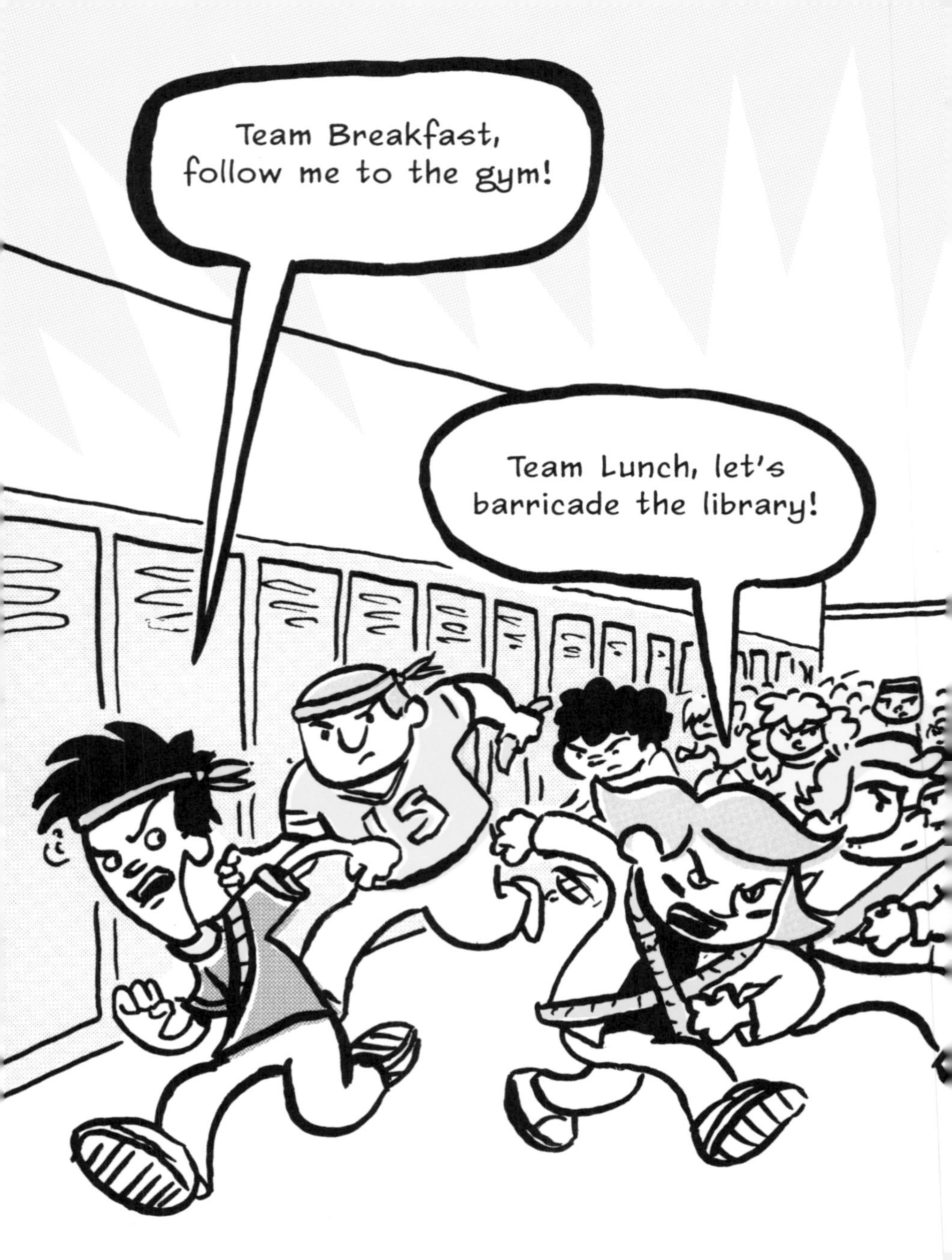
Team Breakfast, follow me to the gym!
Team Lunch, let's barricade the library!

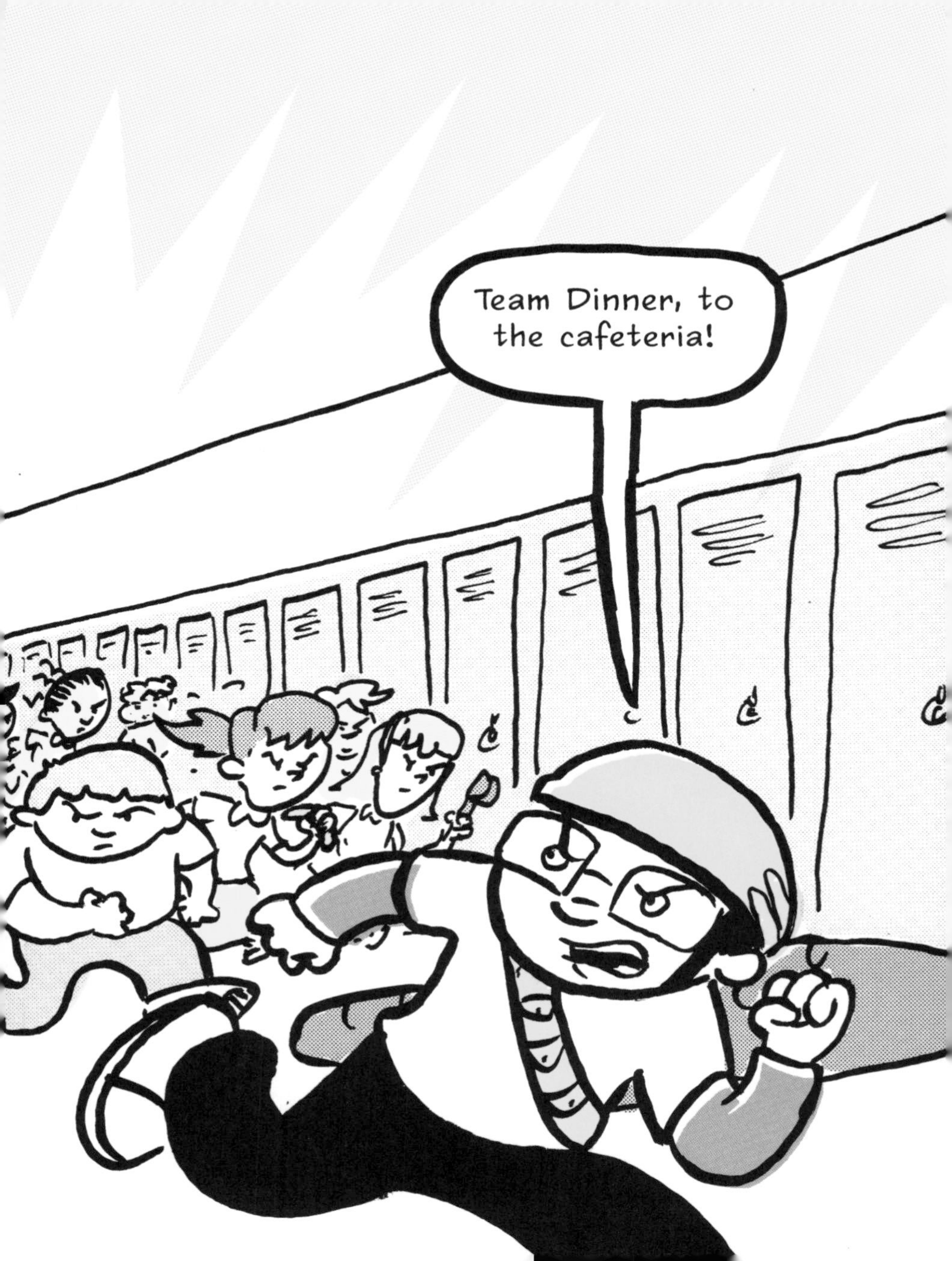
Team Dinner, to the cafeteria!

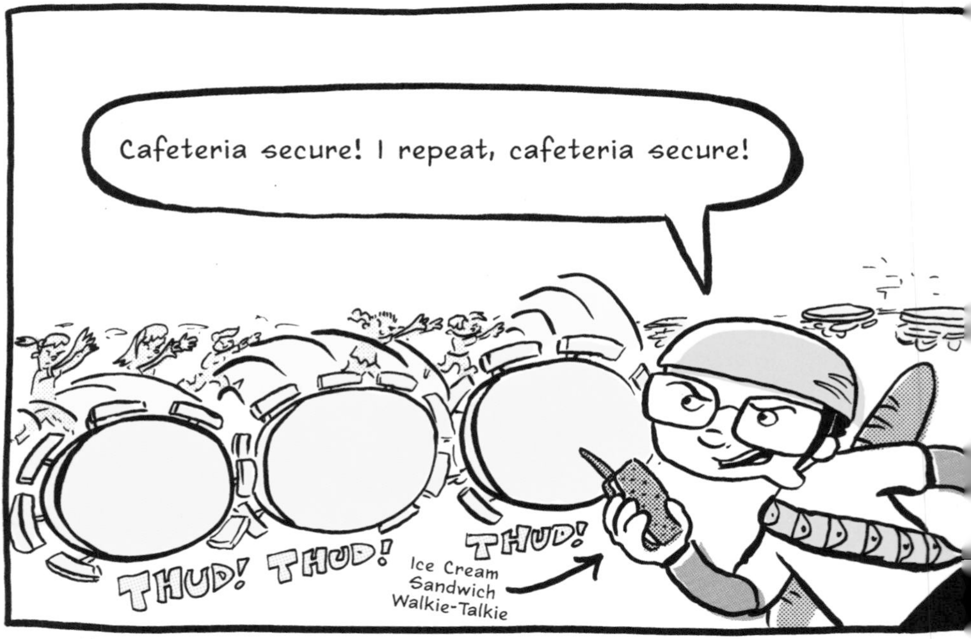
Cafeteria secure! I repeat, cafeteria secure!
THUD! THUD! THUD!
Ice Cream Sandwich Walkie-Talkie

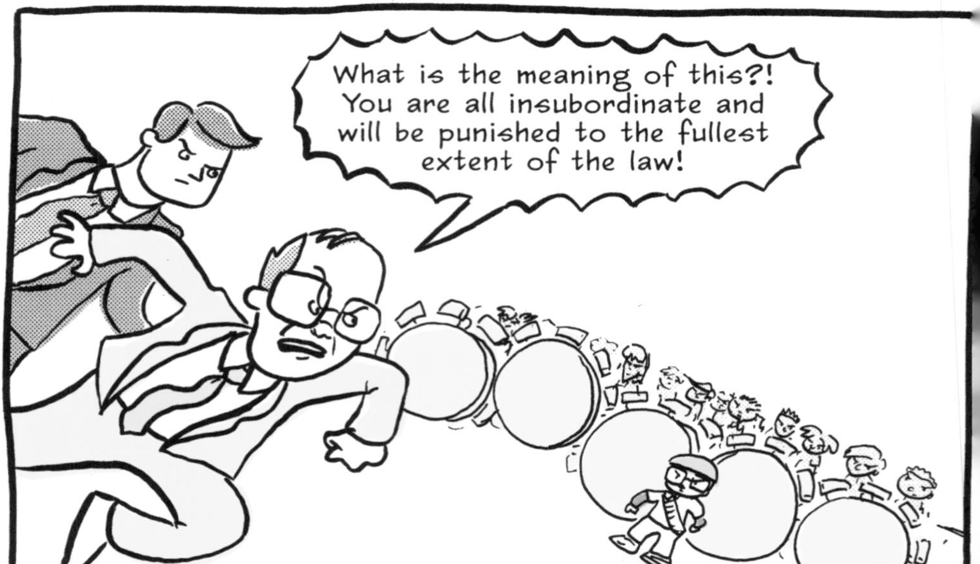
What is the meaning of this?! You are all insubordinate and will be punished to the fullest extent of the law!

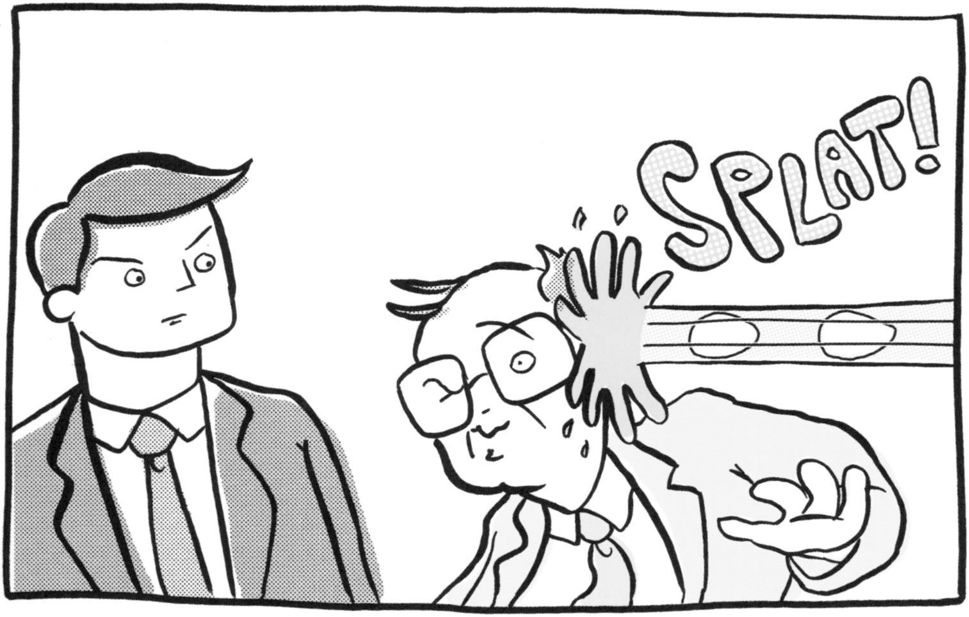
SPLAT!

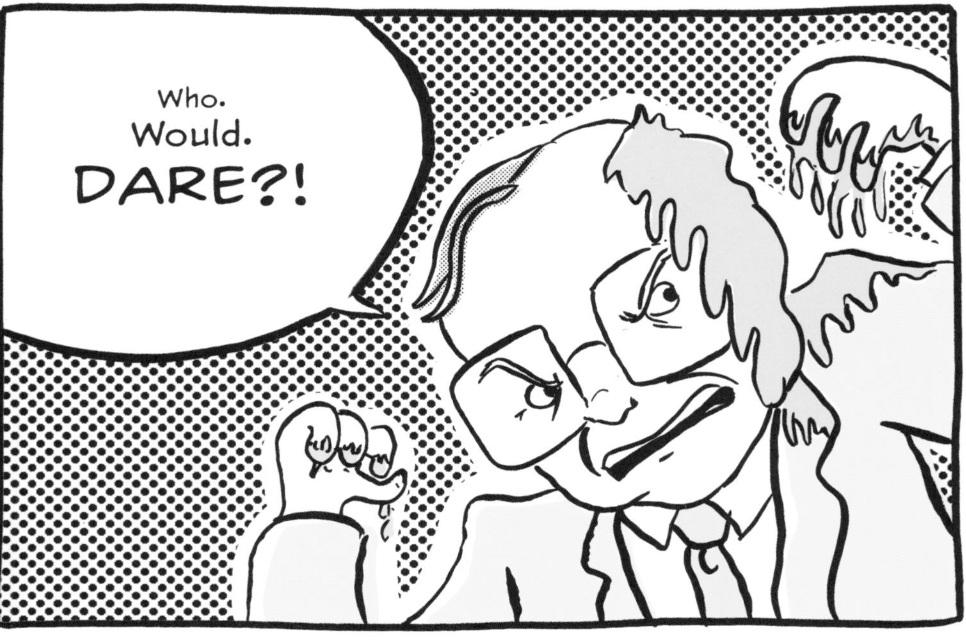
Who.
Would.
DARE?!

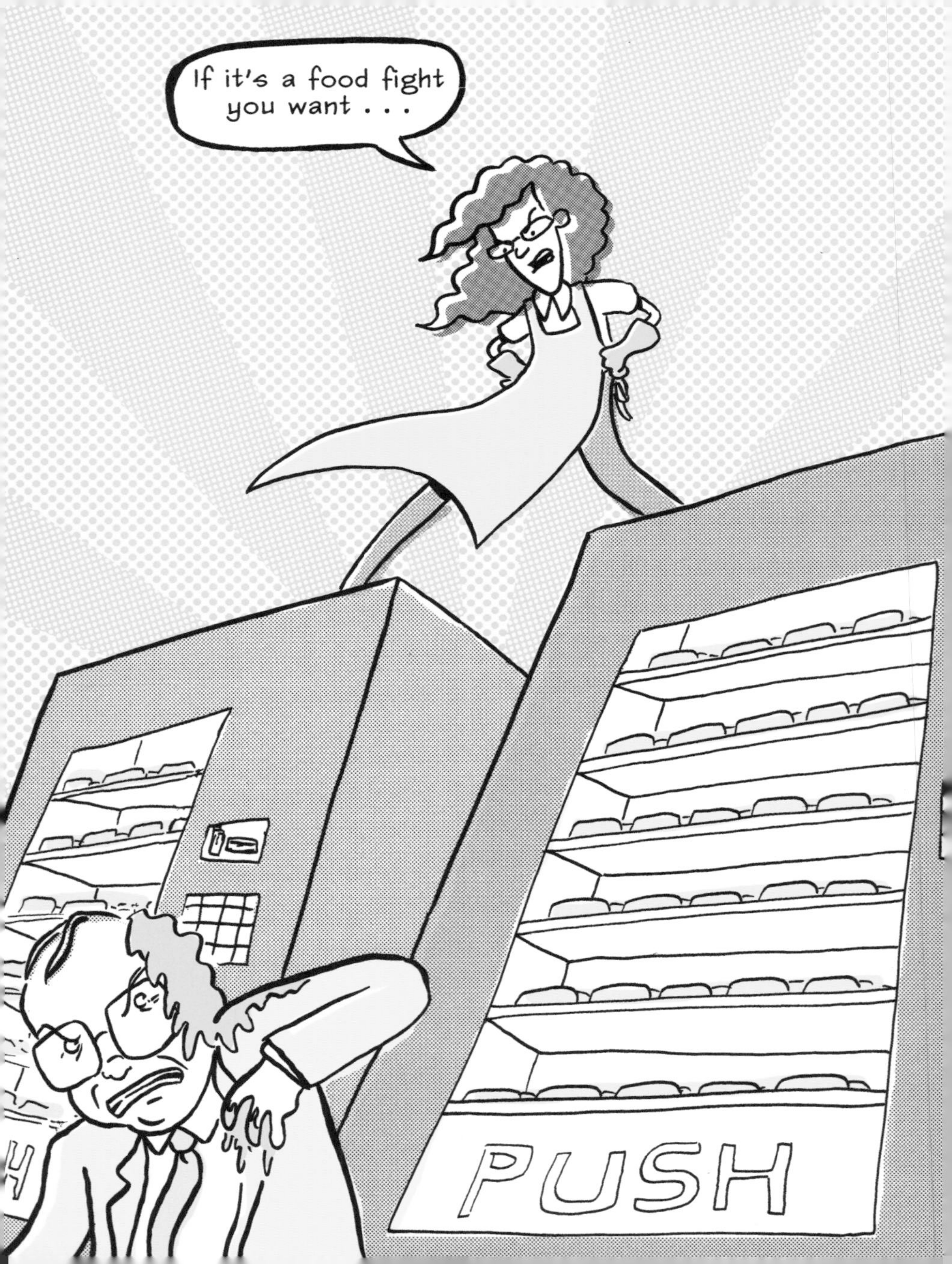
If it's a food fight you want . . .
PUSH

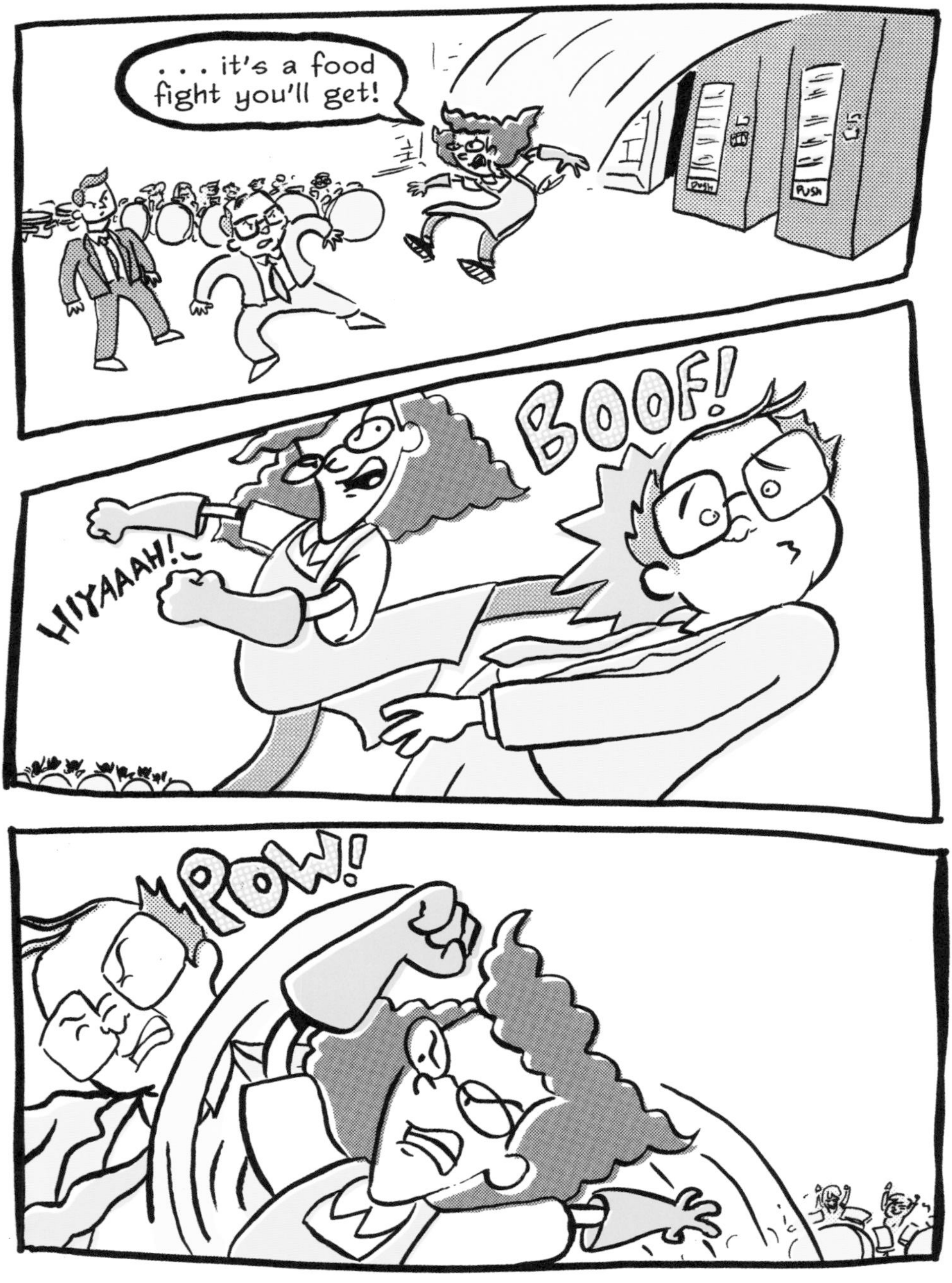
. . . it's a food fight you'll get!
BOOF!
HIYAAAH!
POW!

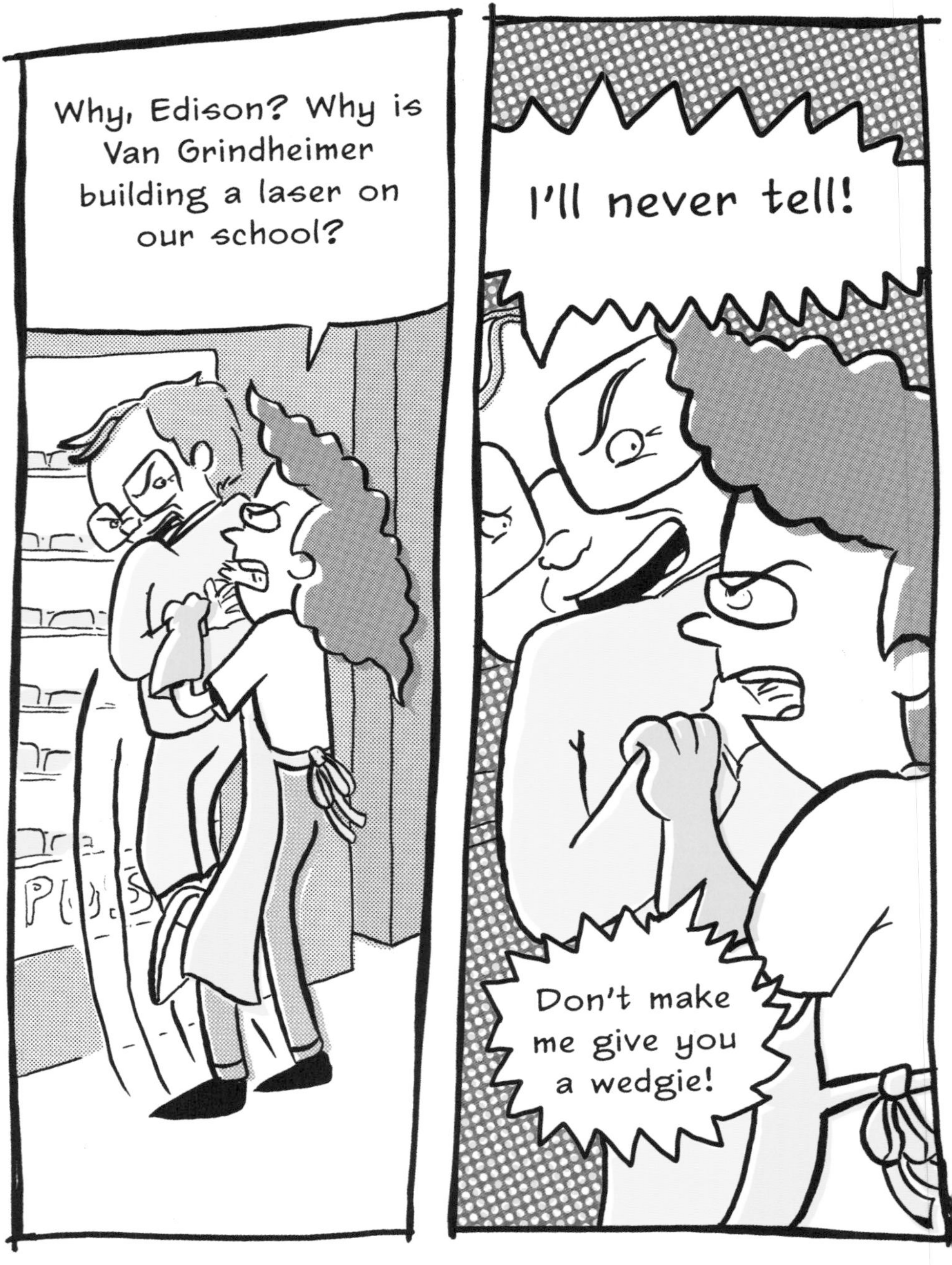
Why, Edison? Why is Van Grindheimer building a laser on our school?
I'll never tell!
Don't make me give you a wedgie!

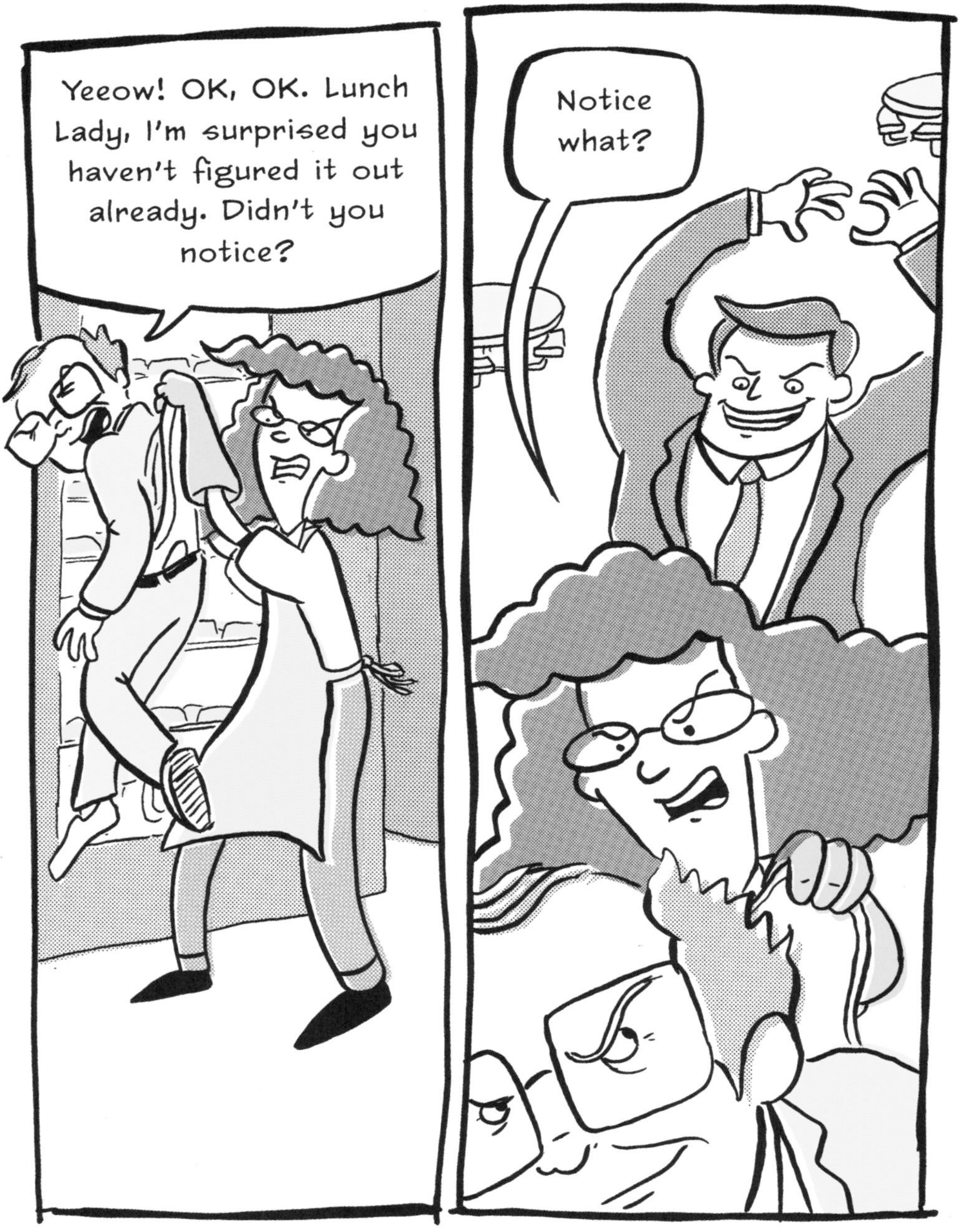
Yeeow! OK, OK. Lunch Lady, I'm surprised you haven't figured it out already. Didn't you notice?
Notice what?

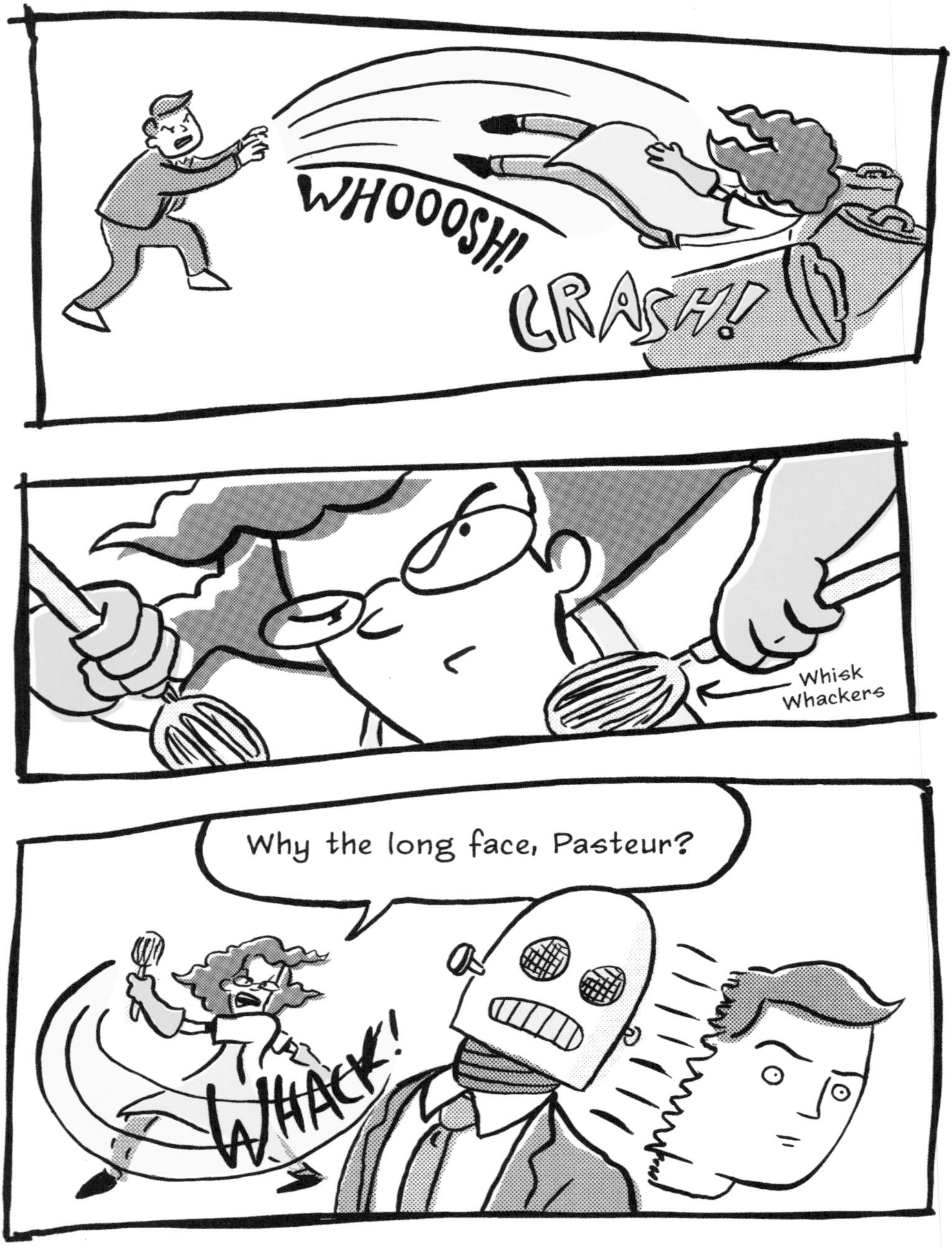
WHOOOSH!
CRASH!
Whisk Whackers
Why the long face, Pasteur?
WHACK!

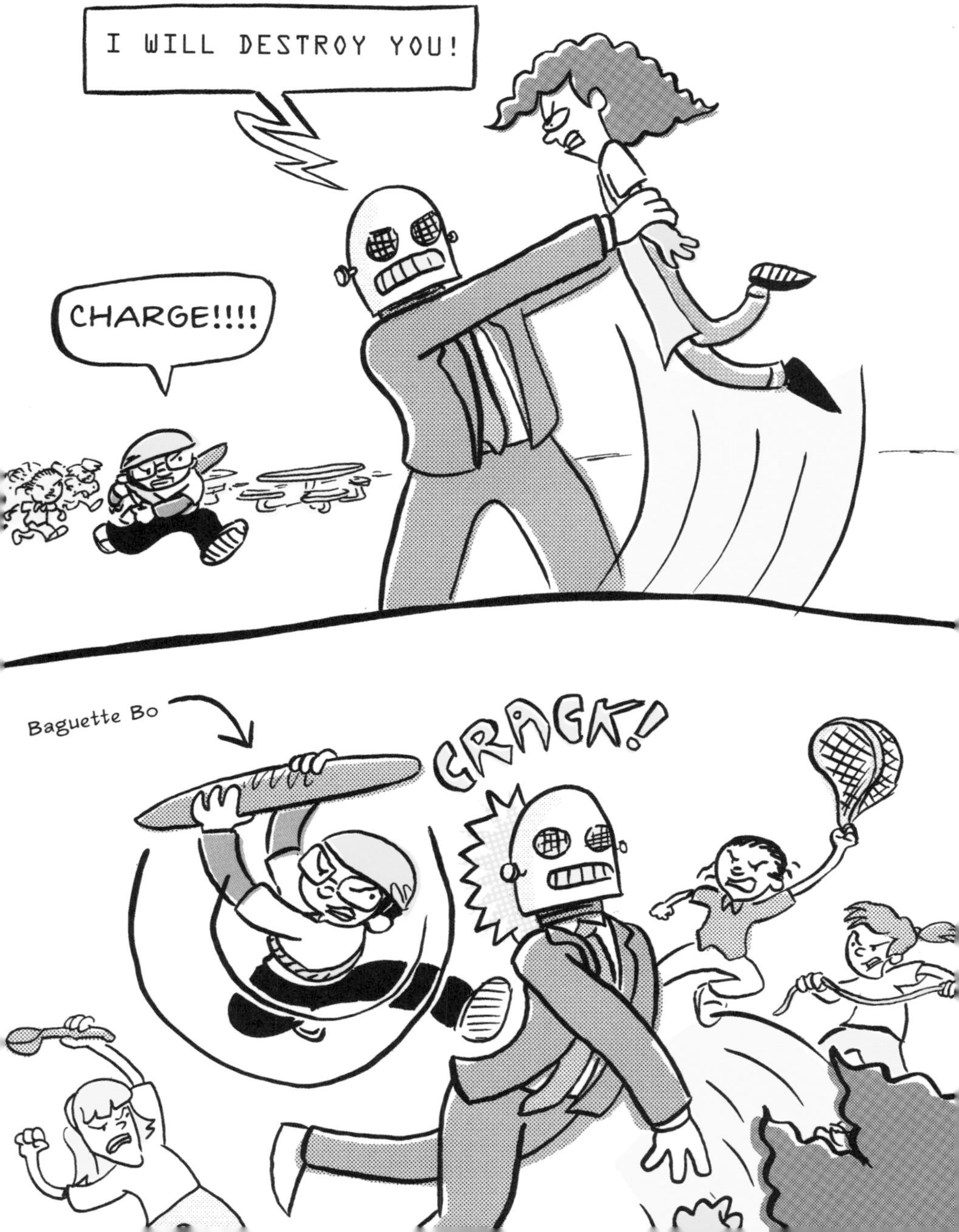
I WILL DESTROY YOU!
CHARGE!!!!
Baguette Bo
CRACK!

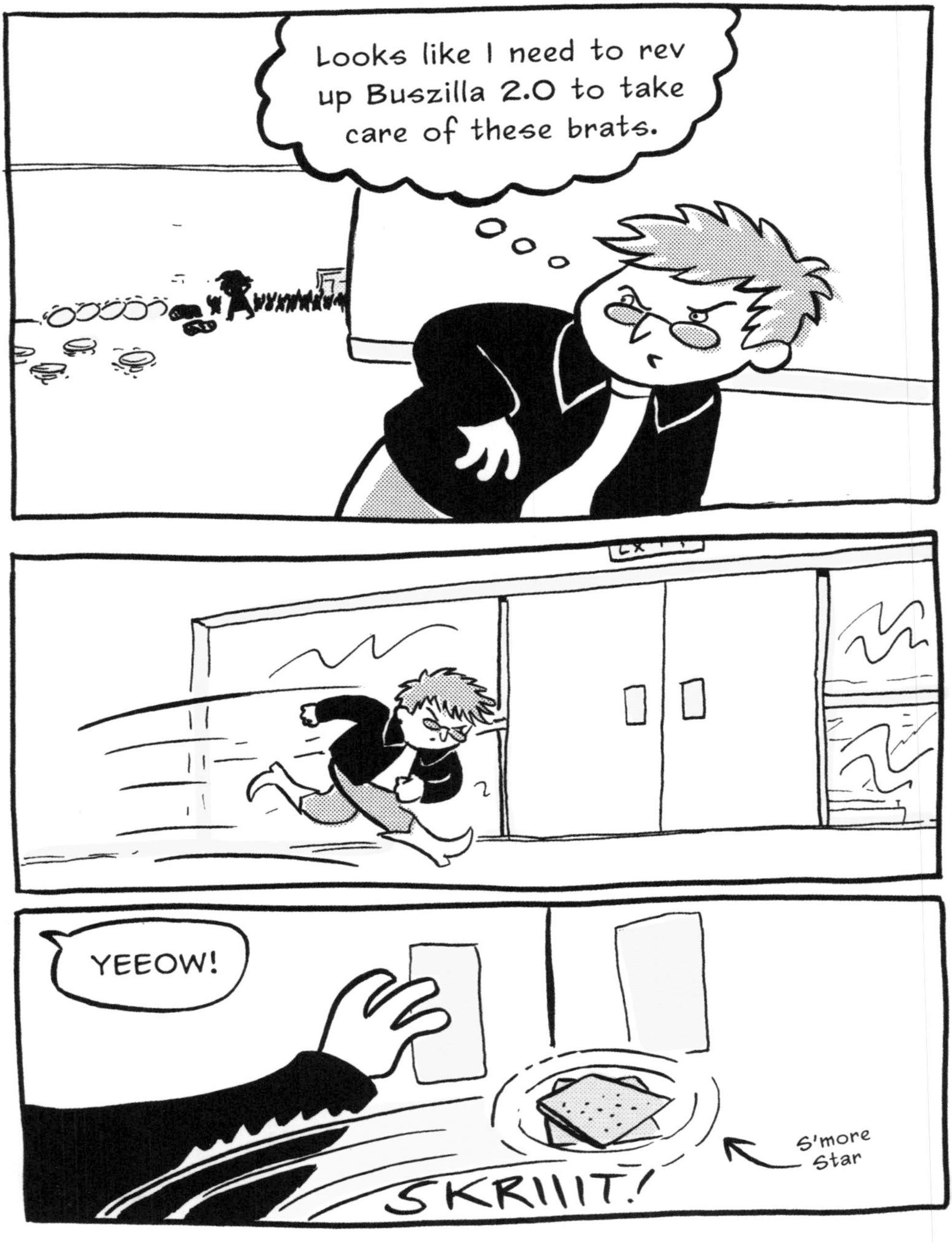
Looks like I need to rev up Buszilla 2.0 to take care of these brats.
YEEOW!
SKRIIIT!
S'more Star

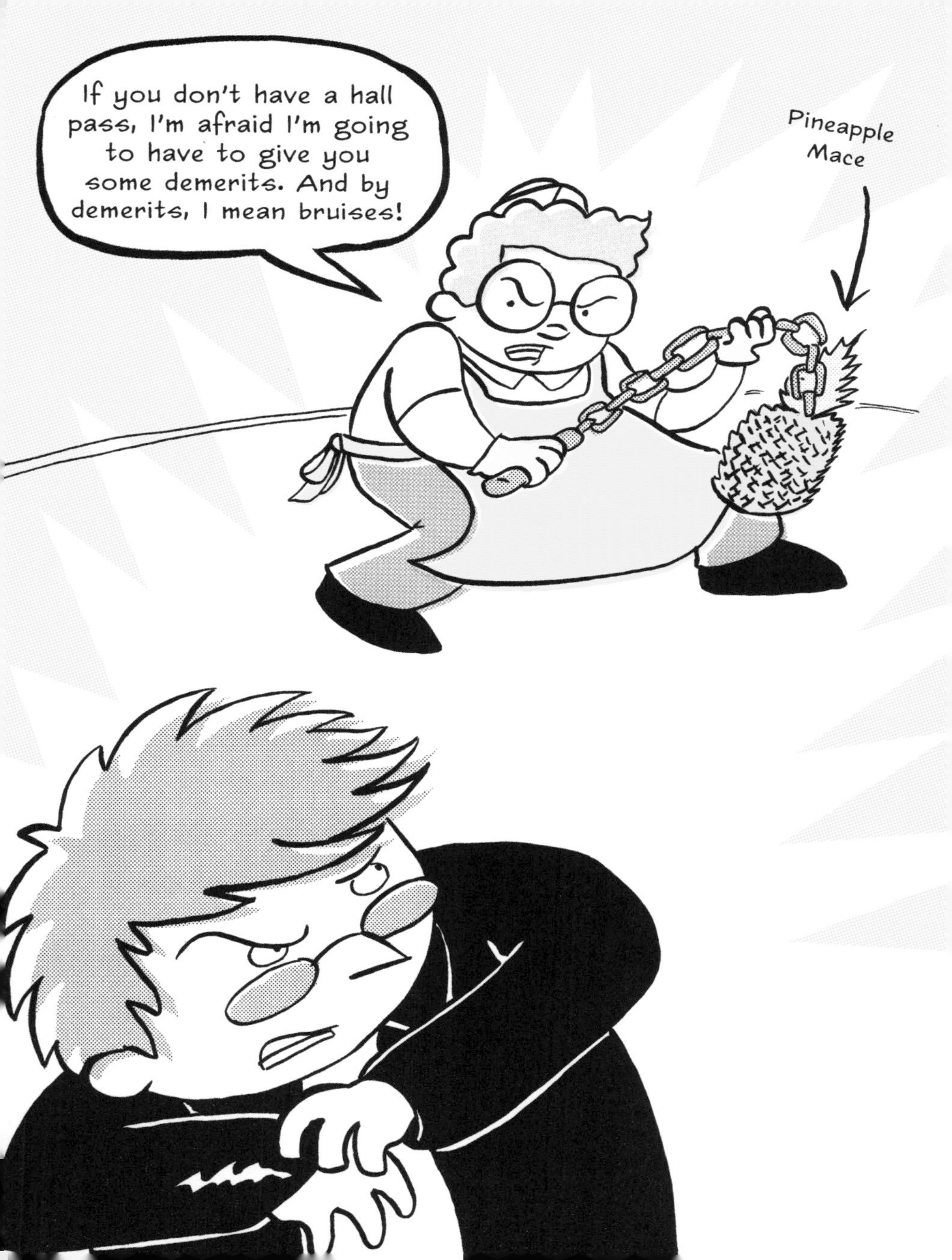
If you don't have a hall pass, I'm afraid I'm going to have to give you some demerits. And by demerits, I mean bruises!
Pineapple Mace

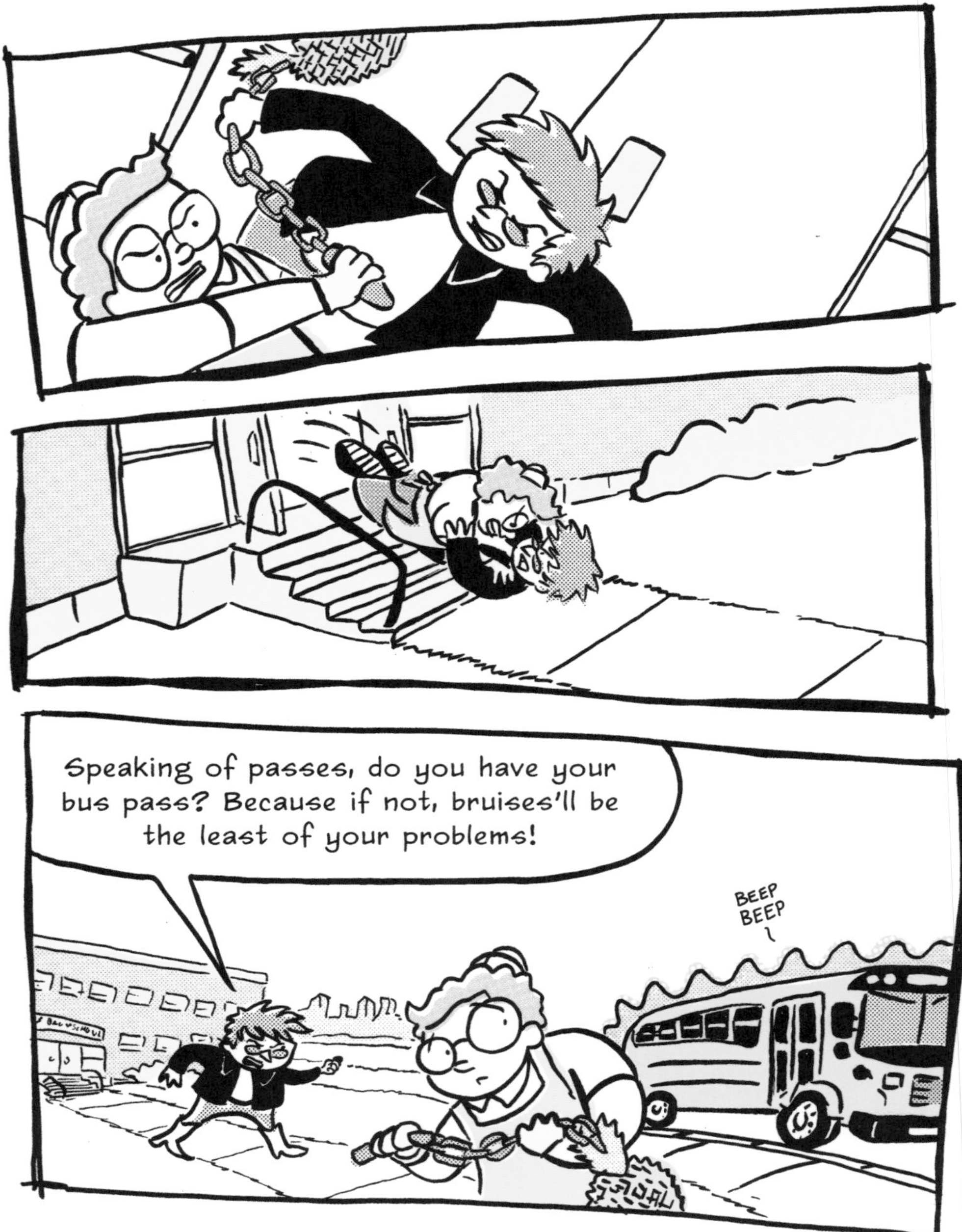
Speaking of passes, do you have your bus pass? Because if not, bruises'll be the least of your problems!
BEEP BEEP

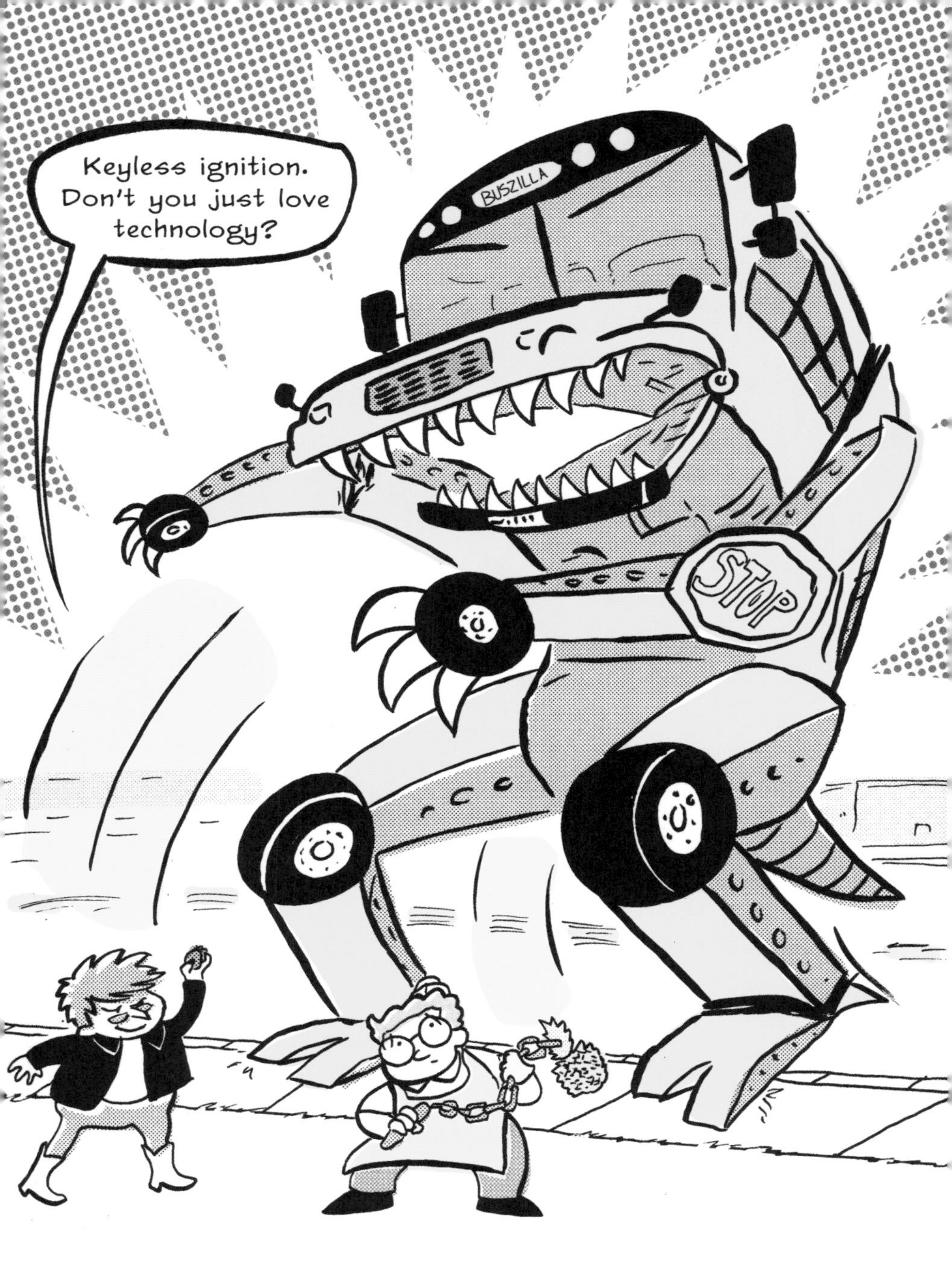
Keyless ignition. Don't you just love technology?
BUSZILLA
STOP

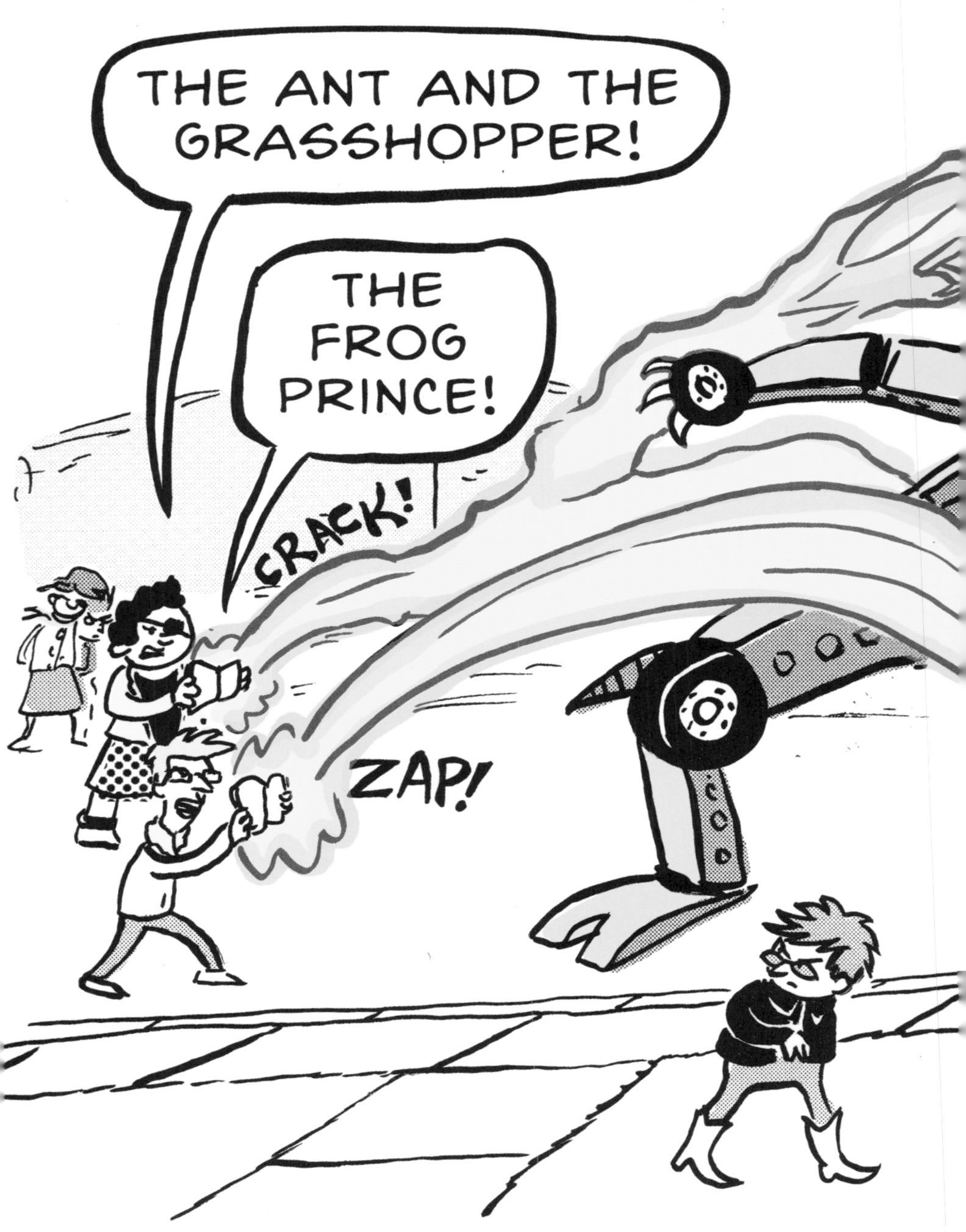
THE ANT AND THE GRASSHOPPER!
THE FROG PRINCE!
CRACK!
ZAP!

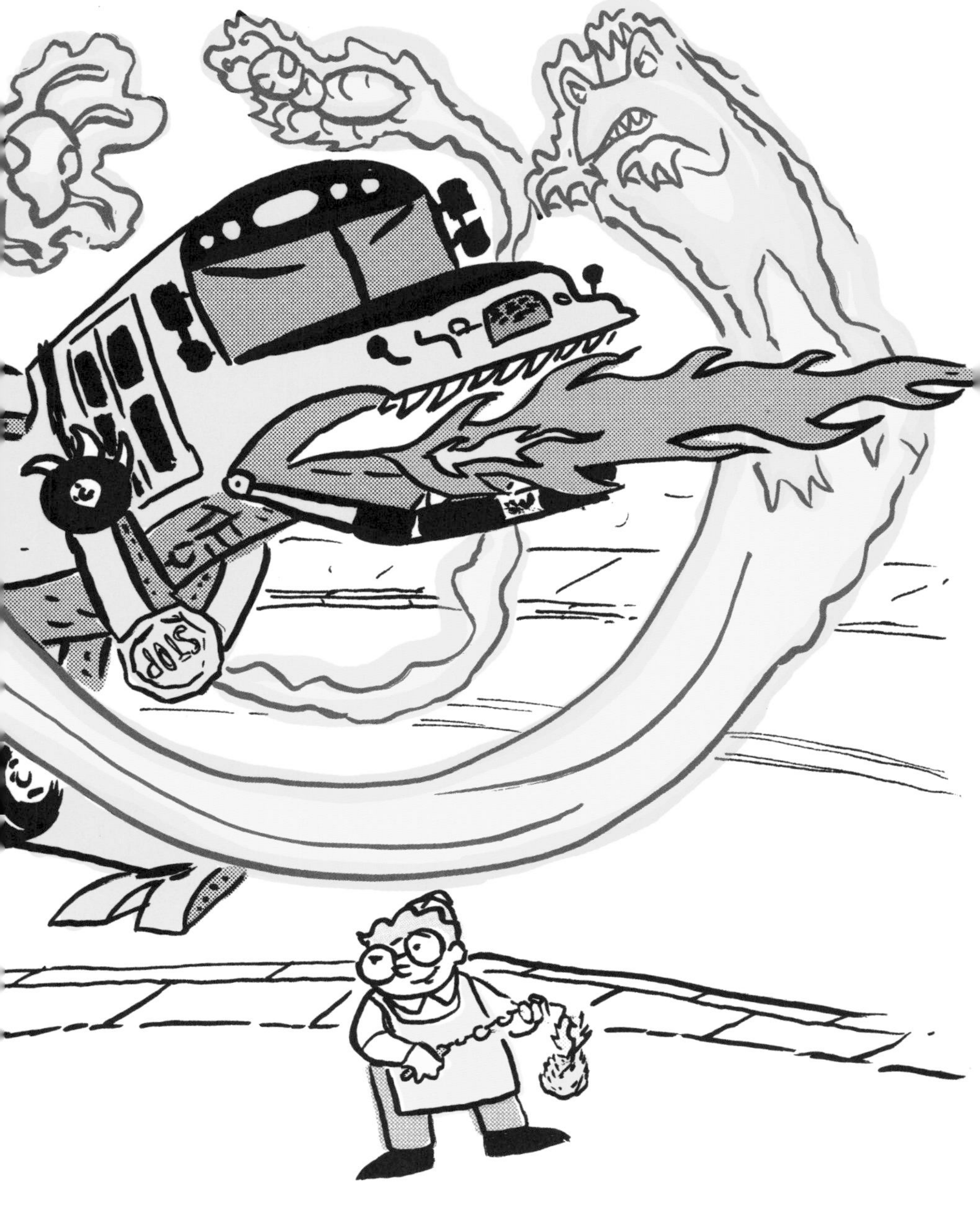
STOP

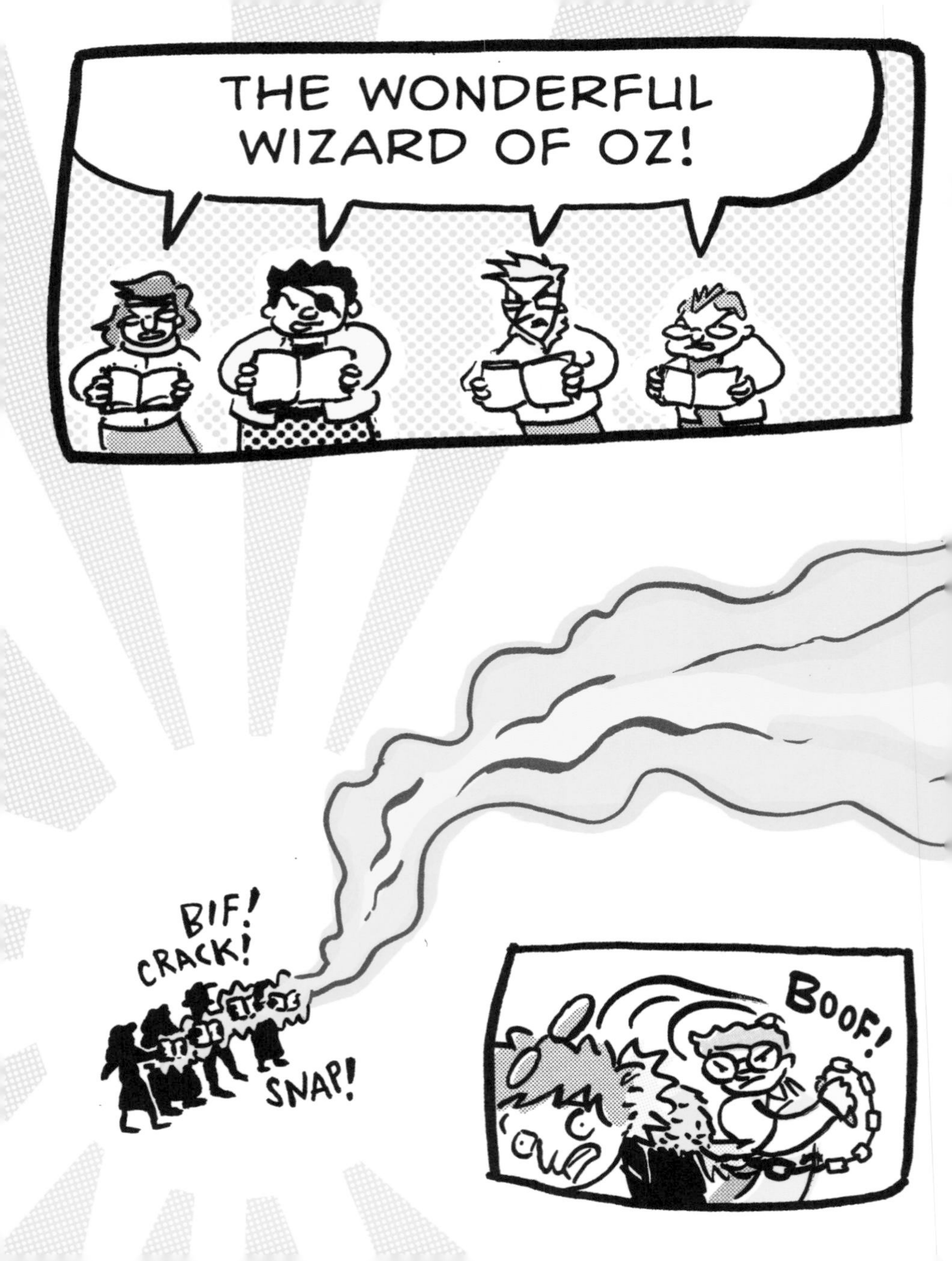
THE WONDERFUL WIZARD OF OZ!
BIF!
CRACK!
SNAP!
BOOF!

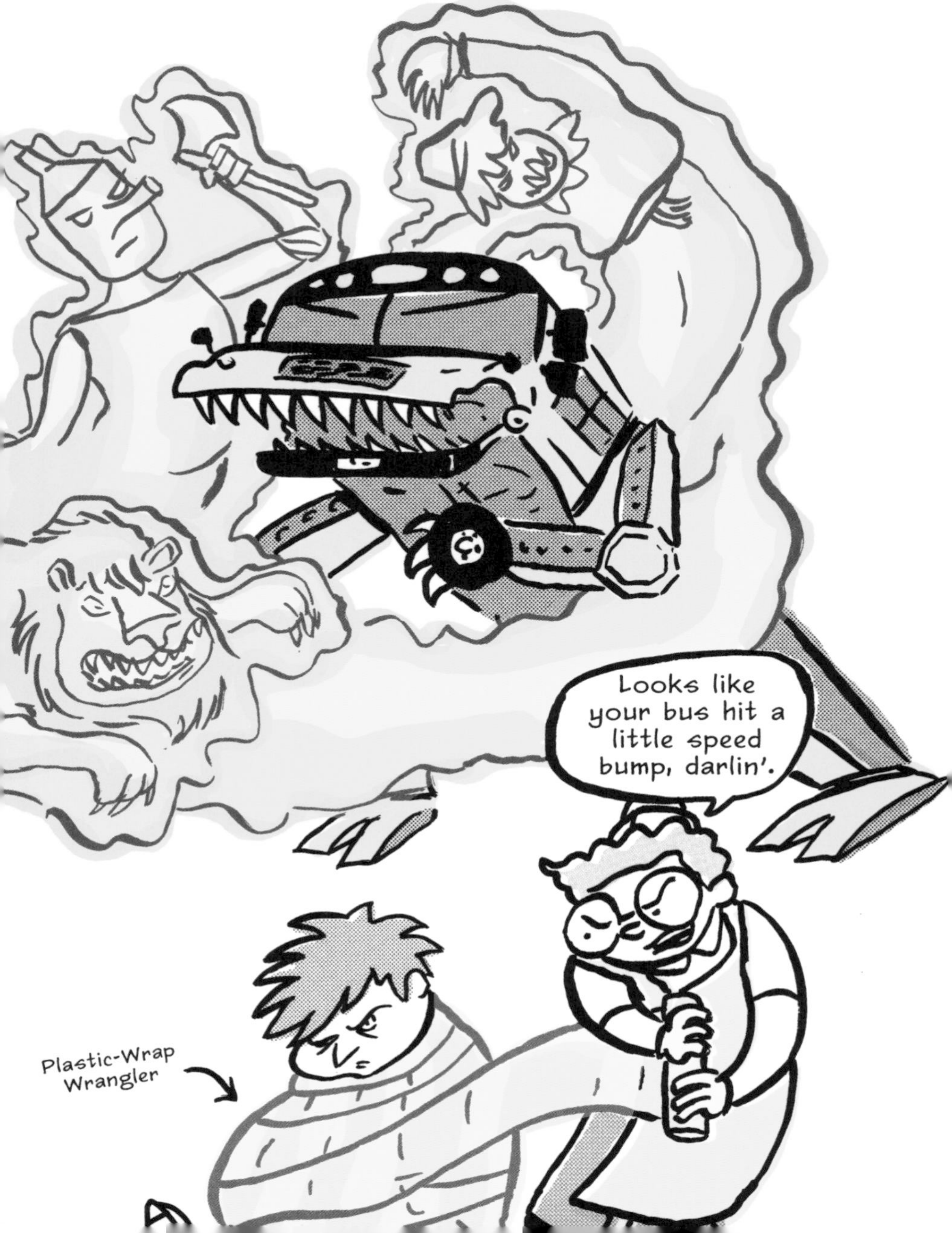
Looks like your bus hit a little speed bump, darlin'.
Plastic-Wrap Wrangler

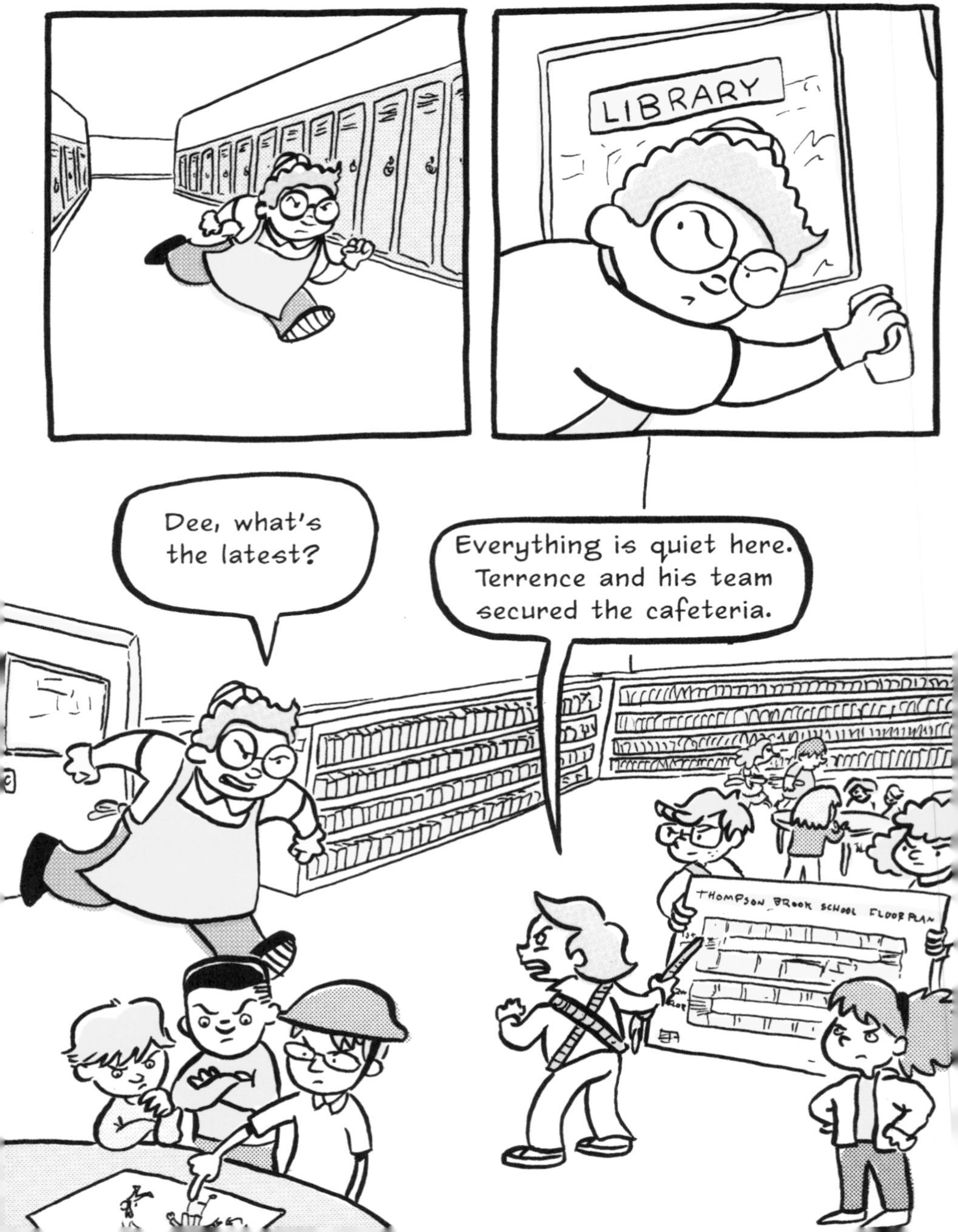
LIBRARY
Dee, what's the latest?
Everything is quiet here. Terrence and his team secured the cafeteria.
THOMPSON BROOK SCHOOL FLOOR PLAN

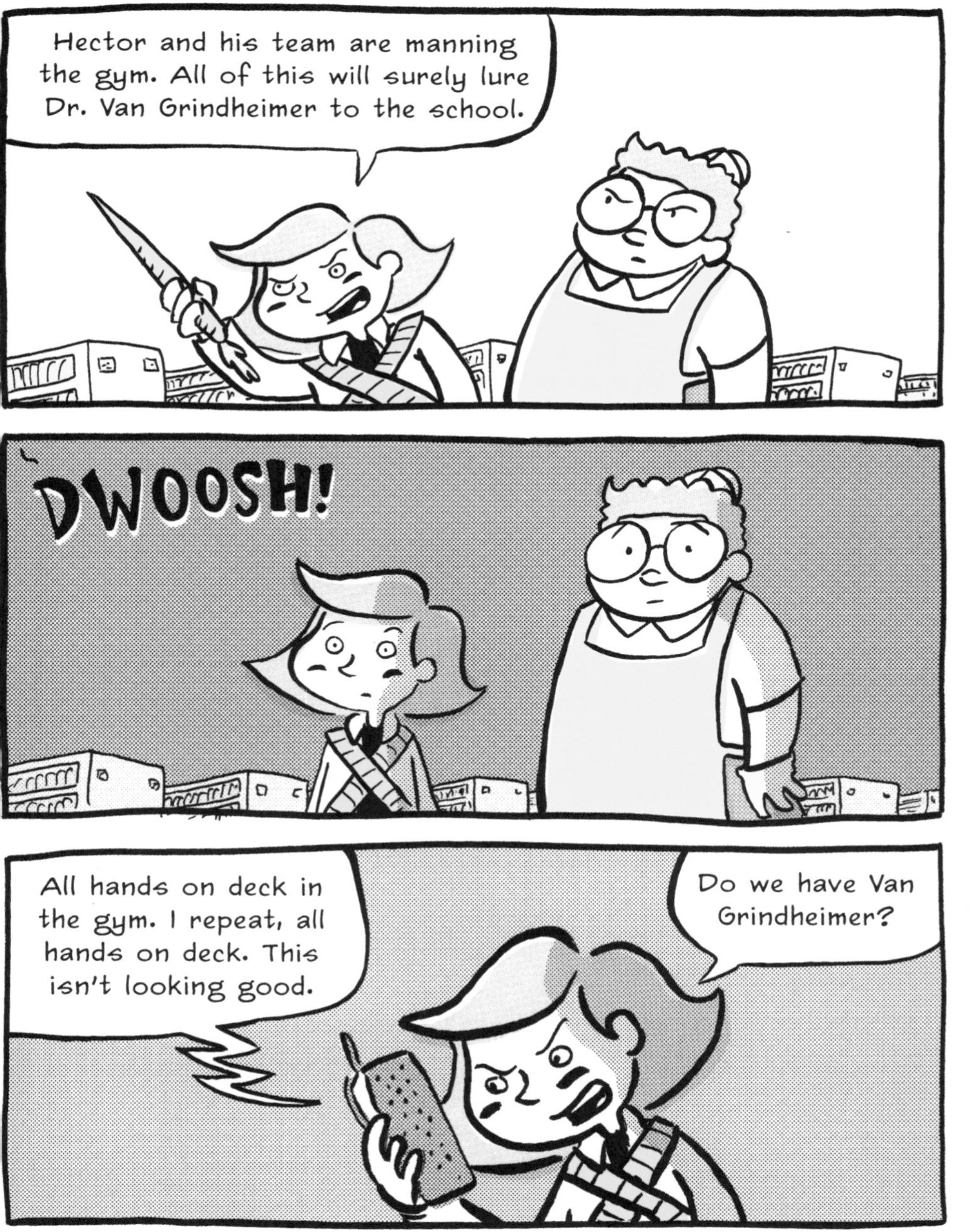

Hector and his team are manning the gym. All of this will surely lure Dr. Van Grindheimer to the school.
DWOOSH!
All hands on deck in the gym. I repeat, all hands on deck. This isn't looking good.
Do we have Van Grindheimer?

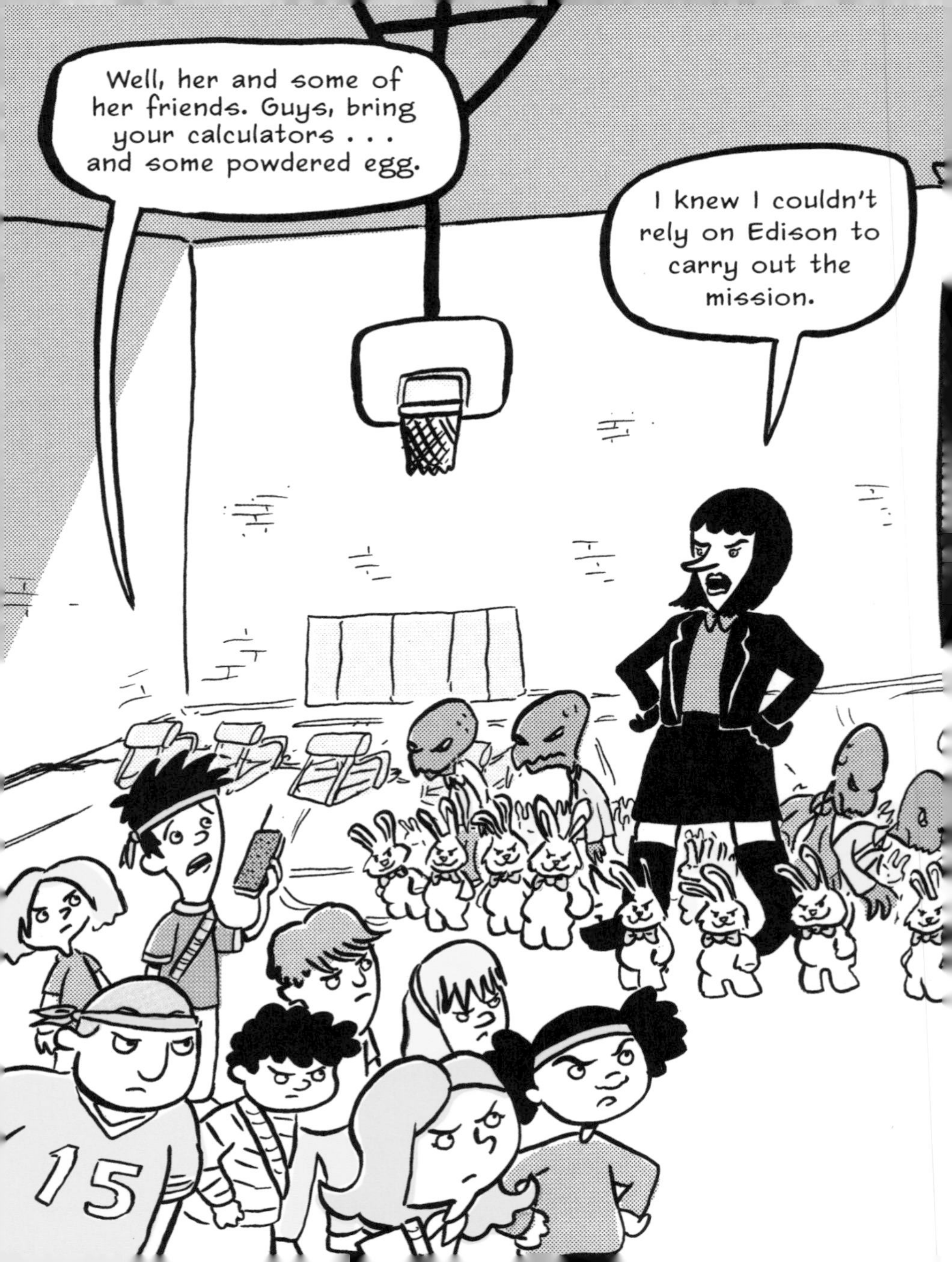
Well, her and some of her friends. Guys, bring your calculators . . . and some powdered egg.
I knew I couldn't rely on Edison to carry out the mission.
15

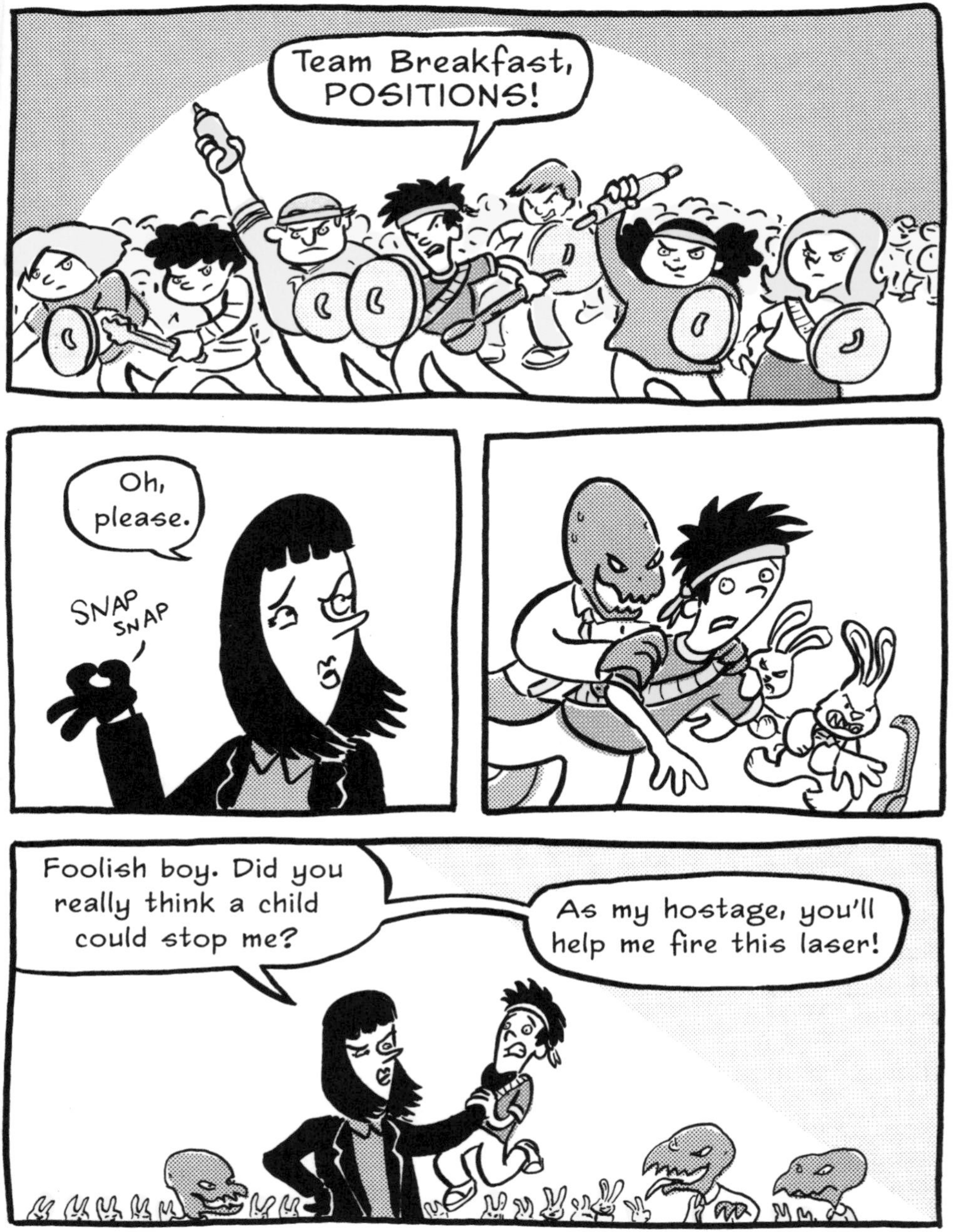
Team Breakfast, POSITIONS!
Oh, please.
SNAP SNAP
Foolish boy. Did you really think a child could stop me?
As my hostage, you'll help me fire this laser!

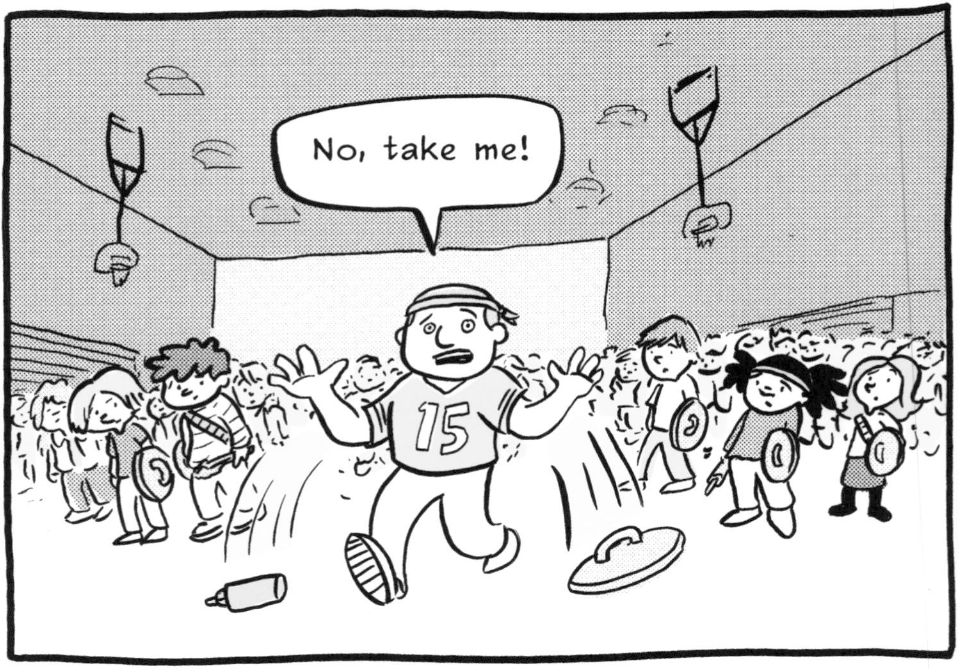
No, take me!
15

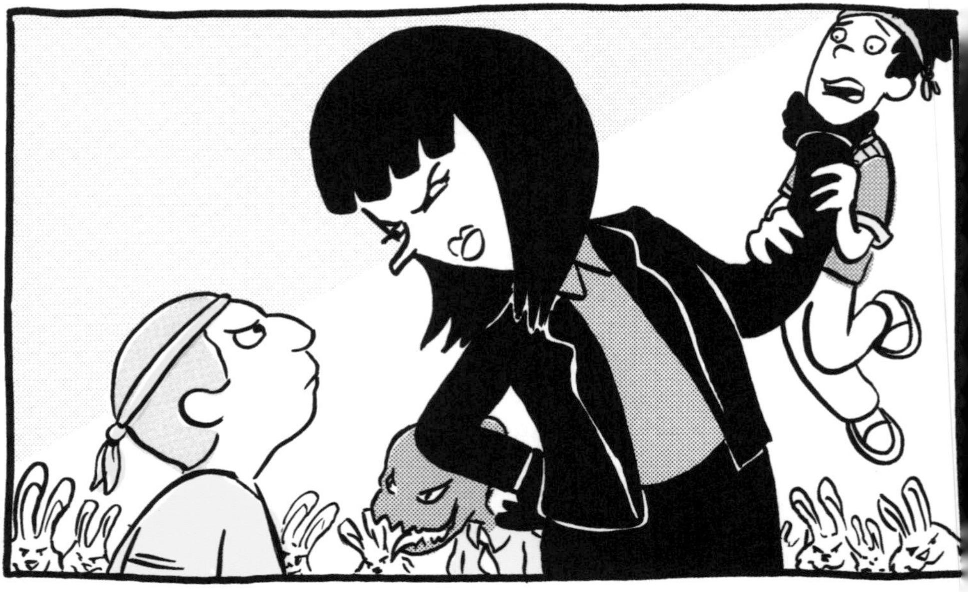

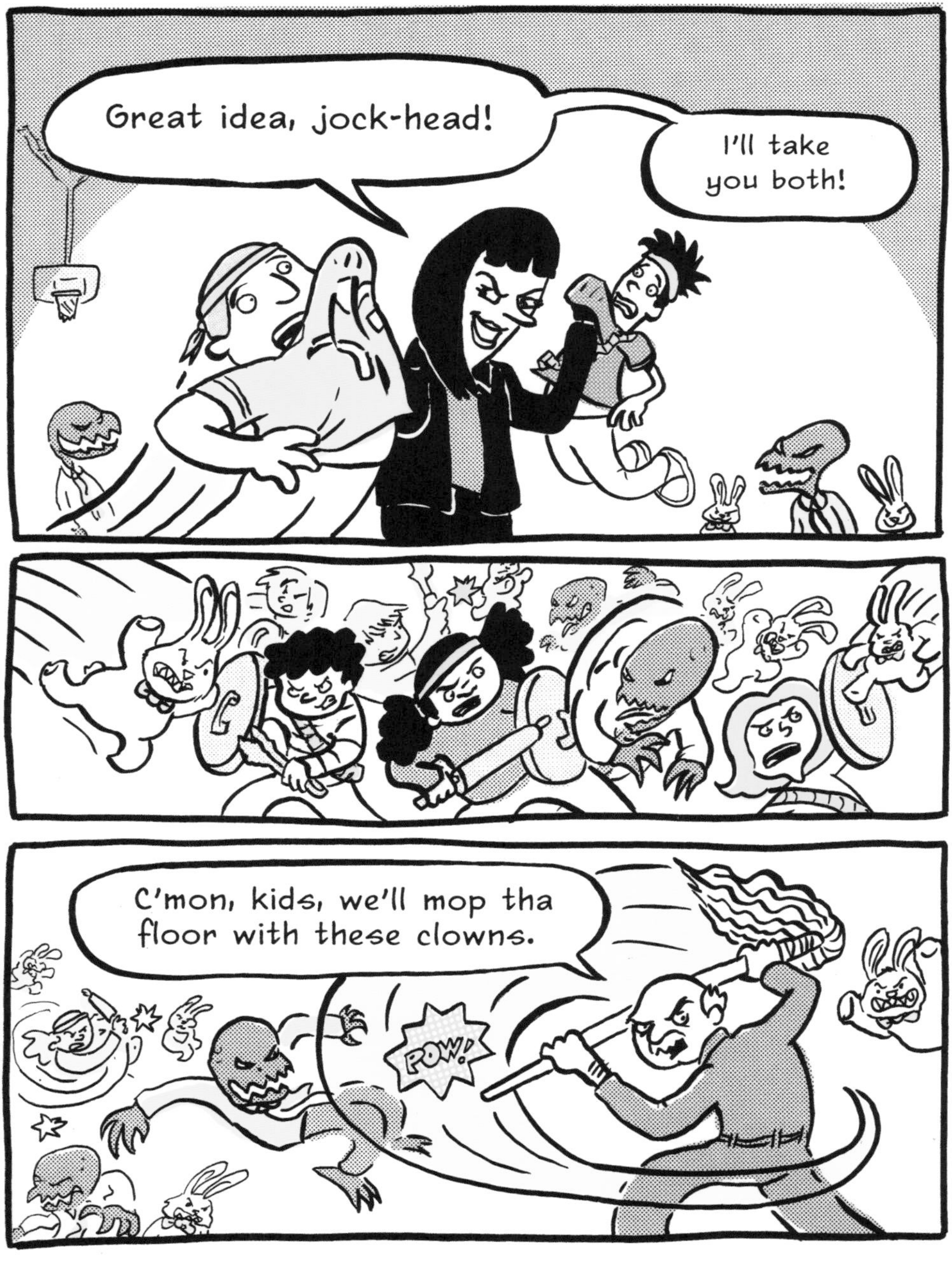
Great idea, jock-head!
I'll take you both!
C'mon, kids, we'll mop tha floor with these clowns.
POW!

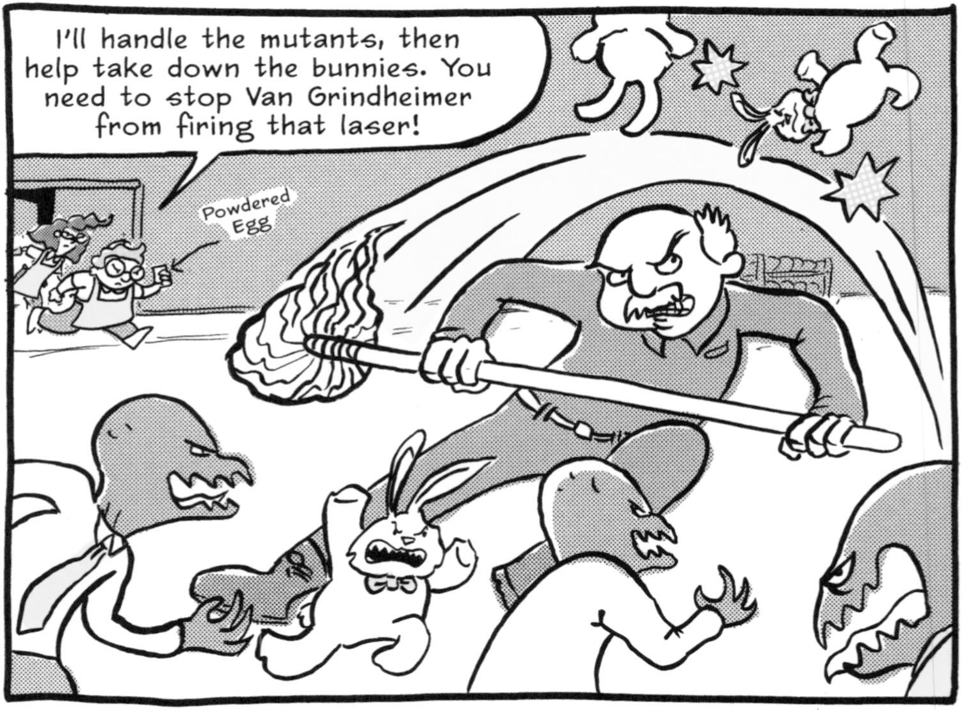
I'll handle the mutants, then help take down the bunnies. You need to stop Van Grindheimer from firing that laser!
Powdered Egg

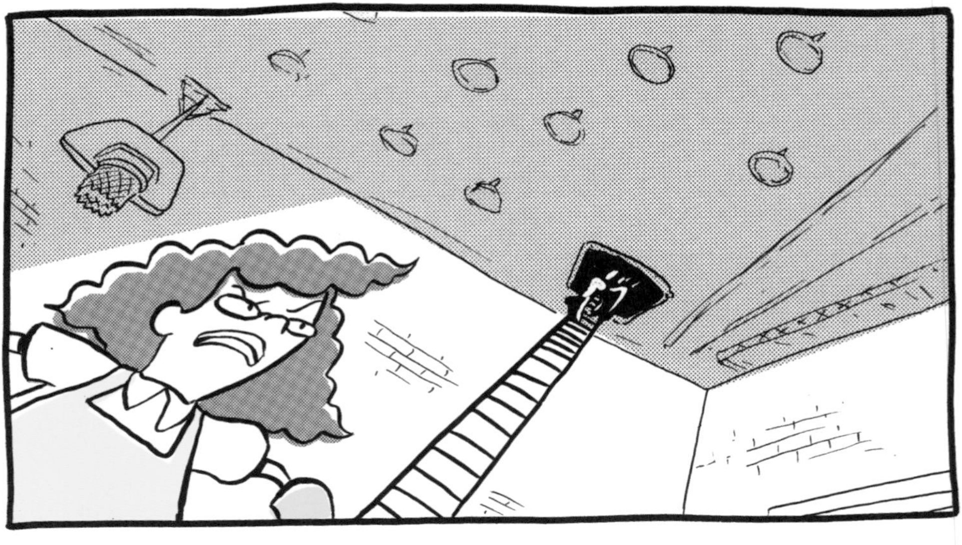

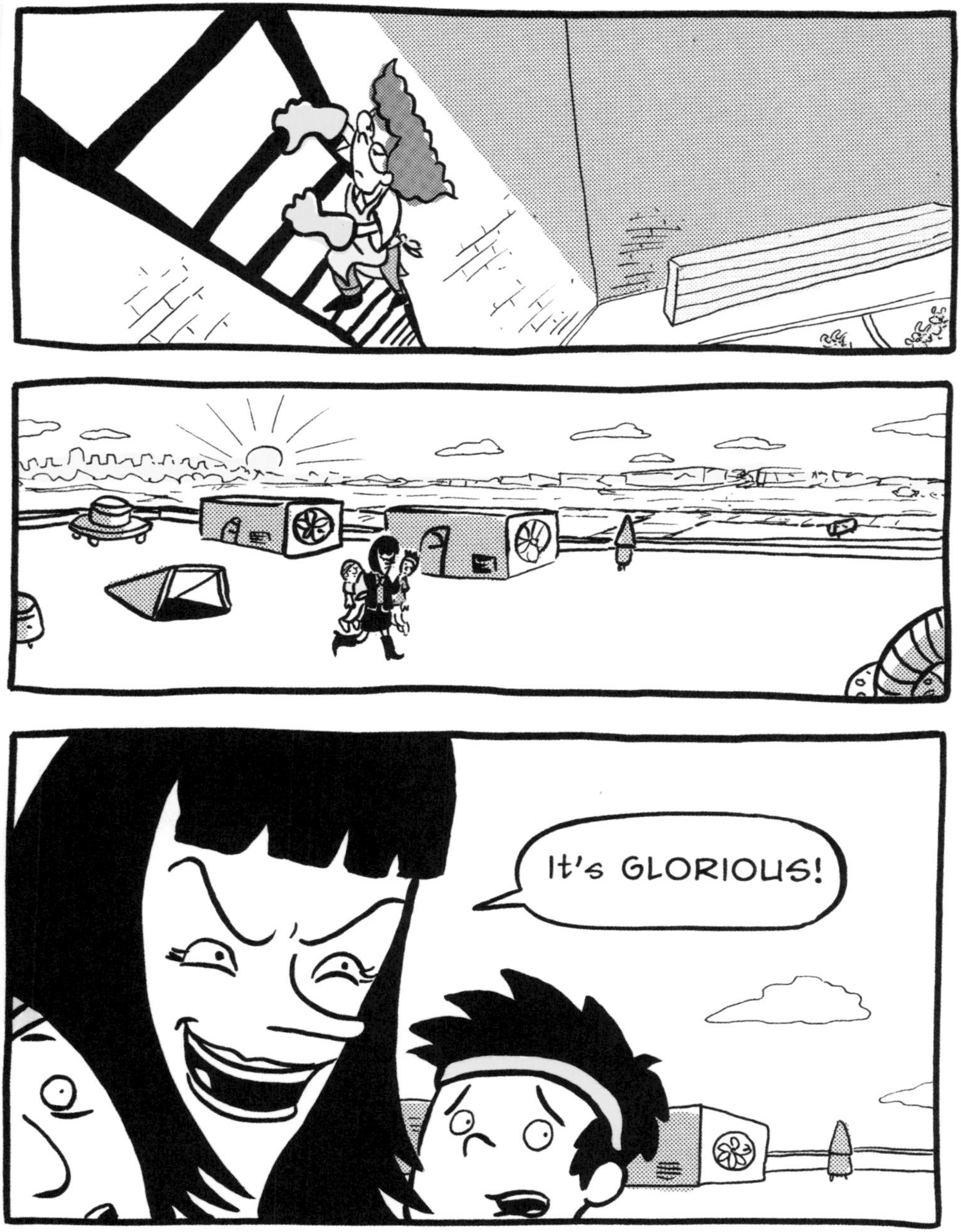
It's GLORIOUS!

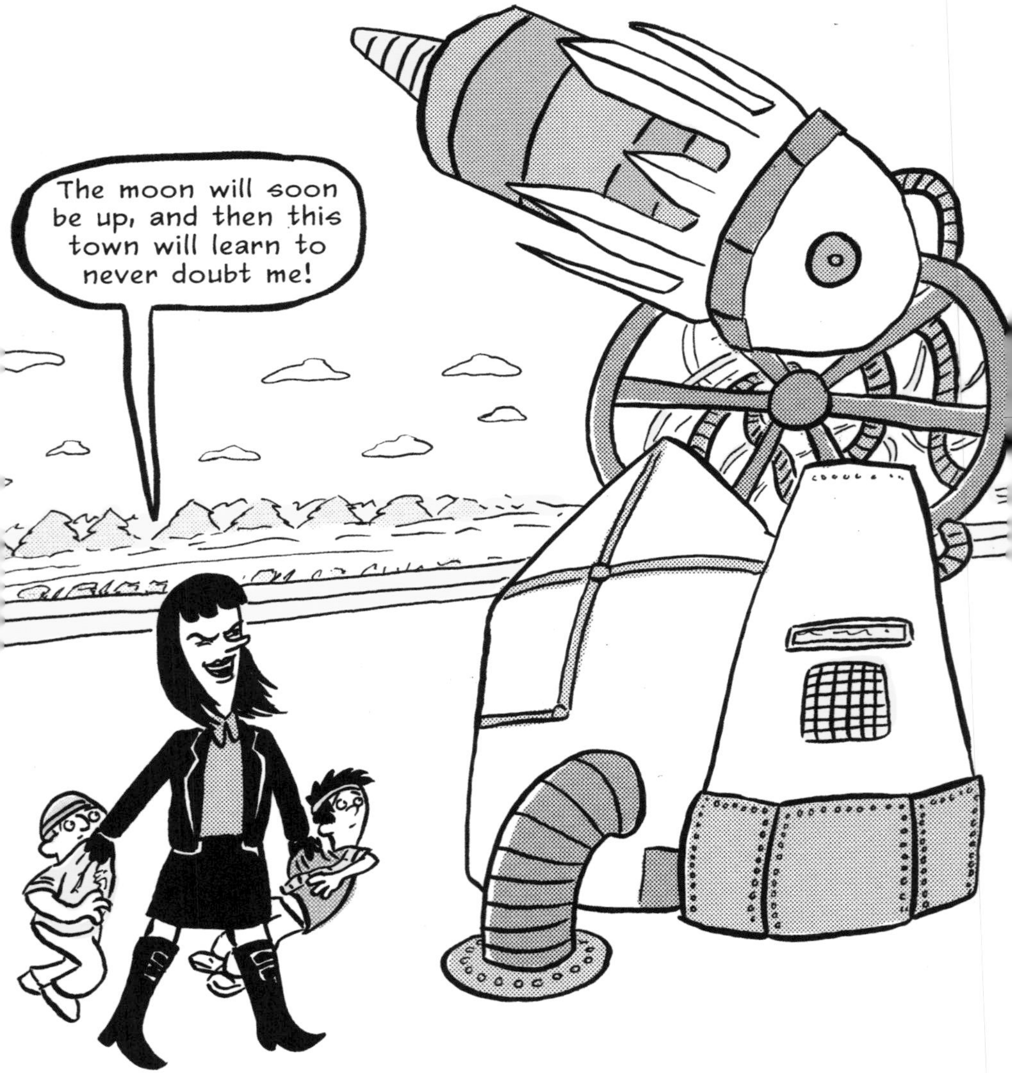
The moon will soon be up, and then this town will learn to never doubt me!

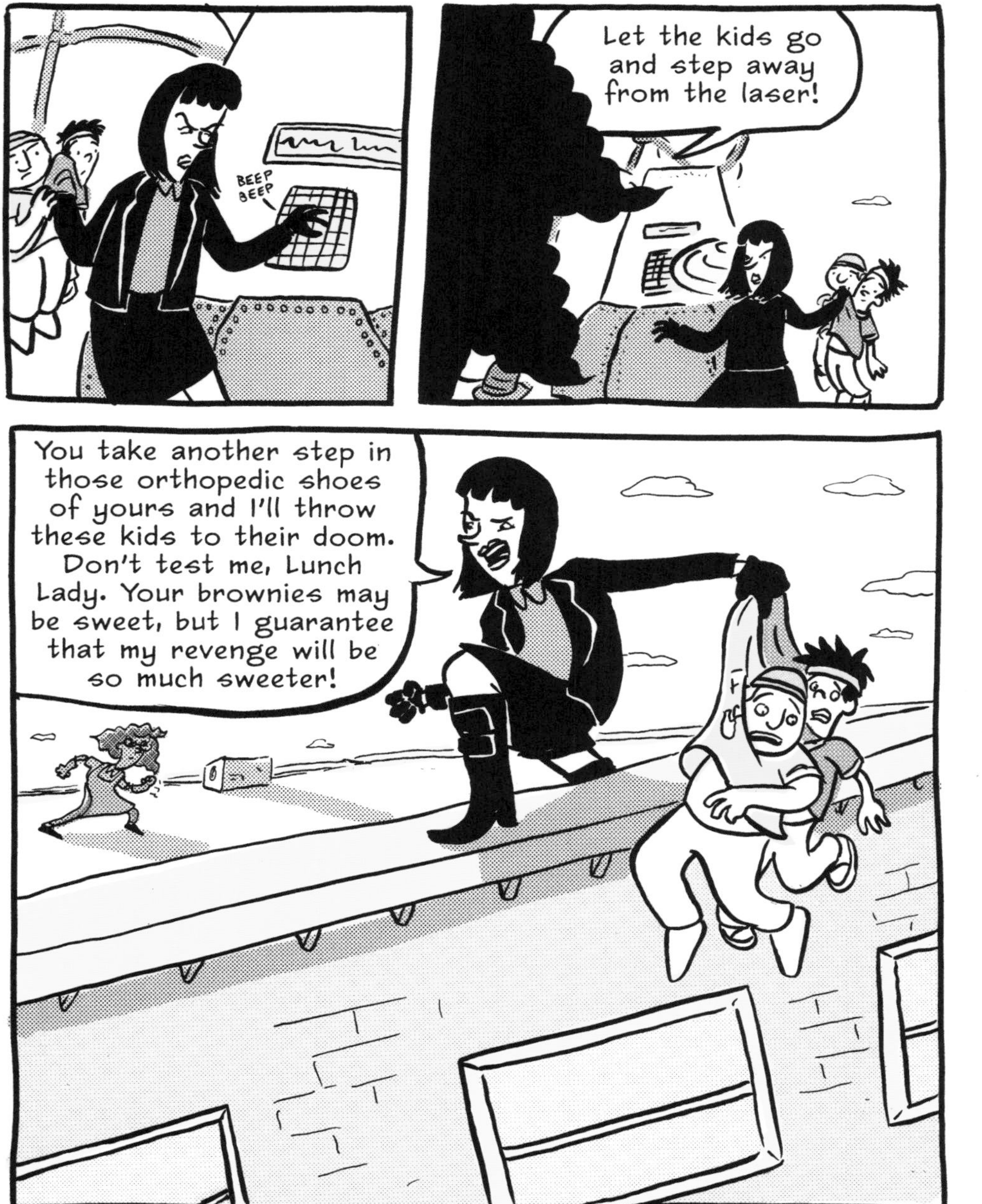
BEEP BEEP
Let the kids go and step away from the laser!
You take another step in those orthopedic shoes of yours and I'll throw these kids to their doom. Don't test me, Lunch Lady. Your brownies may be sweet, but I guarantee that my revenge will be so much sweeter!

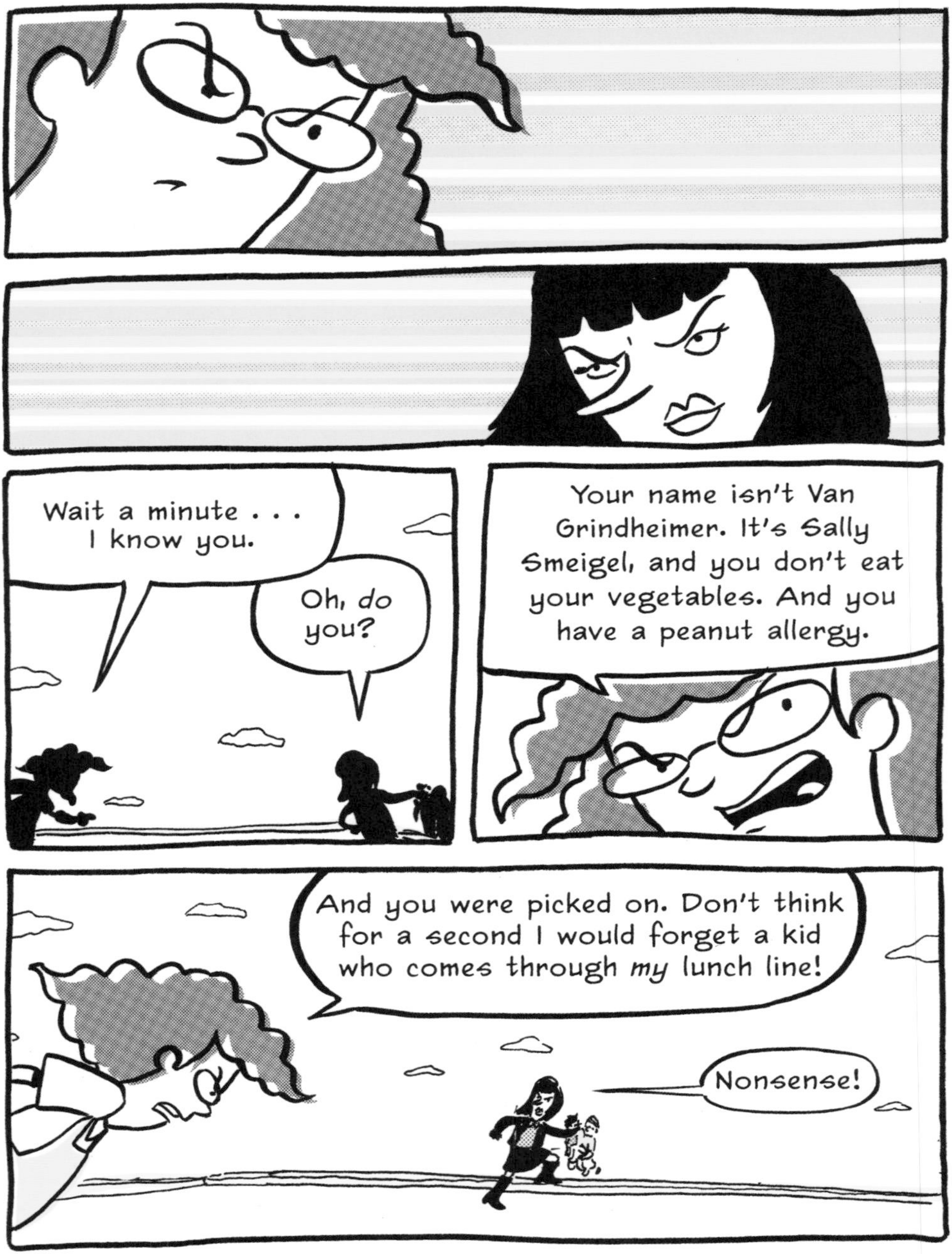
Wait a minute . . . I know you.
Oh, *do* you?
Your name isn't Van Grindheimer. It's Sally Smeigel, and you don't eat your vegetables. And you have a peanut allergy.
And you were picked on. Don't think for a second I would forget a kid who comes through *my* lunch line!
Nonsense!

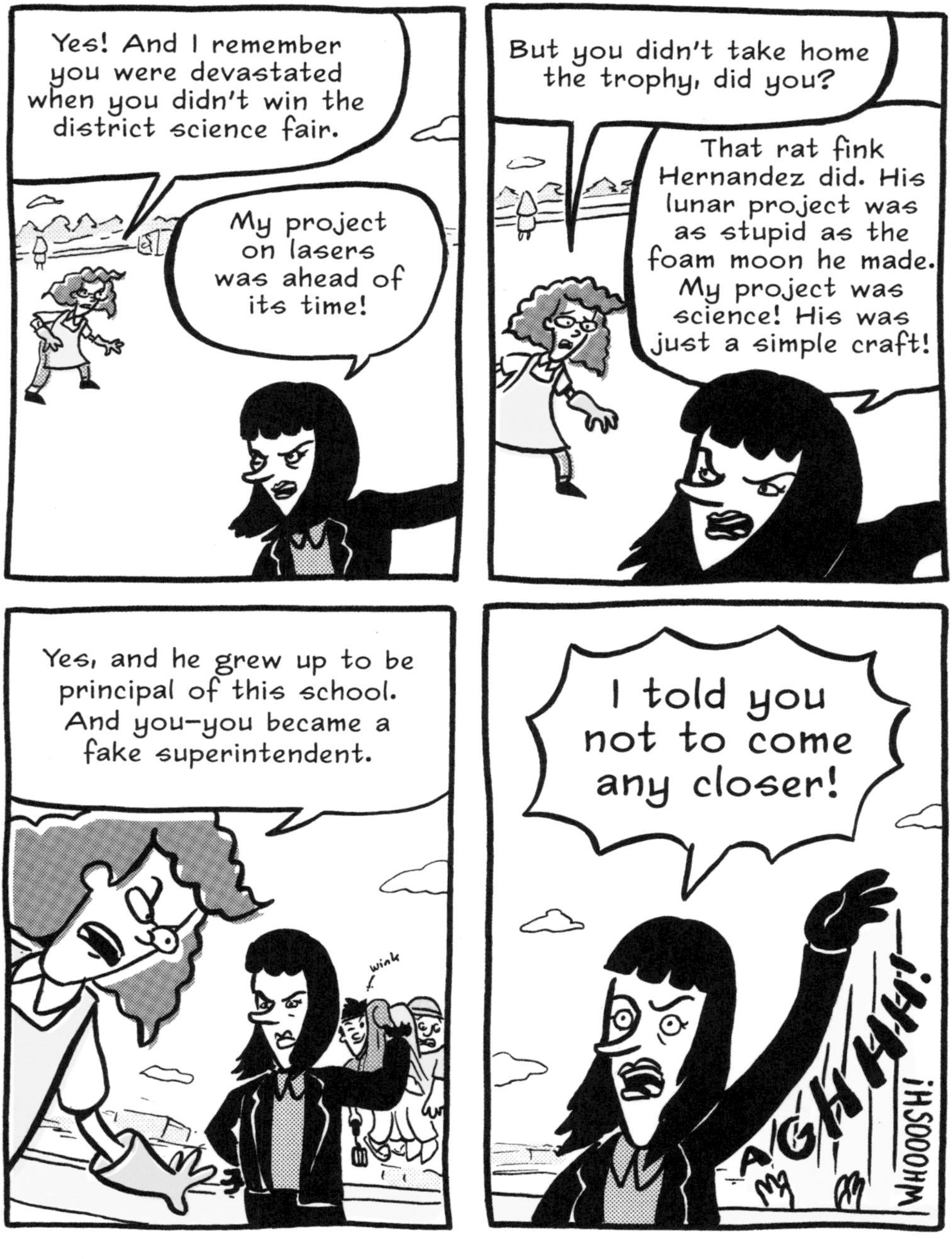
Yes! And I remember you were devastated when you didn't win the district science fair.
My project on lasers was ahead of its time!
But you didn't take home the trophy, did you?
That rat fink Hernandez did. His lunar project was as stupid as the foam moon he made. My project was science! His was just a simple craft!
Yes, and he grew up to be principal of this school. And you—you became a fake superintendent.
wink
I told you not to come any closer!
AGHHH!
WHOOOSH!

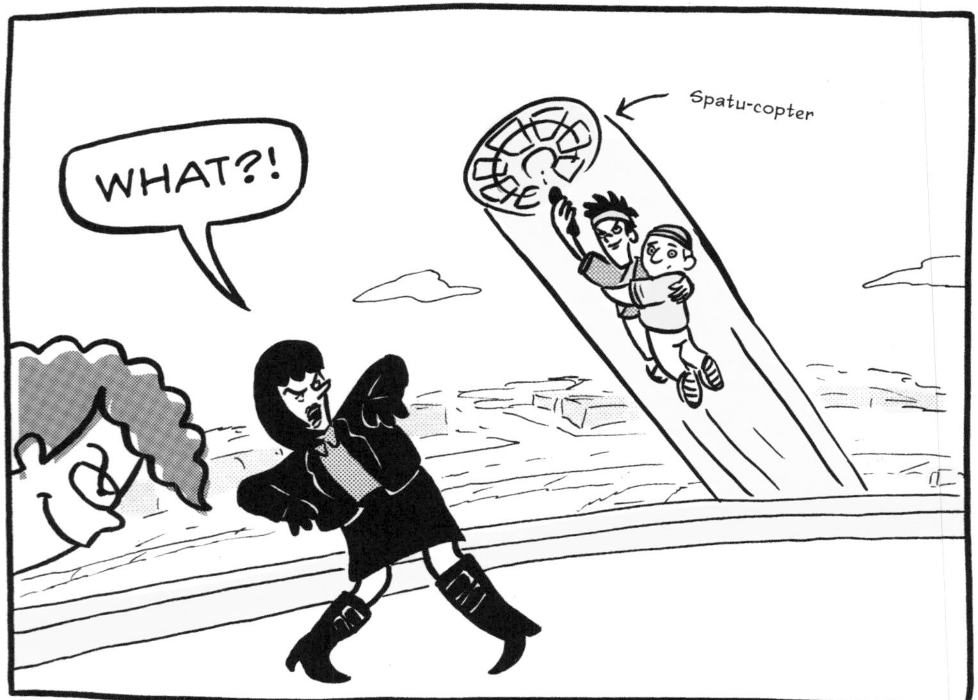
WHAT?!
Spatu-copter

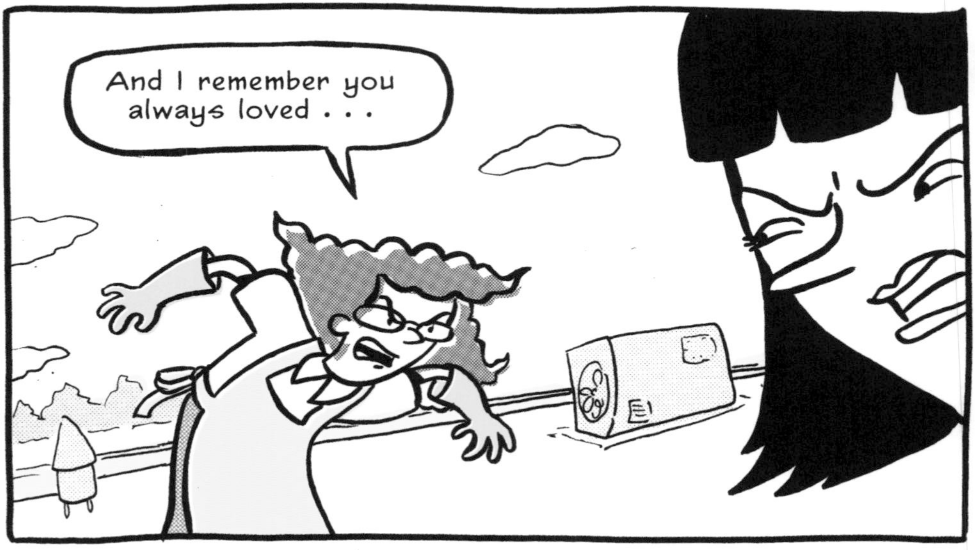
And I remember you always loved . . .

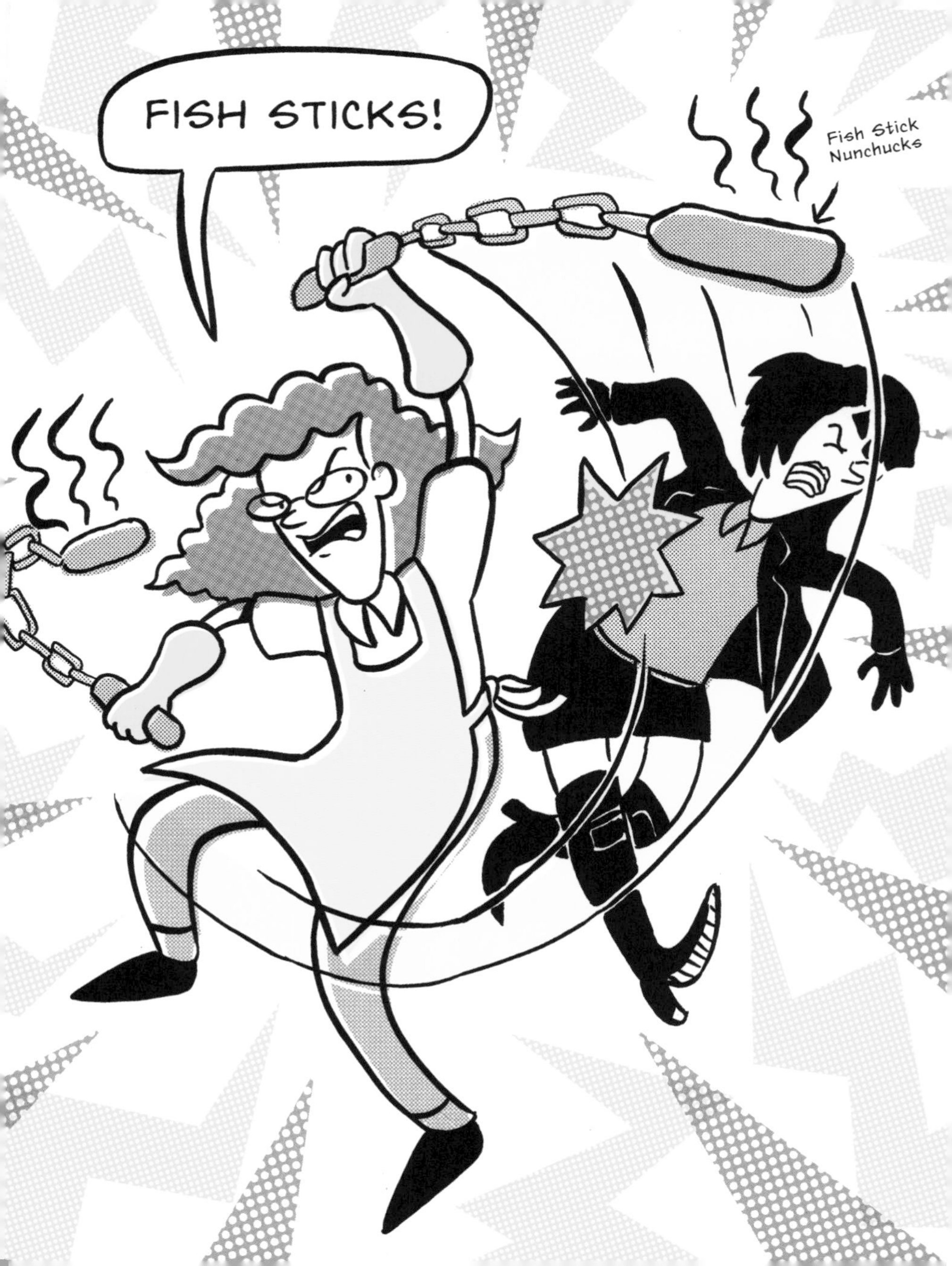
FISH STICKS!
Fish Stick Nunchucks

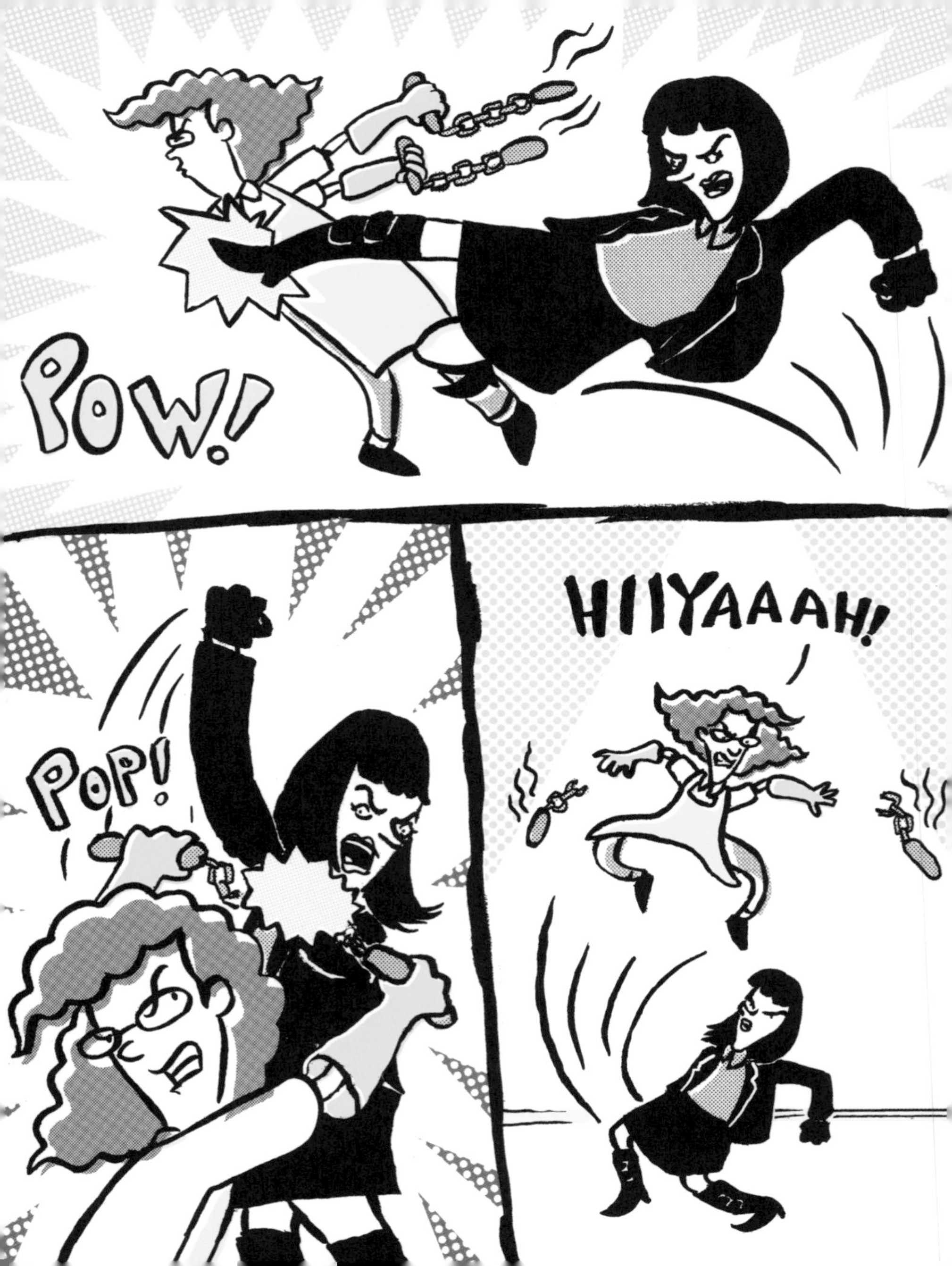
POW!
POP!
HIIYAAAAH!

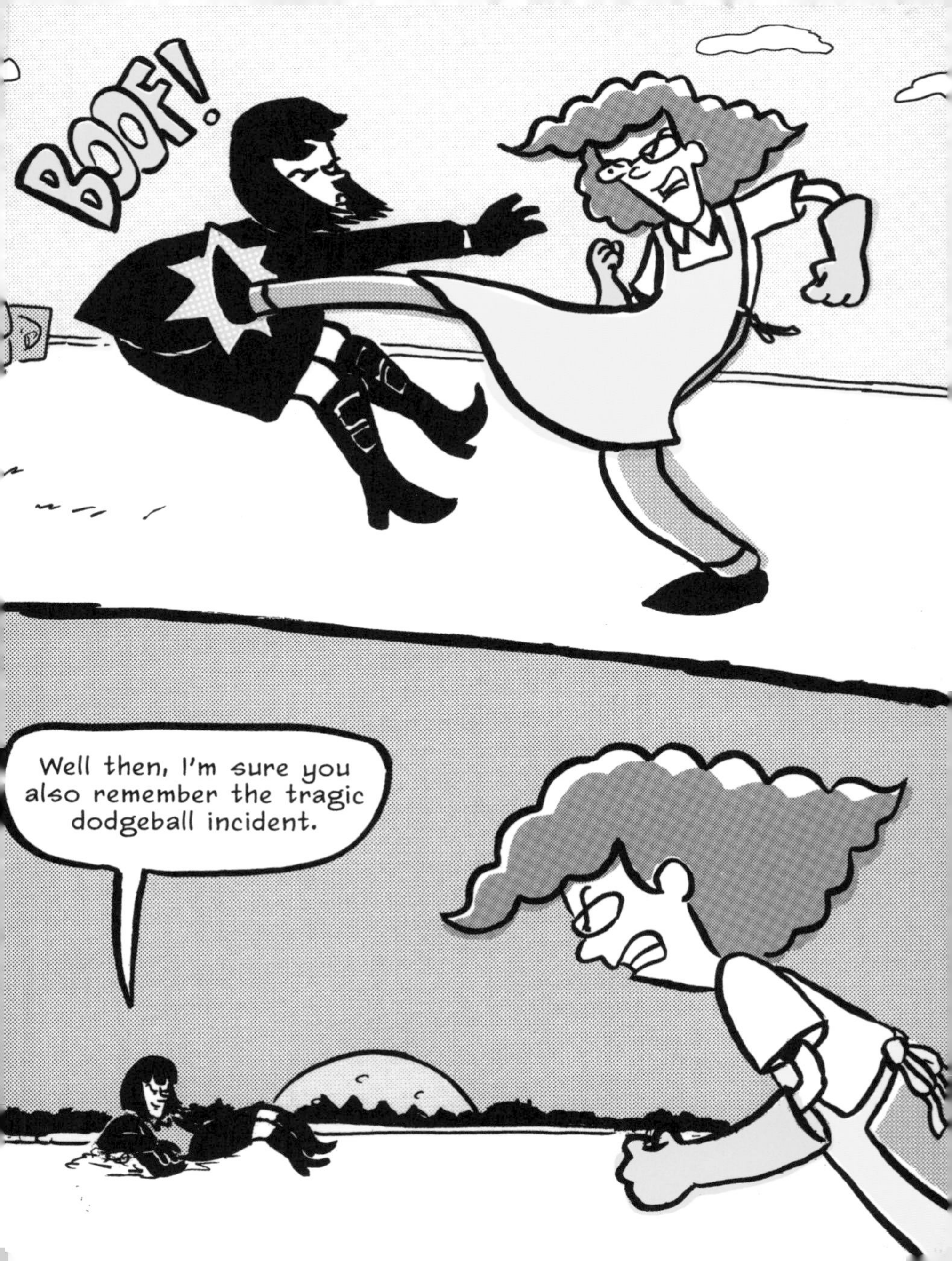
BOOF!
Well then, I'm sure you also remember the tragic dodgeball incident.

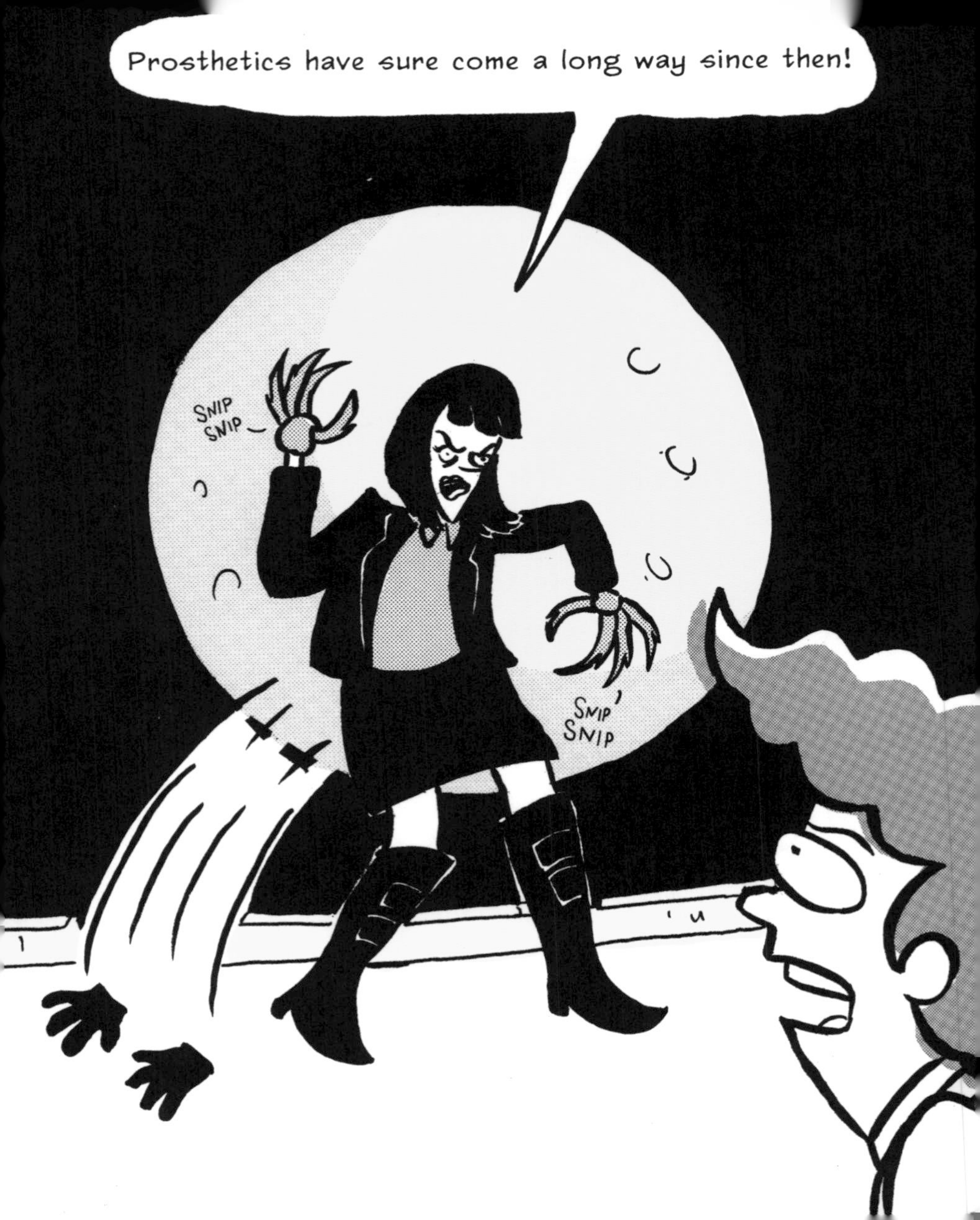
Prosthetics have sure come a long way since then!
SNIP SNIP
SNIP SNIP

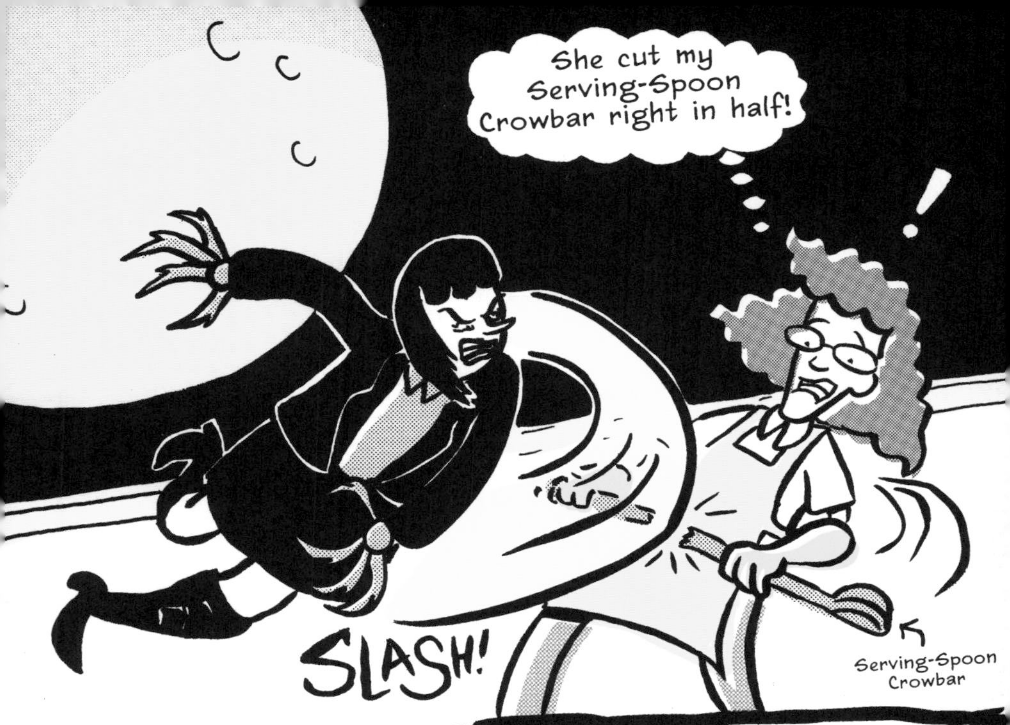
She cut my Serving-Spoon Crowbar right in half!
!
SLASH!
Serving-Spoon Crowbar

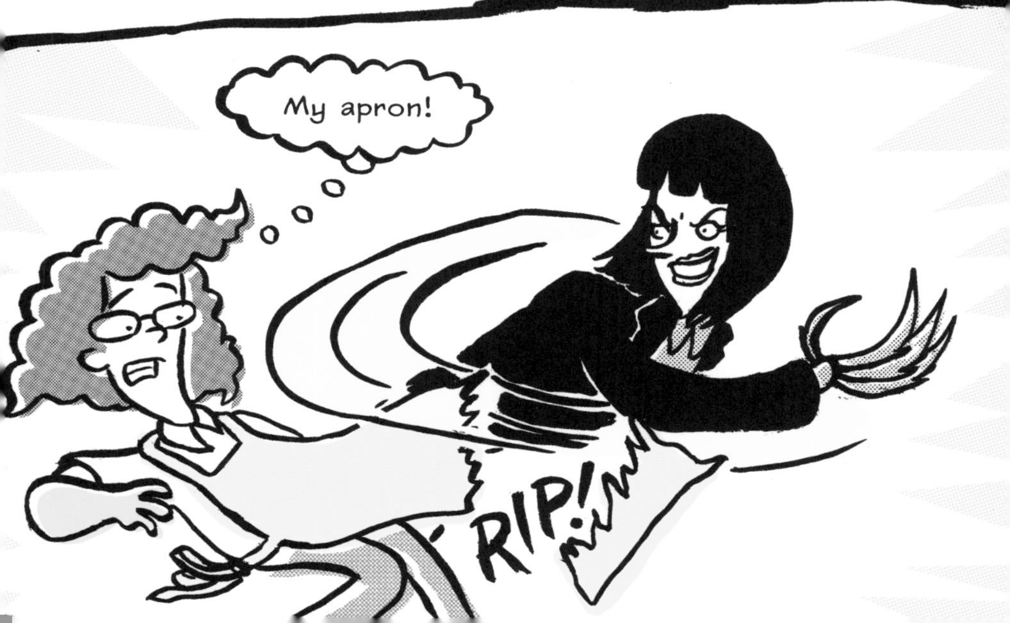
My apron!
RIP!

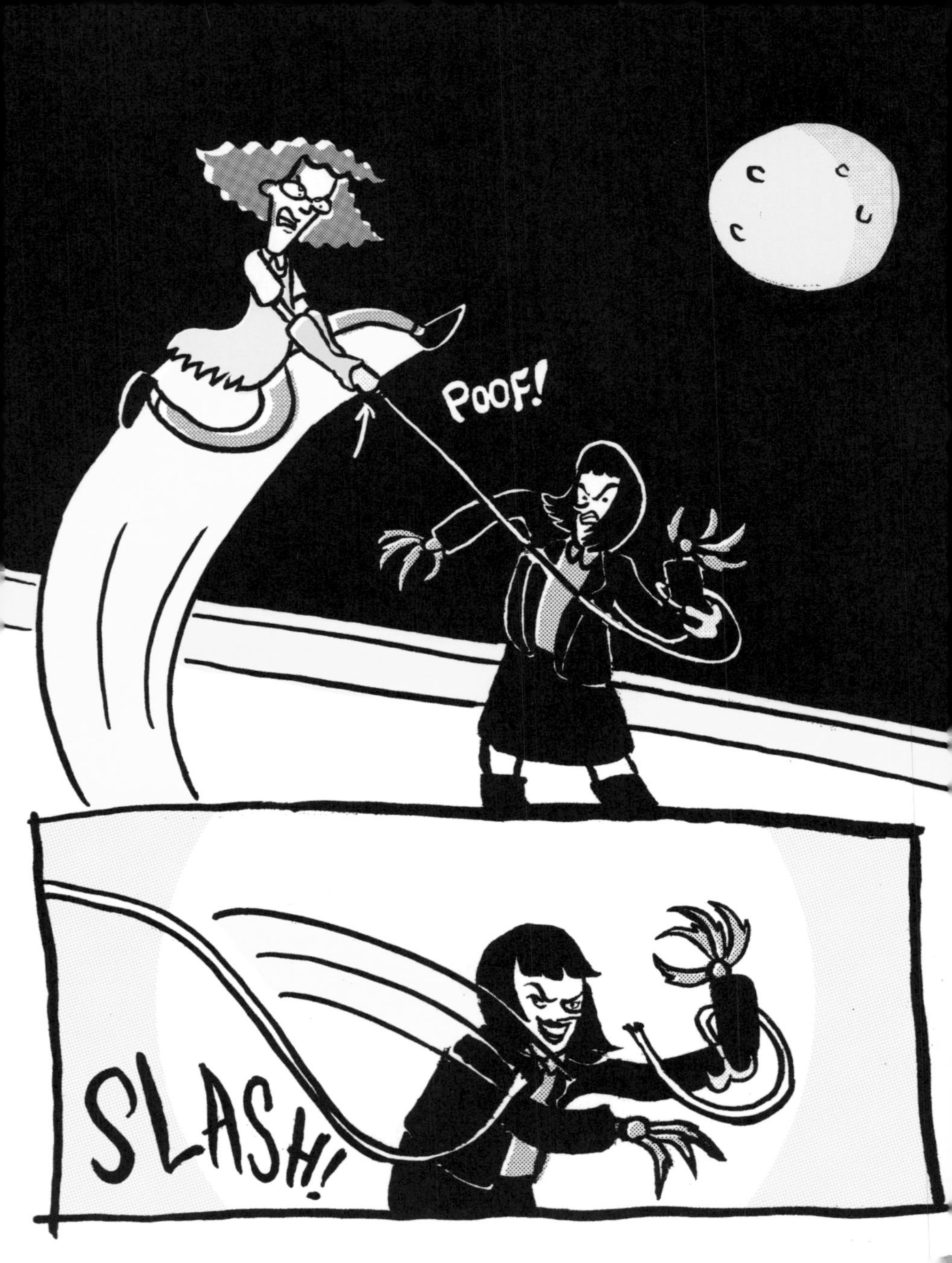
POOF!
SLASH!

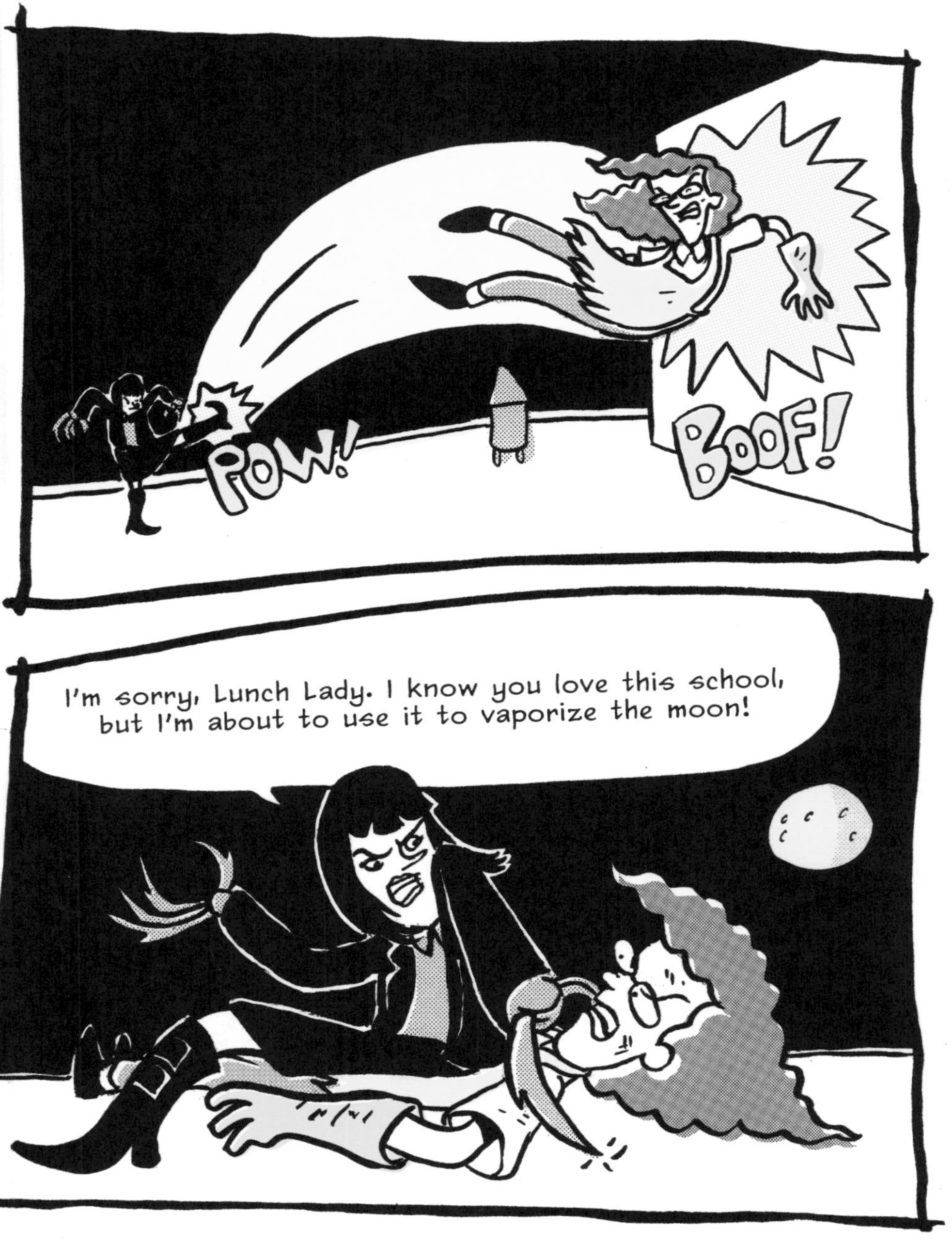
POW!
BOOF!
I'm sorry, Lunch Lady. I know you love this school, but I'm about to use it to vaporize the moon!

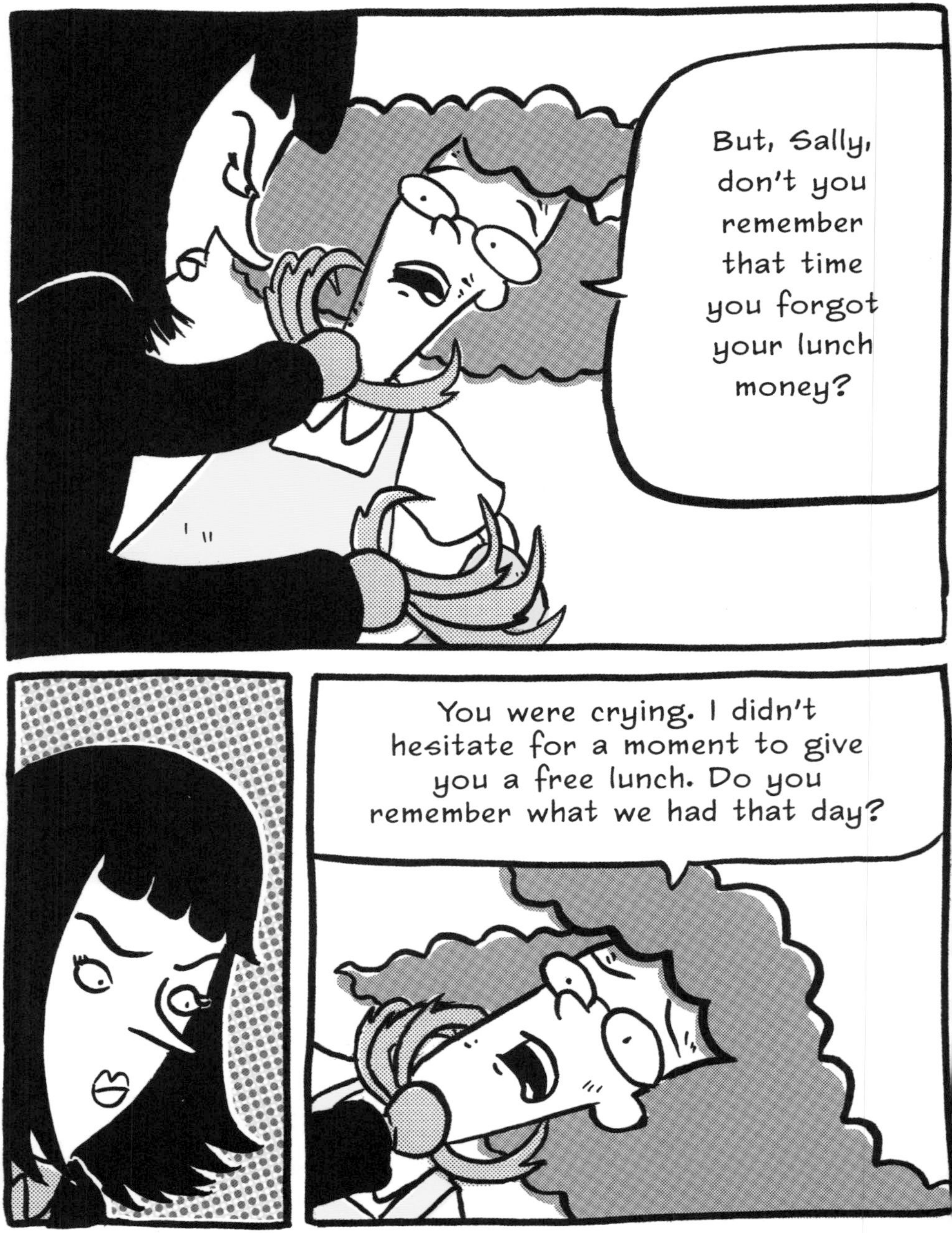
But, Sally, don't you remember that time you forgot your lunch money?
You were crying. I didn't hesitate for a moment to give you a free lunch. Do you remember what we had that day?

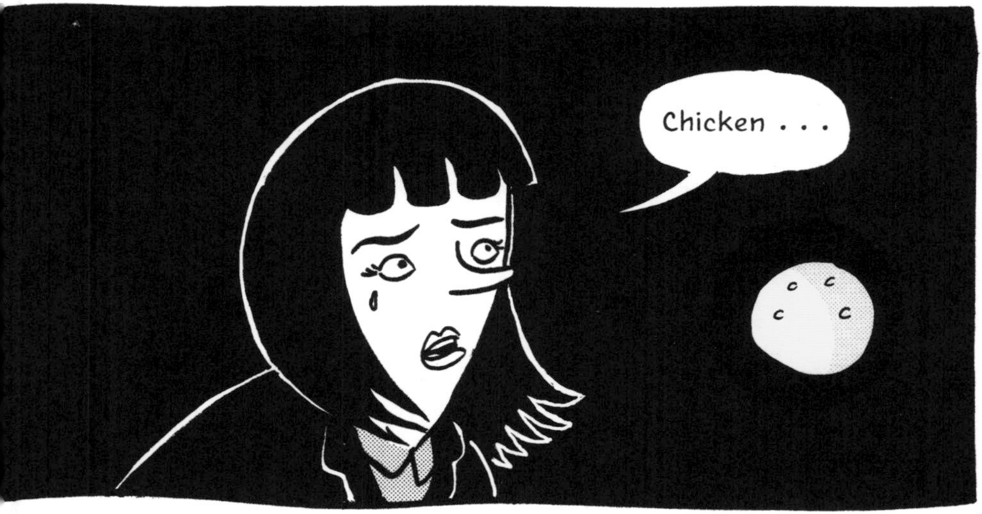
Chicken . . .

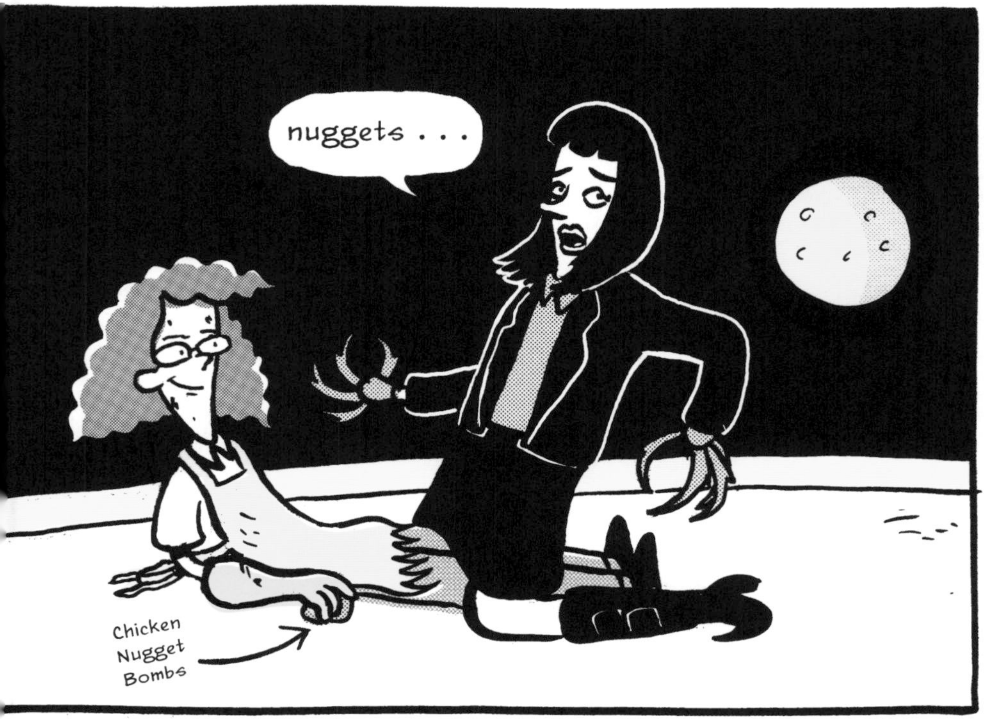
nuggets . . .
Chicken Nugget Bombs

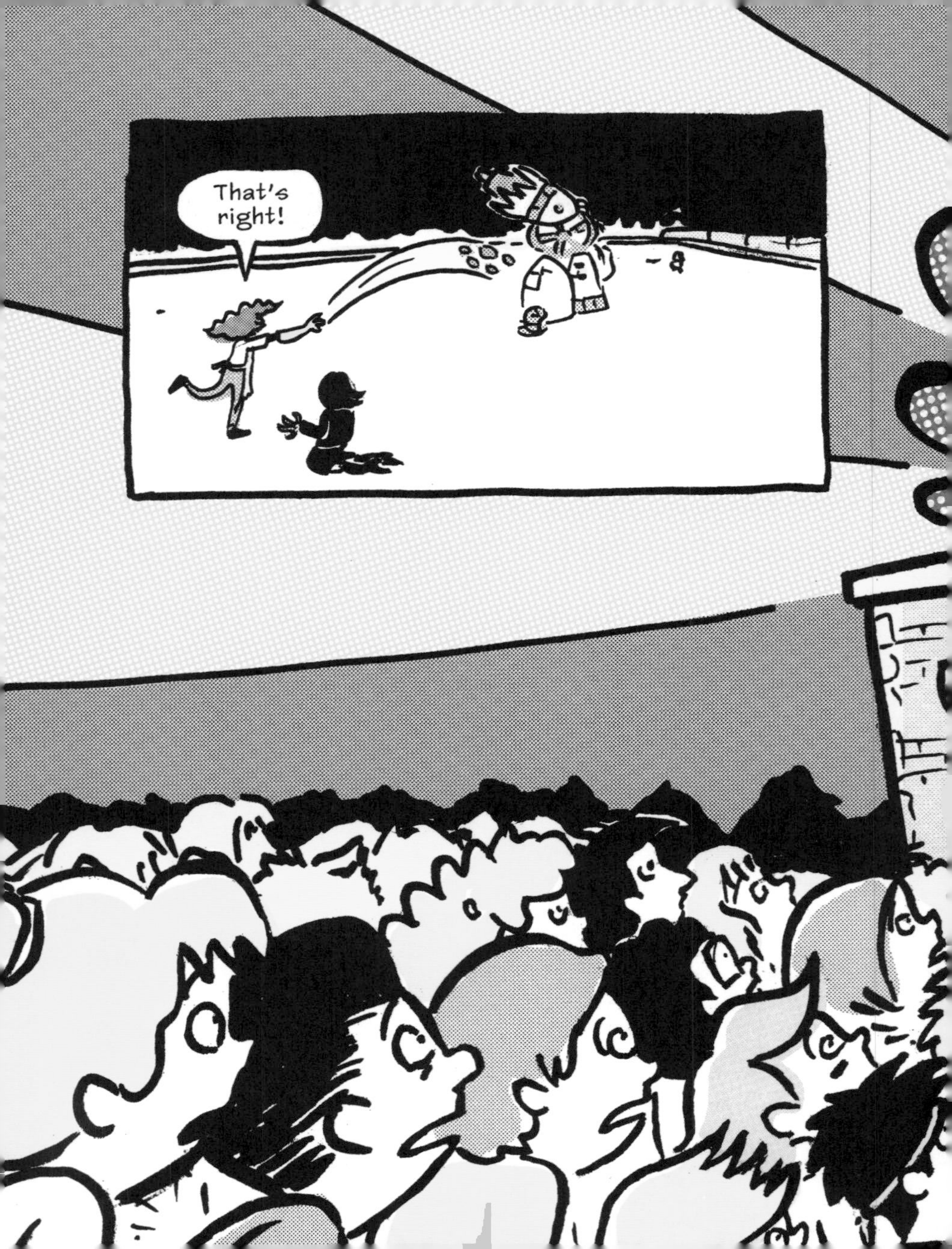
That's right!

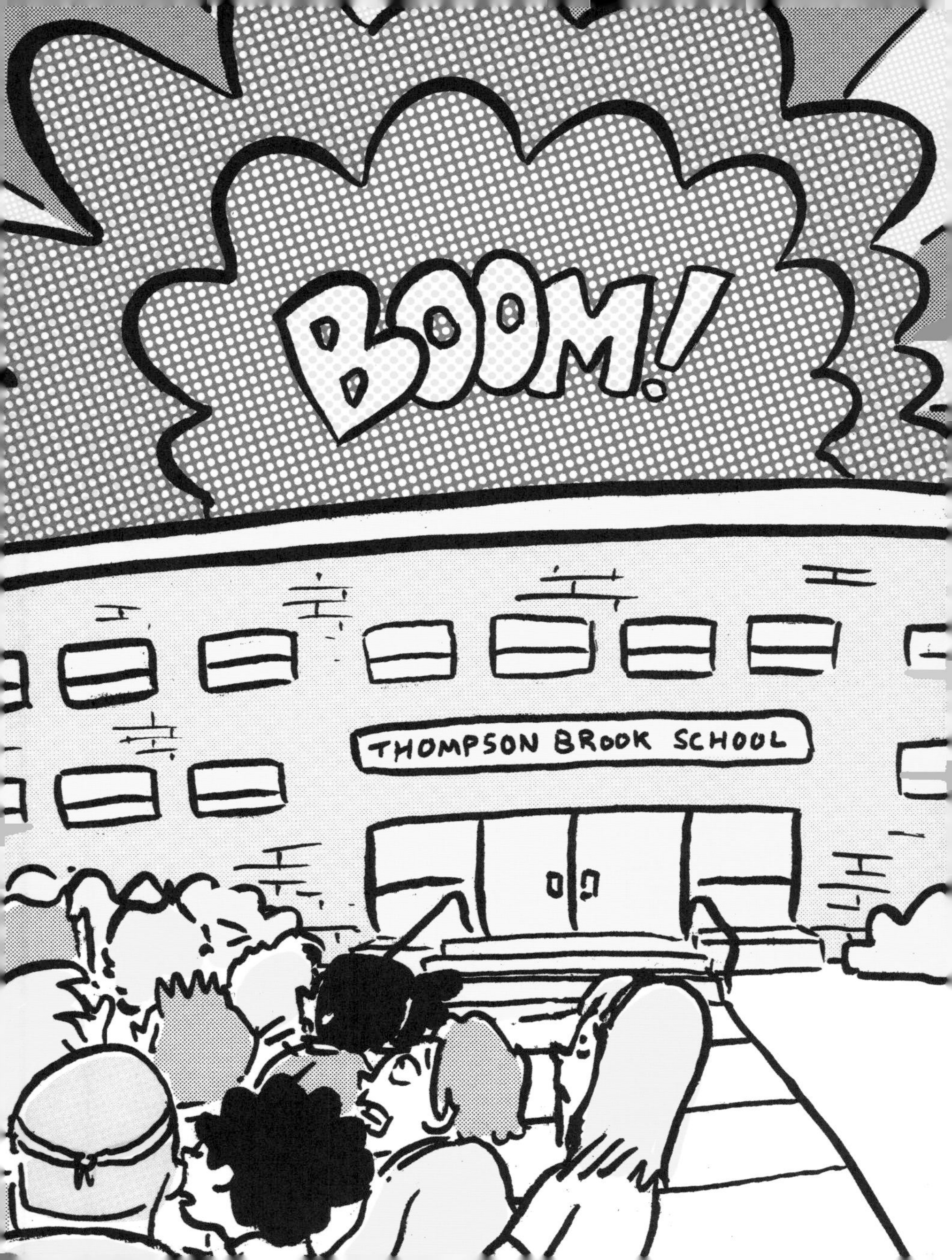
BOOM!
THOMPSON BROOK SCHOOL

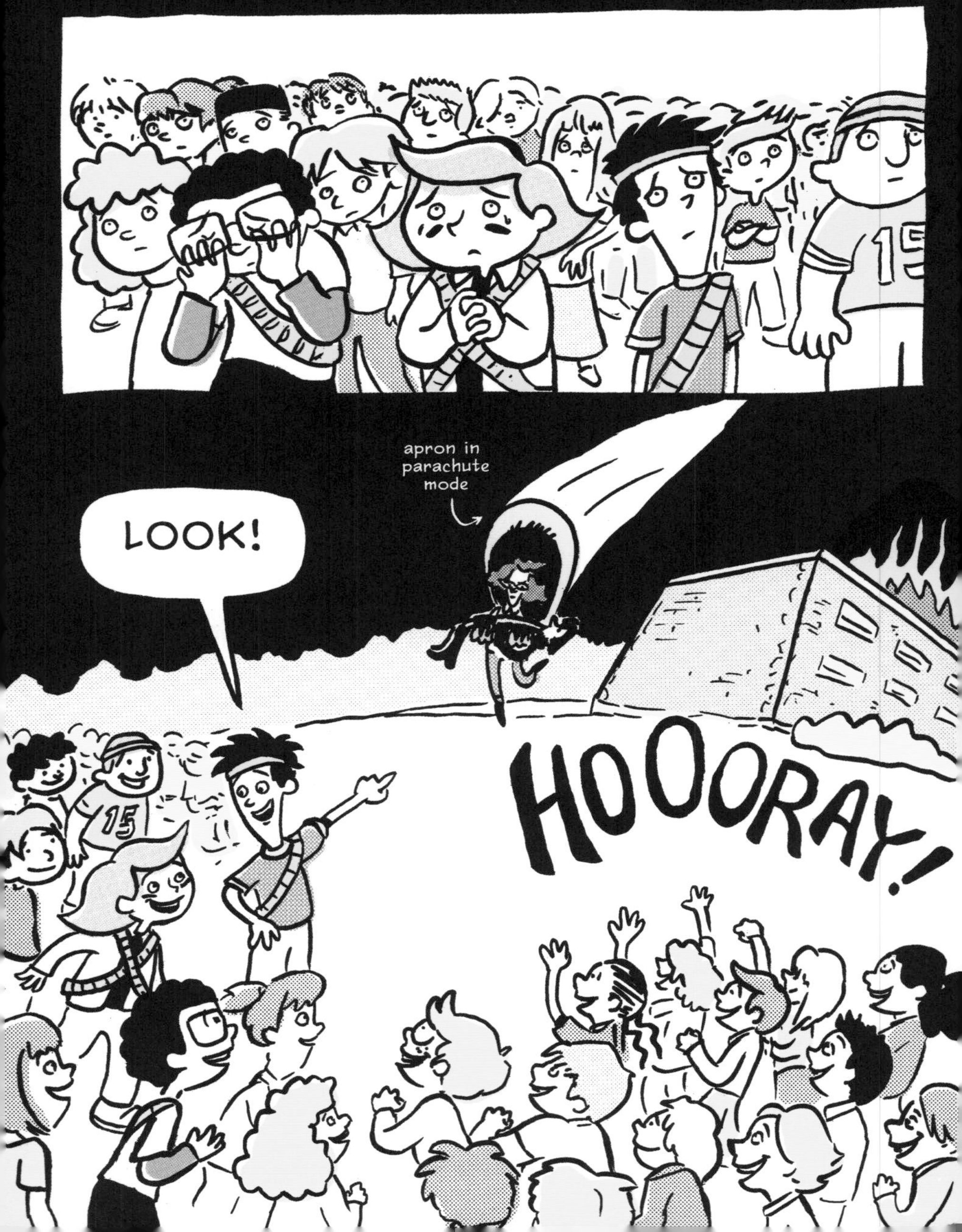
apron in parachute mode
LOOK!
HOOORAY!

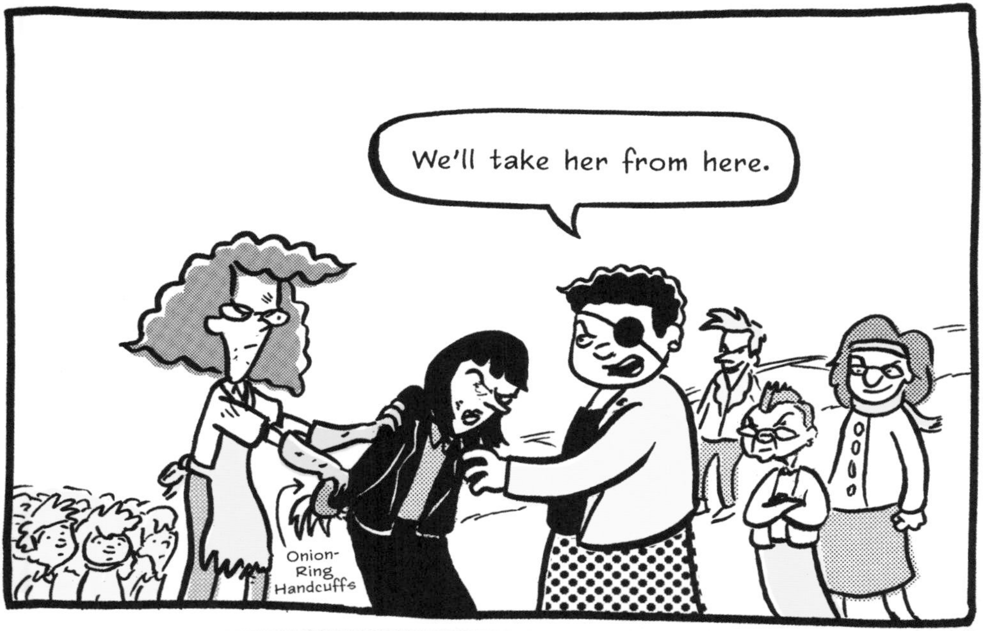
We'll take her from here.
Onion-Ring Handcuffs

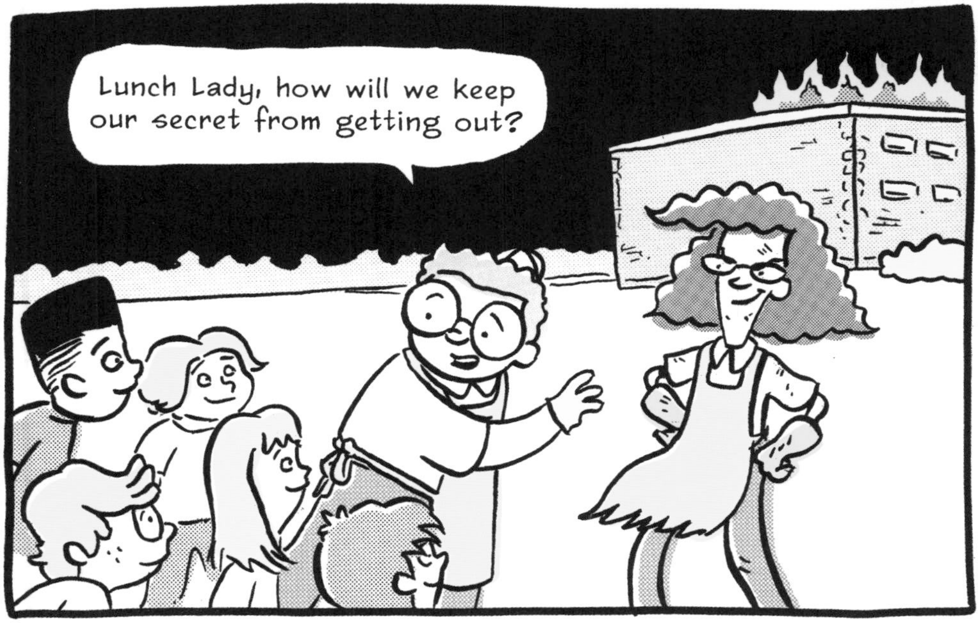
Lunch Lady, how will we keep our secret from getting out?

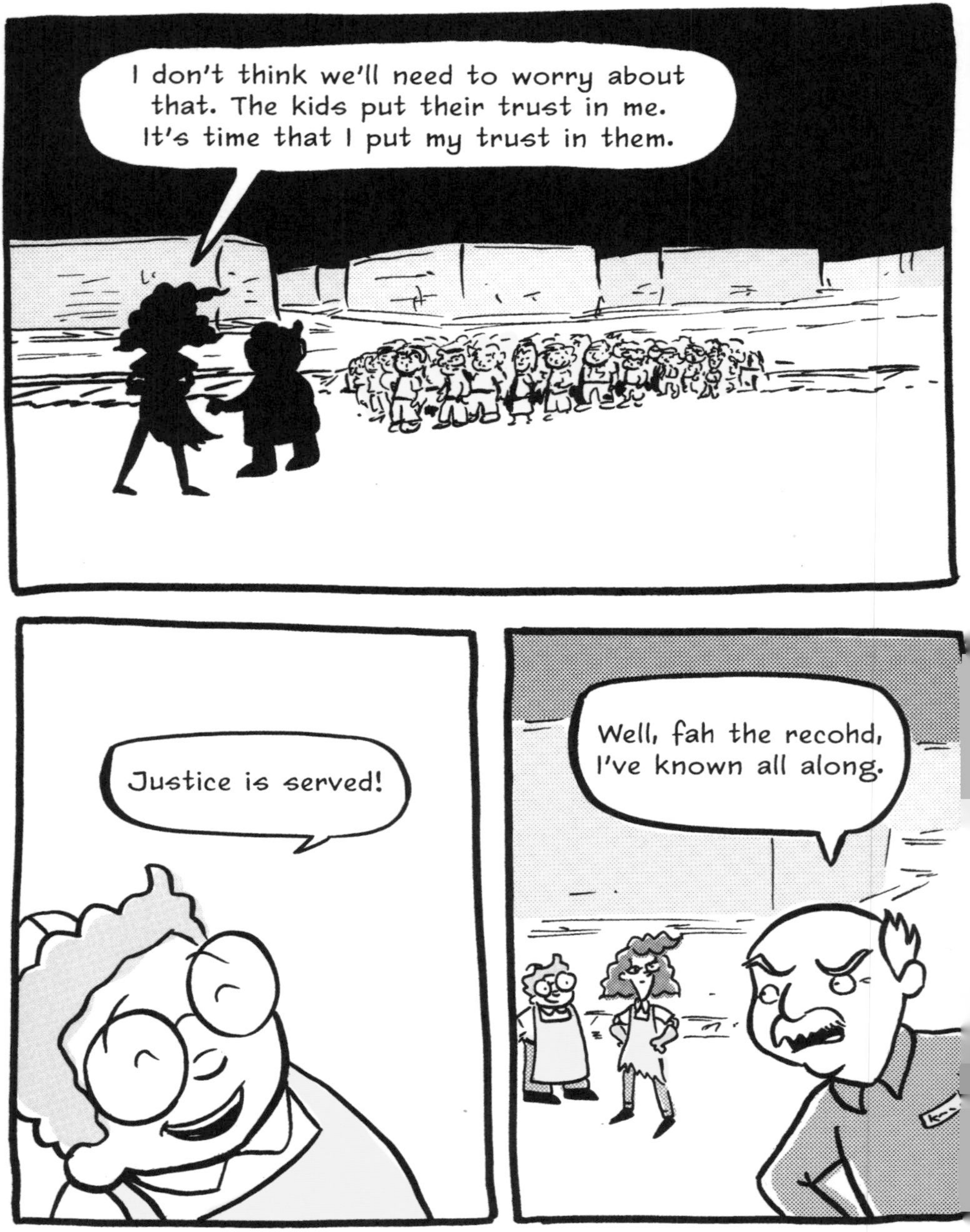
I don't think we'll need to worry about that. The kids put their trust in me. It's time that I put my trust in them.
Justice is served!
Well, fah the recohd, I've known all along.

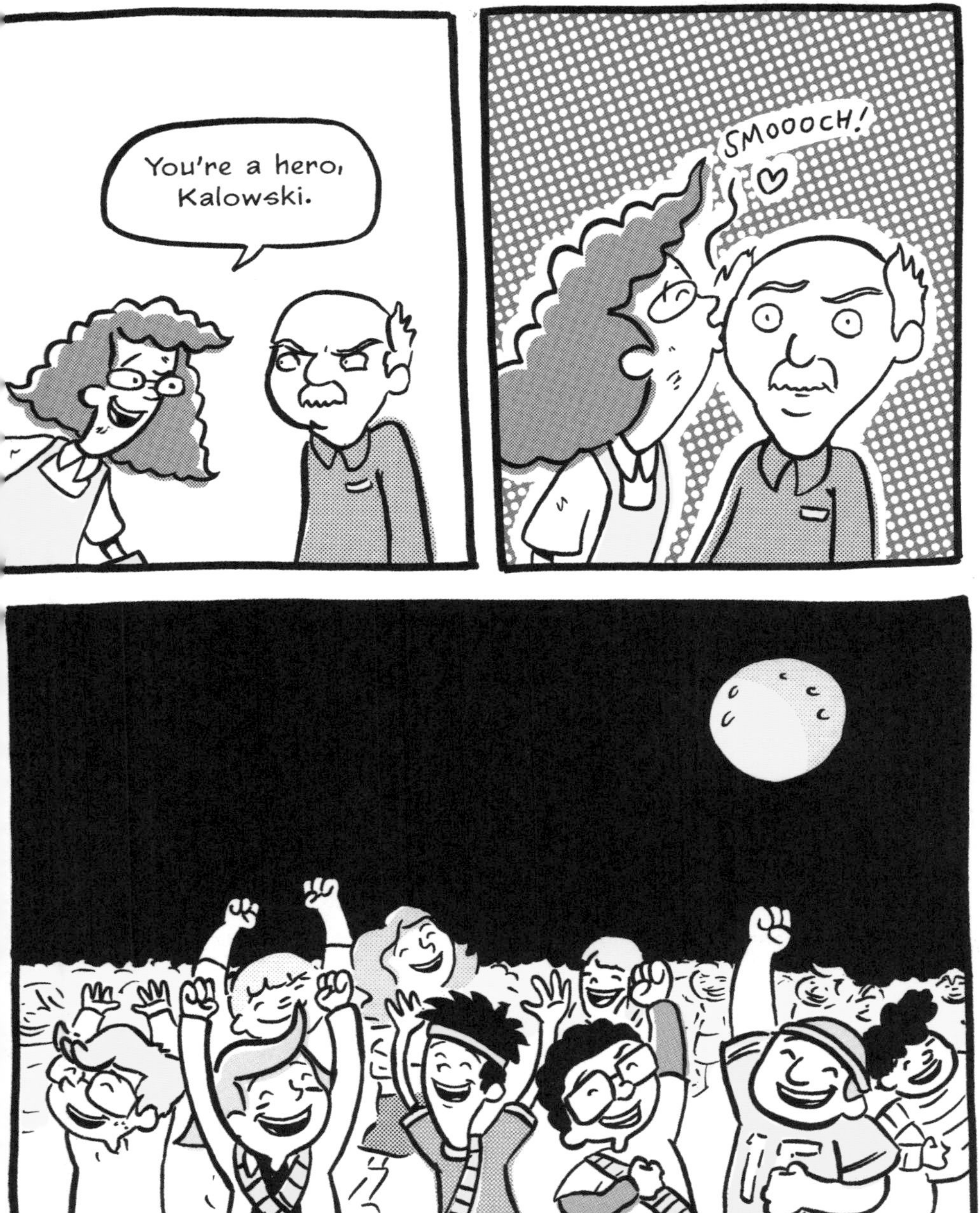
You're a hero, Kalowski.
SMOOOCH!

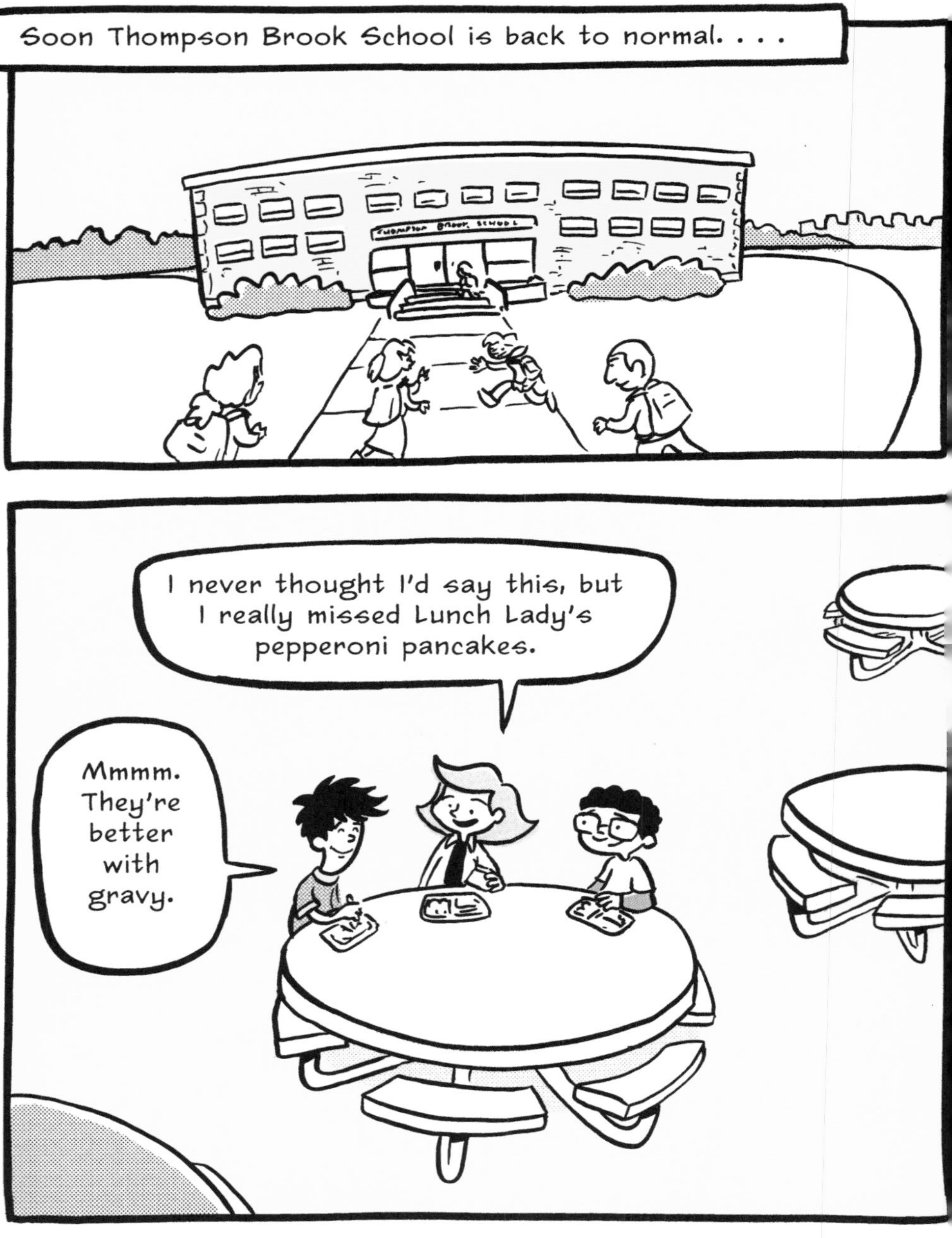
Soon Thompson Brook School is back to normal. . . .
THOMPSON BROOK SCHOOL
I never thought I'd say this, but I really missed Lunch Lady's pepperoni pancakes.
Mmmm. They're better with gravy.

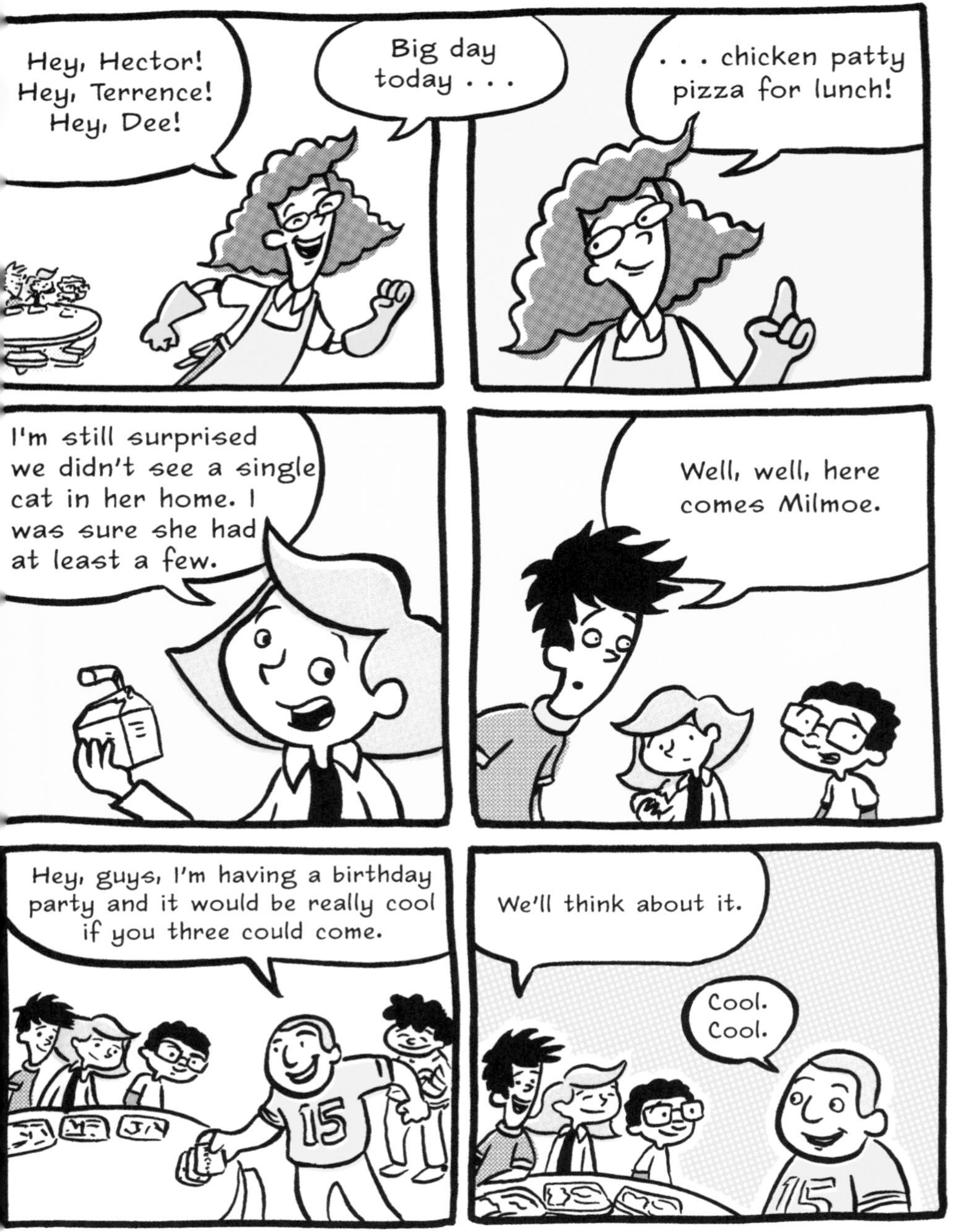
Hey, Hector!
Hey, Terrence!
Hey, Dee!
Big day
today . . .
. . . chicken patty
pizza for lunch!
I'm still surprised
we didn't see a single
cat in her home. I
was sure she had
at least a few.
Well, well, here
comes Milmoe.
Hey, guys, I'm having a birthday
party and it would be really cool
if you three could come.
15
We'll think about it.
Cool.
Cool.
15

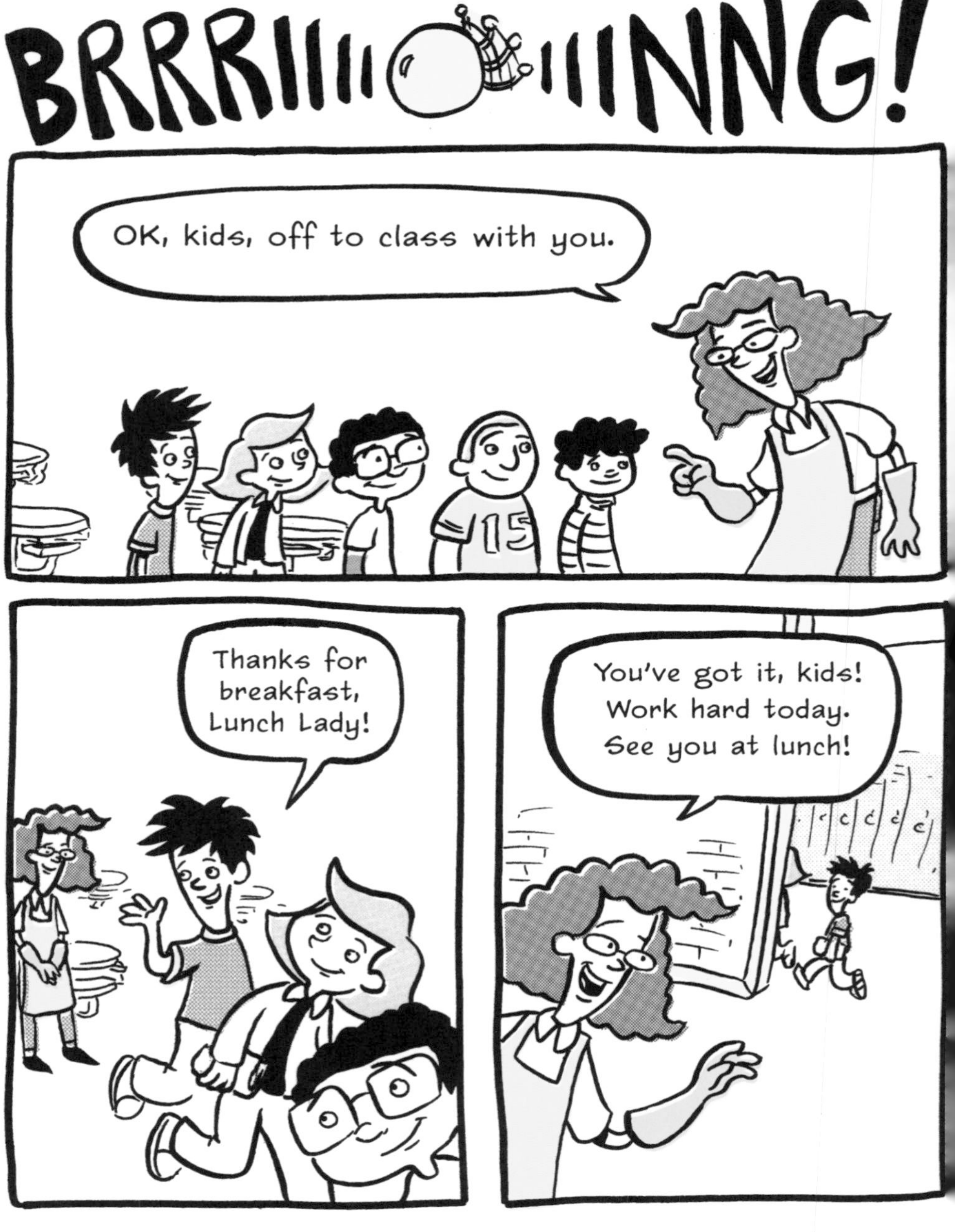
BRRRIIIIIINNNG!
OK, kids, off to class with you.
15
Thanks for breakfast, Lunch Lady!
You've got it, kids! Work hard today. See you at lunch!

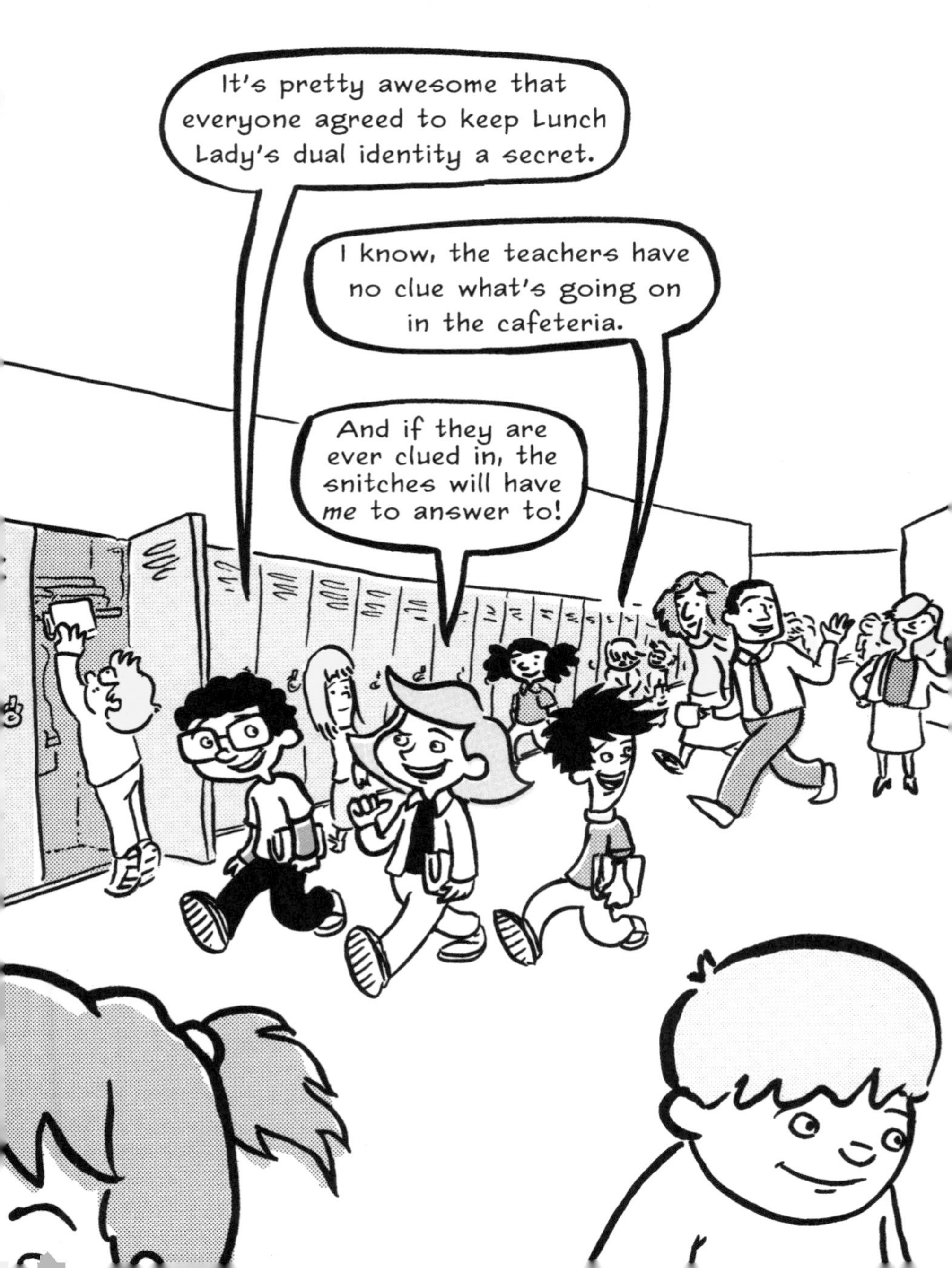
It's pretty awesome that everyone agreed to keep Lunch Lady's dual identity a secret.
I know, the teachers have no clue what's going on in the cafeteria.
And if they are ever clued in, the snitches will have *me* to answer to!

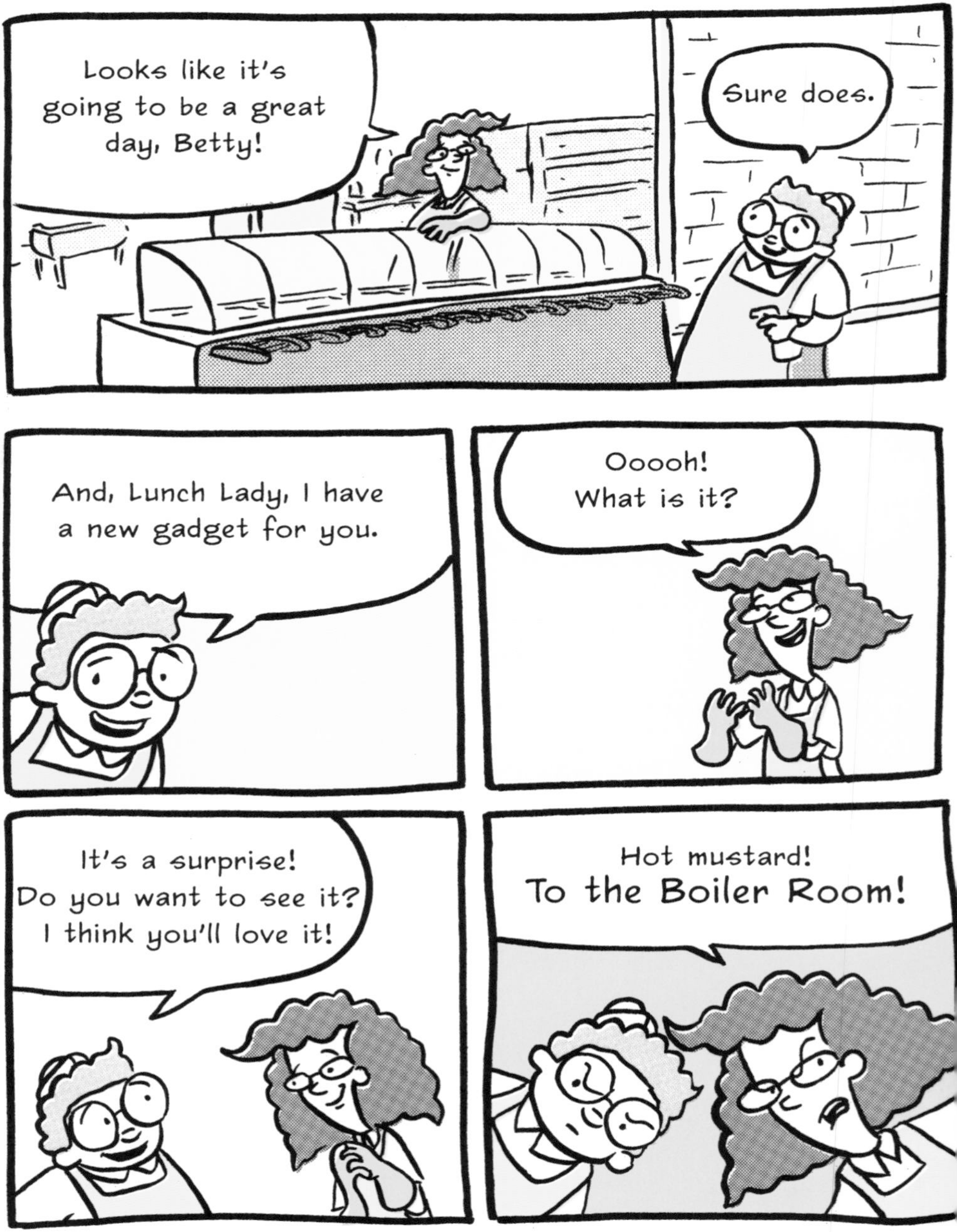
Looks like it's going to be a great day, Betty!
Sure does.
And, Lunch Lady, I have a new gadget for you.
Ooooh! What is it?
It's a surprise! Do you want to see it? I think you'll love it!
Hot mustard! To the Boiler Room!

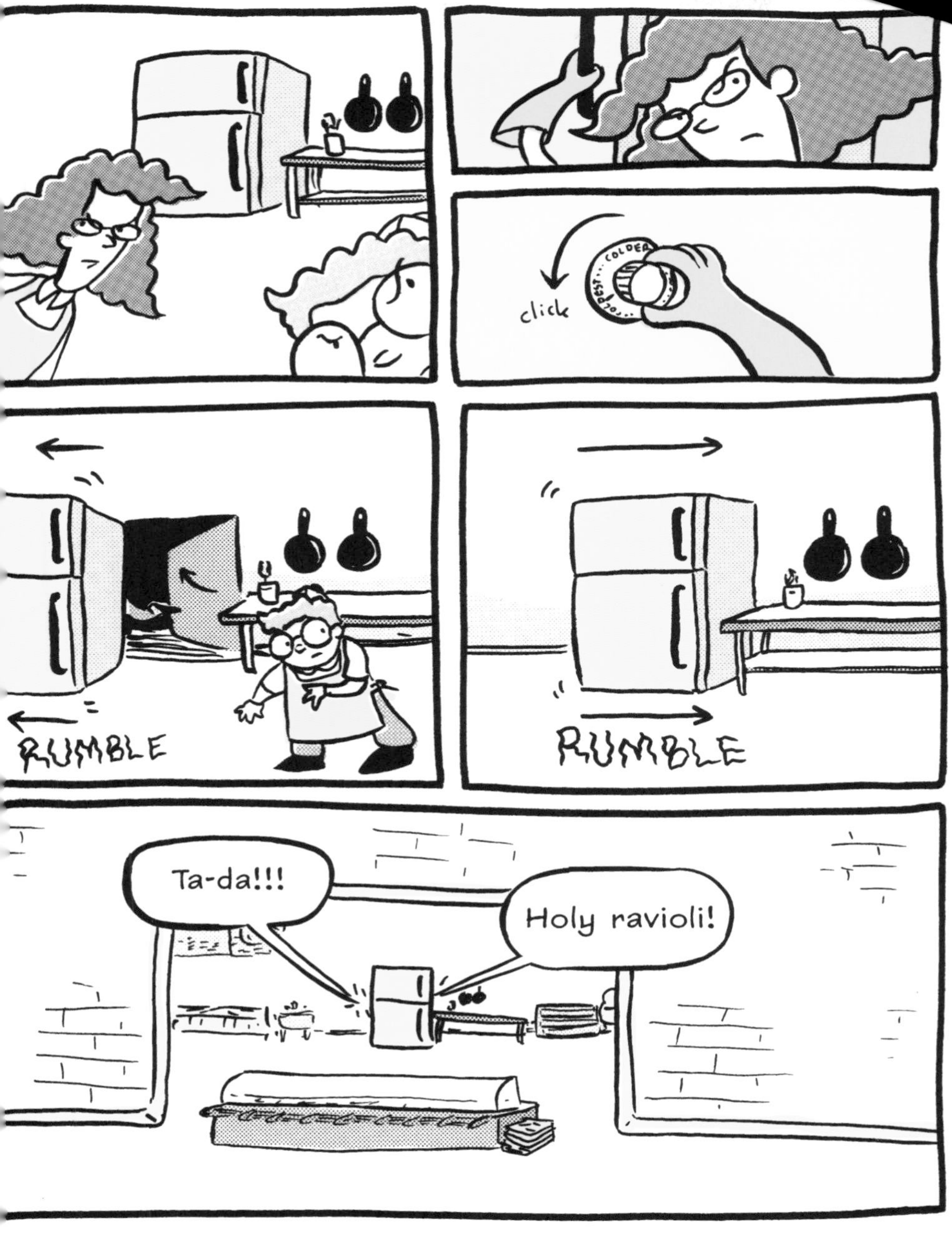
COLDER
click
RUMBLE
RUMBLE
Ta-da!!!
Holy ravioli!

OR MY LITTLE GIRLS, ZOE AND LUCY

The author would like to acknowledge the color work in this book by Joey Weiser and Michele Chidester.

THIS IS A BORZOI BOOK PUBLISHED BY ALFRED A. KNOPF

Visit us on the Web! randomhouse.com/kids

Educators and librarians, for a variety of teaching tools, visit us at RHTeachersLibrarians.com

Library of Congress Cataloging-in-Publication Data
Krosoczka, Jarrett.
Lunch Lady and the schoolwide scuffle / Jarrett J. Krosoczka. — First edition.
p. cm. — (Lunch Lady ; 10)
Summary: Lunch Lady and Betty have been fired but the Breakfast Bunch convinces them to return and stop the school's new superintendent and her minions from carrying out an evil plan for revenge.
ISBN 978-0-385-75279-4 (trade) — ISBN 978-0-385-75280-0 (lib. bdg.) — ISBN 978-0-385-75281-7 (ebook)
1. Graphic novels. [1. Graphic novels. 2. Schools—Fiction. 3. Revenge—Fiction.
4. Mystery and detective stories.] I. Title.
PZ7.7.K76Lur 2013
741.5'31—dc23
2013004886

The text of this book is set in Hedge Backwards.

The illustrations were created using ink on paper and digital coloring.

MANUFACTURED IN MALAYSIA

January 2014

10 9 8 7 6 5 4 3 2 1

First Edition

Random House Children's Books supports the First Amendment and celebrates the right to read.